BADD

Also by Tim Tharp

THE SPECTACULAR NOW
★ "A smart, superbly written novel. . . . Readers will be simultaneously charmed and infuriated by Sutter as his voice holds them in thrall to his all-powerful Now."
—*Publishers Weekly,* Starred

★ "Sutter's lively, humorous narration is deceptively insightful and clever. . . . A sobering look at the rationalizations of a teenage alcoholic."
—*The Bulletin,* Starred

"Sutter is an authentic character, and his unsteady sense of himself, as well as his relationships with his friends, will strike a chord with teen readers." —*Booklist*

KNIGHTS OF THE HILL COUNTRY
★ "Jealousy, rage, and tenderness are wrapped around the story's core theme of self-discovery. . . . This intriguing work demands an audience." —*Kirkus Reviews,* Starred

"Taut scenes on the football field and the dilemmas about choosing what feels right over what's expected are all made memorable by Hamp's unforgettable, colloquial voice that speaks about feelings and football with the same unwavering, fully realized personality. A moving, sensitive debut from a writer to watch." —*Booklist*

"The teen's voice comes in loud and clear, revealing a sensitive, likeable character." —*School Library Journal*

BADD

by Tim Tharp

EMBER

Text copyright © 2011 by Tim Tharp
Cover art copyright © 2011 by Alfred A. Knopf

All rights reserved. Published in the United States by Ember, an imprint of
Random House Children's Books, a division of Random House, Inc., New York.
Originally published in hardcover in the United States by Alfred A. Knopf,
an imprint of Random House Children's Books, New York, in 2011.

Ember and the colophon are trademarks of Random House, Inc.

www.randomhouse.com/teens

Educators and librarians, for a variety of teaching tools,
visit us at www.randomhouse.com/teachers

The Library of Congress has cataloged the hardcover edition of this work as follows:
Tharp, Tim.
Badd / by Tim Tharp. — 1st ed.
p.   cm.
Summary: A teenaged girl's beloved brother returns home from the Iraq War completely
unlike the person she remembers.
ISBN 978-0-375-86444-5 (trade) — ISBN 978-0-375-96444-2 (lib. bdg.) —
ISBN 978-0-375-89579-1 (ebook)
[1. Brothers and sisters—Fiction. 2. Iraq War, 2003—Fiction. 3. Post-traumatic stress
disorder—Fiction. 4. Emotional problems—Fiction.] I. Title.
PZ7.T32724Bad 2011
[Fic]—dc22
2010012732

ISBN 978-0-375-86401-8 (pbk.)

RL: 7.0

Printed in the United States of America
10 9 8 7 6 5 4 3 2 1

First Ember Edition 2012

Random House Children's Books supports the First Amendment
and celebrates the right to read.

BADD

1

Captain Crazy must die.

This might sound like tough talk coming from a girl, but I'm a tough girl. One hundred percent. And my friends, Gillis, Tillman, and Brianna, agree with me about the captain. We trade off ways to do the deed. We'll pickle him in brine, we'll feed him to the blender, the lawn mower, the garbage disposal, the Chihuahua. We'll slice off his fingers and toes like fresh carrots, dice him and mince him and chop off his head. Pack his leftovers in ice, French fry them in a deep-fat fryer. We'll draw and quarter him, go after him with chainsaws and garden shears. We'll stuff him and sell him at the flea market.

No, we won't. Not really. We're not some kind of evil devil cult. But you still don't want to mess with us.

Actually, I'm the only one with a reason to be mad. The

others just want something to happen around here. Anything. But with me it's personal because of my brother Bobby. He's in the army, see, in Iraq. Well, he was in Iraq, but now he's in Germany. We're expecting him home in a month, and we sure don't need Captain Crazy putting a hex on him before he gets back. I mean, this time I know he's coming home. He really is. It's just hard to believe it for sure until he wraps me up in one of his big bear hugs and says, "It's me, Ceejay. Don't worry, little sister, don't worry. It's me and I'm home for good."

The Captain Crazy business starts when me and Brianna are cruising in her car and Gillis calls me up and goes, "Listen, Ceejay, you gotta get over here to the courthouse. Captain Crazy's throwing a Vietnam War protest. It's hilarious!"

Vietnam! Leave it to the captain to go all radical over a war that's been over for thirty-something years.

Two minutes later Brianna and I pull up to the courthouse in her car. That's the one and only good thing about living in a town the size of Knowles. Your friends can call and tell you to come somewhere, and you're there practically before they hang up the phone. So when I get to the foot of the courthouse steps, the captain's just starting to really roll, pacing like a preacher on crystal meth, his face red, his eyes bulging. He's not even Captain Crazy anymore. Now he's *Reverend* Crazy shouting down the devil. And don't you know, if there's anyone who's really seen the devil, it's him.

He's got the usual paisley guitar and the conga drum close at hand but hasn't started in playing them yet. Behind him, three posters on six-foot-tall sticks stand propped against the granite wall, each with flowers painted on them—purple, red, yellow, chartreuse—just like it's really the dead-and-gone sixties hippie days. On the first sign, he's scrawled GET OUT OF VIETNAM NOW! On the second, it's THE PRESIDENT IS INSANE, and the third one says, KISS THE FISH MOUTH! Only Captain Crazy knows the secret meaning of that one.

A couple of women, three old men, and about seven kids from school are watching the show. Nothing much else to do on a late-May afternoon in Knowles now that school's out. A couple of older girls from my high school—the cupcake twins, I call them, because they're all sugar frosting and no substance—look at ugly Gillis, huge Goth-girl Brianna, and scrappy little sixteen-year-old pit-bull me with these expressions like, "Oh God, there *they* are."

Next to the fish-mouth sign, Mr. White stands with his arms crossed like he's the captain's bodyguard, and I have to admit I'm as bad as the cupcake twins because I can't help thinking, Oh God, there *he* is.

Mr. White. He's even weirder than we are—the long-haired, stick-figure guy from my English class who never says a thing. The new kid in town. Well, actually he's been here a whole year, but in a town where everyone's known you since you were a zygote, you're still the new kid until you've lived here for at least five years.

His real name's Padgett Locke, but we call him Mr. White because he always dresses completely in white. Probably never been in a fight in his life. Today he has on a plain white T-shirt, white shorts, white socks, and white tennis shoes. His skin is almost as white as his clothes. It's like he finally broke out of his room, where he's been cooped up reading books and listening to alternative bands that no one ever heard of, and now he thinks he's at Wimbledon. The only thing not white about him is his long, stringy brown hair and his black-framed glasses. Anyway, I'm not surprised he hooked up with the captain. Maybe he thinks he'll be like an apprentice and take over the job of town eccentric when the captain retires.

Gillis is standing in the front row of the small crowd, grinning like an evil leprechaun. I don't call him a leprechaun because he's short. I mean, he's around my height, five-six, but he's real solid, about as wide as he is tall. No, the leprechaun thing comes from his Irish pug nose and that sparse red wreath of a high-school-boy beard. Not a pretty sight, but he's my buddy, so who cares?

He waves me and Brianna over and goes, "Check this out, Ceejay. The captain's finally lost it all the way down to his socks," and I'm like, "What socks?"

That's the captain for you—ankle-high corduroy pants, ancient ruins for shoes, and no socks. He's a mess. A scraggly sixty-something-year-old reject from a mental ward with a beat-up baseball cap and a beard that doesn't look so much like he grew it as like it exploded out of his face.

To tell the truth, I always liked the captain all right until today. My dad says he's bipolar. My big sister says he's schizo. I say he's probably both, but I don't care if he's a leper. He's a lot more interesting than the rest of the humanoids we have around this town.

I don't know how many times I've stopped off at Corker Park and watched him play his guitar and drum and sing his bizarre songs about Martians, chicken teeth, and blue cockatoos. What else am I going to do, go see the six-month-old Disney movie at the Apollo? Maybe go to the senior center and watch the clog dancers?

For the last couple of years, Captain Crazy has been about the best entertainment we have in Knowles. The story around town is that he moved here from California, probably from some crazy street-person shelter, after his mom, the cat lady, died two years ago and left her farmhouse to him. The place is a dump, hasn't really been a farm for years, but supposedly the captain's brother, Richard, is jealous because he didn't get it.

None of that is the reason why people are fascinated with the captain, though. Supposedly, he used to be semi-famous, had a handful of underground cult records out in the psyche-delic sixties and seventies. "Sliced Penguins," I think, was the name of his big song. It's from his album *Captain Crazy's Crash Landing on Pluto*. Hey, we didn't make the name up. That's what he calls himself. Sometimes he wears a T-shirt with his own picture on the front and the words CAPTAIN CRAZY spelled out in snakes.

Some people think he's not fit to walk our streets, like our streets are paved with platinum Communion wafers or some-thing. Captain Crazy's a menace, they say. Not me. I like people who are different most of the time. That's why I'm so pissed today. I was a supporter, a cheerleader for the cause of crazy. But then he goes and double-crosses me and my family and, most of all, Bobby.

At first, the protest is entertaining—the captain does have a sense of humor about how crazy he is—but things go bad when he picks up the guitar and starts singing about the war. I mean, you can't even call it a song so much as it's just howl-ing to two chords with an occasional whack on the drum for an exclamation point. He's all about tanks and bombs and children running down the street naked, on fire. Grue-some stuff. And then it's white coffins rolling off of air-planes like widgets down a conveyor belt, and soldiers getting their faces blown off or trying to run for cover on bloody stumps. Screaming for medics, and the medics are already dead. And after all that, he howls what I guess is supposed to be the chorus:

Look out for the Nogo Gatu.
They're coming for me, they're coming for you.
Never give in to the Nogo Gatu!

This is too much. I see what he's doing now, and it's not funny. He's not really protesting Vietnam. That's just a cover-up. He's talking about the war in Iraq. If you knew me, you'd know I'm not about to put up with this crap about soldiers getting their faces blown off. I mean, what if Bobby was coming home today instead of next month? What kind of welcome home would that be?

No one could get the better of Bobby here in Knowles, and no one in some small-time foreign country will ever get the better of him either, but crazy or not, the captain's not going to get away with yelling garbage like that at me. That is totally unacceptable. I don't need images like that in my head, with Bobby still out there trying to make it home. It's not like I believe in hexes or anything, but there's no reason to take chances.

And that's not even the worst of it. Next, he starts spewing this trash about how war is the coward's way. The president's a coward, the vice president, the secretary of state, the secretary of war. And okay, I don't really care about that, but then he goes and starts yelping about how anybody who is afraid to turn off their TVs, get off their big, fat couches, and stand up to the warmongers is a coward.

"You are a coward if you don't stand up here with me," he howls, and I swear he's looking straight at me. "You are a coward just like the cowards who didn't say no to Genghis Khan or Attila the Hun or Alexander the Runt or that nasty little tramp Adolf Hitler-Schmitler. Cowards, cowards, one and all!"

A coward! Nobody calls me a coward and gets away with

it. I have never been afraid of anything! Bobby taught me how to kick butt, and he was the best this town's ever seen. And maybe the captain is including Bobby in with the cowards too. Like he should have just run away instead of going to war. It's ridiculous.

I yell at the captain to shut up and that if he doesn't lay that guitar down now, I'm going to wade straight into his business. "Don't be fooled because I'm a girl," I holler. "I've beat on guys bigger than me all my life."

No chance to prove it, though. The cops show up just as I'm getting started. Officer Larry and Officer Dave. After what they did to Bobby back in the day, I hate the sight of these two bastards, but for right now I'm on their side. I'm thinking, Here it comes. Let Captain Crazy get smart-ass with these two mutants, and they won't think twice about pulling their batons.

The captain howls his chorus again, his face red, spit glinting in his beard. "That'll be enough, Carl," says Officer Dave in his matter-of-fact cop voice. The captain's real name is Carl Monroe, and the police have gotten to know him very well since he took over the farmhouse.

"You know the drill," says Officer Larry. "Disturbing the peace."

But the captain keeps singing, so the cops, trading tired expressions, go right to work, Officer Larry taking the captain's right arm and Officer Dave clamping down on the neck of the guitar.

"Show's over," says Officer Dave.

"This is a peaceful protest, man," sputters the captain. "You can't halt a peaceful protest. This is the United States of America."

"You have to have a permit," Officer Larry tells him. "You know that."

"A permit to speak the truth?" The captain's eyes bulge. Actually, they always bulge some, but now they look like they could pop out and go rolling down the courthouse steps. "What are you, storm troopers of the Nogo Gotu?"

"Come on, Carl," says Officer Dave. "No one in this town wants to hear this crap. Either you pack up and go home or we're hauling you in."

The captain just throws back his head and starts in singing again.

Jesus. I could spit on him. But with the captain still wailing, the cops drag him to the squad car and shove him inside. Officer Dave goes back to pick up the drum while stupid Larry gathers the protest signs.

"What are you gonna do to that douche this time?" Gillis shouts to Officer Dave.

"Same as usual, I guess."

"You heard what he was yelling, didn't you?" I say, still really heated.

"I heard."

"Well, you didn't hear the part about soldiers getting their faces blown off. That's bullshit. What if my mom or my little sister had been here?"

He gives me his squinty cop stare. "Go home, Ceejay." Then he looks around at the rest of the crowd. "Everybody go about your business."

"You need to get him out of town," I say. "He shouldn't even be around normal people."

Officer Dave stops right in front of me, the conga drum tucked under his arm. "I'm not gonna tell you again, Ceejay. You don't listen and you're gonna be sitting in that car next to the captain."

I stare back at him, my skin on fire. My brother's been out

there putting his life on the line. The way I figure it, I wouldn't be worth much if I wasn't one hundred percent ready to stand up for him here.

Officer Dave seems to read my mind. Maybe he feels guilty for what he helped do to Bobby after all. His eyes turn sympathetic, and he puts his free hand on my shoulder. "Look, Ceejay, I understand why you're mad. But don't worry, we're gonna take him down to the station. He won't be doing any more protesting. Okay?"

I keep my stare going full blast. "Okay. But I don't even want to see that asshole in town anymore."

The officers return to the squad car, and as they get in, I hear the captain yelling, "Kiss the fish mouth! Kiss the fish mouth!"

The car pulls away, heading for the jailhouse, but I know what will happen, the same sick thing that always happens. The captain's brother will show up at the station and bail him out before dinner.

But this time I'm not going to let him off so easy. I have a plan. Revenge is for the mighty. Time to dust off my armor.

2

If the captain wasn't crazy, I'd just gather my crew, kick his butt, and be done with it. But you know how it is—you can't really go around kicking crazy guys' butts. It isn't sporting. People come to expect certain things of you when you're the little sister of a legend like my brother Bobby. Back in his high school days, he was wild and he was B-A-D-D, *BADD*. People all over the county told stories about him. But he was never a bully. He had ethics. He took up for the weak, and he told me to do the same. It didn't matter that I was a girl, he said. I was the same as him. My big sister isn't, my little sister isn't, and my little brother—he's too young to tell yet how he'll be.

I was never too young, though. I got into my first fight with a boy the summer before third grade. It was on the playground of our elementary school, not long after the Fourth of July. I was still little enough then and had such pretty blond hair—before it turned dingy brown—that you might have thought I still had a chance to turn into a girly-girl one day like my sisters. But I knew different.

Jared Jones and a couple of littler kids were squatting in the dirt behind the backstop. They were mean kids with mean parents. Jared had a string of Black Cat firecrackers—that's the kind of parents he had, letting him run around the neighborhood with his own firecrackers—and he and the others were using them to blow up an anthill.

Did you ever watch ants when you were little? I'm sure you did. I'm sure you sympathized with them like I did. They're so small that a hard wind can pick them up and blow them a million ant-miles away from home, but still they just buckle down to business and make the trek back through mighty forests of grass blades with all sorts of trouble lurking to take them down. And you'll see them with these huge, boulder-like crumbs on their backs, hauling them back to the hill, where all of them are working together, making this pyramid, this colossal wonder of the world, to keep them safe from sand lions and grasshoppers and toads. They're amazing.

And Jared Jones was stuffing Black Cats down the door to their pyramid and blasting it to pieces.

"Yeah!" they all yelled as another firecracker exploded. "Kill those little suckers."

There wasn't any question in my mind what I had to do. I walked right up to those boys and slapped Jared hard across the back of his fat head and told him to stop it if he didn't want to end up eating a handful of dirt.

He rose up with this look in his eyes like he was ready for

World War III, but when he saw me, the fierceness pulled up short. "You're lucky you're a girl," he said. "I'd feed you one of these Black Cats if you weren't."

I just stared him down and said, "You're gonna stop blowing up those ants." It wasn't a question.

"I doubt that," he said.

I put out my hand. "Give me those firecrackers."

"Why don't you stick one up her butt," said one of his buddies.

I left my hand where it was.

"What are you gonna do?" Jared asked, sizing me up. "Go tell your big brother on us?"

"I don't need to tell my brother," I said, and before I even finished, I whipped my hand over and grabbed the string of firecrackers away.

Of course, he wanted them back, said he'd forget I was a girl if I didn't hand them over. I didn't say anything. I just turned around and started to walk away. I knew what would happen, though. I'd seen the same situation with Bobby. He had some words with this guy Ally Taylor, and just when Bobby turned around to leave peacefully, Ally rushed him from behind. I learned something important from Bobby that day. Movie fighting is crap. You don't need spinning kicks and fancy karate fists of fury. You just need to get the other guy on the ground as quick as possible and don't let him up till he knows he's beat.

So I did just what I saw Bobby do. As soon as I sensed Jared coming at me from behind, I whirled around low, under any punches that might be coming, and tackled him at the waist. In the next second, he was on the ground and I was sitting on his chest, slapping his face. His friends just laughed.

Fat tears boiled out of Jared's eyes, and as much as I despised him, I couldn't help but feel sorry for him. Beat up by a girl. His friends would spread the word around like a bad case of the bird flu. But I guarantee you, they didn't want any piece of me either.

After that, I wasn't just the badass's little sister anymore. I was a badass in my own right. That's a lot different from a bully. Bullies start things. Badasses finish them. And as the baddest girl in Knowles, there are certain things I'm bound to do.

Dealing with Captain Crazy is one of them. He started something, and I'm going to finish it.

3

It's me and my two main boys, Gillis Kilmer and Tillman Grant. Gillis and I grew up two houses apart. Tillman joined up with us as soon as we hit first grade. Whereas Gillis is stocky and hard, Tillman's tall and lean and twice as hard. Black-haired, brown-eyed, dark-skinned. He looks Italian, but he's not. From that Adam's apple of his, you'd think he got a hand grenade stuck in his throat. He's the kind of kid who never has you over to his house and doesn't hang around there much himself if he can help it. It's a dump. His dad's long gone, and his mom's kind of a tramp. Tillman would probably be in reform school by now if it wasn't for us. Who knows, our whole group may still make it. I'd probably fit in better there than in this town anyway.

I don't ask my girl Brianna along. She's too big and clumsy, and for someone who tries hard to look scary, she gets too nervous to drag along on a mission like this. Anyway, she's the worst paintballer in town.

That's the plan—to wreak paintball devastation all over Casa Crazy. Gillis is an okay paintballer, but Tillman and I are heroes. Not that we have an official paintball field in Knowles, but that's all right. It's probably better in the woods anyway. We play a couple of times a month with two teams of five. Our team is me, Gillis, Tillman, Brianna, and either Charles Lyman or Kelli Sundy, depending on what day it is. Tillman keeps trying to get me to kick Brianna off our team because she always gets tagged in about thirty seconds, but I say no way. She's a friend and we're sticking. Besides, I'm good enough for two people.

At dusk, all decked out in our camo, we load our gear into Gillis's car and head off on our mission. On the way to the edge of town, I lay down the strategy. We already know the basic lay-out of Captain Crazy's place, a crumbly old ex-farmhouse on the outskirts of town. Just about everybody within fifty miles stops by there now and then so they can look at the sculptures the captain makes out of junk—the fat boy, the giant robot, the two-headed lady, the twenty-foot-tall winged giraffe, all constructed of old tires, washers and dryers, car fenders, rusted farm equipment, aluminum guardrails, paint cans, and warped shingles. They're not bad for something made by a lunatic.

"First," I explain, "we'll park in the woods on the other side of the captain's place, about a hundred yards away. Then we'll split up and each take a different line of attack. Wait till I give a whistle, then we'll come screaming in from three sides."

"We gonna light this dude up?" asks Tillman, grinning maliciously.

"No," I tell him. "No body shots, just property. Hit the house hard. And that old lime-green pickup."

"How about the sculptures?" asks Gillis.

"Hit as many of them as you can."

"Hell, Ceejay," says Tillman. "We need to put some bruises on this dude. What good's marking his property gonna do? He'll just wash that off."

I'm like, "That's the point. While he's washing up, he'll have plenty of time to think about things."

Once we get parked in the woods, we pull out our rifles and helmets and put on our fingerless gloves. Since real Spider rifles are too expensive, we have semiautomatic Spider clones with ported barrels for quieter firing. You might think we wouldn't really need the helmets since we're not shooting at each other, but they're important for getting into the warrior spirit.

Gillis heads for the right flank, and Tillman takes the left. Me, I want to come roaring straight down the middle of the yard, just like Bobby would do if he was here. The sky is mostly dark by now, but the stars are coming out and the moon hangs over the trees. It's eerie. I've never looked at the captain's sculptures at night, but as I sneak up to the far edge of his yard, they seem like dark, intergalactic demons standing guard.

Off to the right, something crashes in the brush and then Gillis lets out a *goddamn*. I freeze. Stupid Gillis, tripping around and making noise. He's sure to give us away. Silence is key. We need to get a lot closer before letting the hellhounds loose.

I study the dark windows, checking for any sign of movement, but everything remains still. Lucky for Gillis. I'll blast him in the butt if he screws up this mission.

The captain's weathered old lime-green truck sits about thirty yards from his front porch. I crouch behind it and check my rifle to make sure it's ready to shoot. Captain Crazy deserves our fiery wrath. I have no doubt of that. He sinned against us.

And really, we're doing it for Bobby, who's halfway around the world and can't do it for himself. Still, I hesitate. I can't help wondering if maybe I should try to talk to the captain first. Isn't that what Bobby would do?

But I'm here. And Gillis and Tillman are out in the woods waiting, expecting things from me. I can't cut and run.

The dark shapes of the sculptures gaze down on me, giving off this feeling like the captain is judging me through them. I stare back hard, determined, and the captain's song bursts back into my brain—*War is the coward's way.* Well, my brother's no coward and neither am I.

I'm right to be here, I tell myself. It's too late for doubts. Like I said, Revenge is for the mighty.

I whistle the attack signal as loud as I can.

Gillis and Tillman charge from the woods, and I dart out from behind the truck, firing one ball after another, splattering the fat boy and the robot, the front of the house, and the porch steps. Globs of orange paint blossom everywhere, like mutant peaches. We're all laughing, but at the same time, ready to run into the sanctuary of the woods if Captain Crazy tries to chase us.

Then the lights in his house flick on.

Expecting the door to fly open, I half turn toward the tree line, but nothing happens. Inside the house, a dog barks like wild, but everything else is as still as a tombstone. None of us fire another shot. Something's up. We can feel it—some kind of Captain Crazy weirdness.

Suddenly a voice rises up over the dog's bark, a long, ripping cry, so loud and metallic it must have come through a bullhorn. "Yaaaahhhhhhh!"

"Holy crap," says Gillis.

Then the bullhorn voice goes, "Stop in the name of the

17

nine prophets of the Yimmies. You are surrounded by titanium angels. There is no escape."

I look at the silhouettes of Gillis and Tillman.

"I'm gone," says Tillman, and just that fast his silhouette tears for the trees.

"I'm behind you," says Gillis, and there he goes too.

Me, I'm not backing down so easy. Besides, I haven't achieved my main goal yet—to smack a big orange splotch dead in the middle of the front door. I raise my rifle to take aim when the bullhorn screeches again.

"Search yourself for your inner heaven or end up stuck in limbo!"

This is weird. Now the voice is coming from a new place, somewhere near the fat boy, just behind it, maybe. I can't figure out how he could have got there so quick.

I fire my last shot, but I don't know whether I hit the door because I'm too startled by that weird voice crying out again, a long wail like something dead and come back, and this time it sounds even closer. Fast as I can, I sprint to the lime-green truck and crouch by one of the tires. Footsteps crunch in the gravel close by, and the dog's bark starts up again, only he's not in the house anymore. I can't tell exactly where he is, maybe behind me. Maybe the captain is closing in from one side and his dog's coming from the other. They're tricky, but I'm trickier. I slide under the truck, where nobody can see me from either side.

For a long time, the place is quiet. Then I hear the soft trot of the dog's feet, probably about ten yards away. He circles the truck once and stops. I know he's sure to smell me, but I don't know which side of the truck I should scramble out from without running into the captain.

The dog begins to growl, the kind of low growl that starts

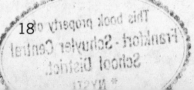

way back in the throat and gets louder as it rumbles forward. The next thing I know, he's at the side of the truck, his muzzle thrusting in next to one of the tires, the growls busting into full barks. He paws at the dirt and snaps in my direction. From what I can tell, he's not too big to crawl right under here with me and have my face for dinner.

There's nothing to do except explode out from the other side of the truck and make a run for the trees, hoping the captain won't see me. The dog squeezes his head and shoulders under the truck as I roll out the other side. I hop up and run, dodge around the winged giraffe, and smack hard into Captain Crazy's chest.

He grips the bullhorn in one hand and, with the other, he grabs hold of my arm. I've never stared into his eyes this close before. It's like five hundred years of the world's insanity staring back at me.

"Let go of me," I demand, trying to wrench my arm away.

His grip only squeezes tighter, and he sticks his face so close to mine I can smell the unexpected scent of his breath—Cocoa Puffs.

Looking hard through my paintball goggles and into my eyes, he goes, "You are not who you think you are."

That's all: "You are not who you think you are."

Then he smiles.

He lets go of my arm, and for a moment I just stand there staring at him like I'm hypnotized. Then my brain kicks into gear, and I take off across the yard and into the woods, dodging around trees, jumping over shrubs, never looking back. The dog's barks are far behind me. No one can catch me now.

But all the way to the car those words keep banging around in my head. *You are not who you think you are, you are not who you think you are, you are not who you think you are.*

Gillis and Tillman are lucky they had the sense to wait for me with the car. They'd have a lot to answer for if they left me stranded in the forest of craziness. Driving home, we laugh and replay the invasion, and talk about how much scrubbing the captain will have to do tomorrow. We don't worry about him calling the police. They aren't likely to pay attention to him if he does. Still, even when I get home, I can't help but think about how he looked at me and what he said. *You are not who you think you are.*

How does he know who I am? He doesn't even know who he is.

4

The thing is, growing up, I was always one hundred percent sure of who I was—Bobby McDermott's little sister. That was a great thing to be. It didn't matter that he was six years older. We were tight. He was the one who started calling me Ceejay way back when I was only two years old. He knew Catherine Jameson was no name for a warrior girl. The two of us just laughed at how corny and goofy our parents were, but we had each other, so it was fun. It was like we were both changelings, brought up in the wrong family together.

You should see my mom. She's so bubbly, it's like her cork could pop any second. And she's always that way—upbeat and perky as the "Happy Birthday" song. I don't understand it. How great can life be when you're a bookkeeper at a body shop? The biggest things that ever happen to her are church and a trip to the hairdresser. But even when Bobby had to go into the army, she acted like it would be great for him, like God was dripping golden blessings on us instead of dumping a truckload of crap on our heads.

Now her mom, Grandma Brinker, is sick—cancer—but Mom swears it's not serious. That's right—cancer. Not serious. Weekends, she's been making the hour-and-a-half drive to Davenport to help Grandma take care of her house, and every time she comes back, she's all positive and glowing. "They got it in time," she says. "Just a few more treatments and she'll be back to her old self. We'll all go over for a visit then." That's Mom. She can even find the silver lining in cancer.

My dad's not much different. He's just the male version, grinning like *hearty* is his middle name, slapping people on the back, calling them *bud*, shaking hands with his hand-of-steel death grip. And the jokes. If he ever comes up to you and says, "Have you heard the one about . . . ," run the other way as fast as you can. They're the lamest. To hear my uncles' stories, Dad used to be a pretty big badass himself back in the day, but now he's just a jolly, fat tire-plant foreman who gets all sentimental over hokey songs and Christmas movies.

My big sister's a replica of Mom. In fact, since she's eight years older than me, she seems more like an aunt than a sister. My little sister's a stuck-up priss, and my little brother's a captain second grade in Halo, so I've barely seen him since he got the Xbox. I don't even know how we ended up with so many kids in our family. Can you imagine my parents having sex? *Errrrg.* All I can figure is that every once in a while, during sleep, my dad accidentally rolls over on my mom, and presto, nine months later, there's a new baby squalling around the house. It's ridiculous. Why would you want to bring a bunch of kids into this messed-up world? I mean, wake up! Bobby's in the war, for God's sake. He's in the frigging war! And it's all my parents' fault.

Some of the idiots at school say they could see trouble coming for Bobby a mile away, but that's just because they don't know the difference between *bad* and *BADD*. The first one is small and mean. The second one is vast, like a wild continent. That's Bobby. Sure, he did crazy things, but he never hurt anyone that didn't deserve it. Well, except maybe himself.

When he was ten, he rode his bicycle off a park-pavilion roof and broke his arm. We still have the pictures of him with his arm in that cast, a big smile on his face like he's showing off the Congressional Medal of Honor. In junior high, he jumped out of a second-story window at school, just sailed out like Superman because someone told him he couldn't. He held the record for climbing the highest on one of those high-voltage towers in the alfalfa field off Highway 9, and once, on his motorcycle, he held a wheelie the entire length of Marshall Drive, around the curves and through the intersections. He was wild but always in a fun way.

Then, when he was just out of high school, he went a little too far. He stole a car, not to keep for himself or to profit from in any way, but just to cruise in, to be a free man in at four o'clock in the morning while his motorcycle was in the shop. No doubt he would've brought it back, too, parked it just where he found it, but this time his famous luck let him down.

The cops spotted him speeding down Gunderson Road on the outside of town and took after him with red lights flashing. Of course, Bobby being Bobby, he gunned it and would've lost them, too, if it hadn't been for that sharp curve and the bald tires on that stolen Ford. Instead, the rear end got away from him, and he ended up plowing through a fence and straight into the water hazard on the seventh hole of Knowles' shaggy little nine-hole golf course.

He didn't even try to run anymore—he just stood there in the knee-deep water with his hands over his head, ready to surrender. Still, Officer Dave and Officer Larry made him lie facedown in the rough and handcuffed his wrists behind his back. "Your joy-riding days are over, Bobby," they told him. And then they found that baggie of weed in his pocket.

Things get a little murky from there. I don't pretend to know a whole lot about how the law and the government and all that work, but the deal they gave Bobby had a real bad smell about it. The lawyers and the judge, the cops, and the guy whose car Bobby stole got together with my parents and chiseled out this deal that allowed for a choice between jail and joining the army.

I'm not going to lie and say Bobby hadn't become pretty well acquainted with the police in our town over the years, but he never got in any serious-serious trouble. Wouldn't you think they'd just give him probation? Of course, I didn't want to see him go to jail, but sending an eighteen-year-old just out of high school into a war for having a little bit too much fun doesn't seem nearly fair. In fact, I have to wonder if it's even legal.

That's what happened, though. My parents didn't even fight for him—just the opposite. Talk about cowardly. I didn't know if I'd ever be able to forgive them for that. They even tried to act like the army was going to be the greatest thing in the world for Bobby. Sure, the military would straighten him right out. First time he came home in uniform, my dad was so proud, you'd have thought Bobby was a five-star general. Of course, the war had only just got started then. Dad told me they wouldn't need that many soldiers over there. Bobby probably wouldn't even have to leave the States. There would just be one big raid. *Bam!* Saddam would go down and that would be it. Mission accomplished.

But it didn't happen that way. More and more soldiers had to go. And they didn't come back like they were supposed to. The president kept sending them in again and again and again. And every time, I got madder and madder at my parents and at this whole stupid town with its so-called upright citizens—the lawyers and the judge—who took Bobby away and stranded me here, the only real human being left in this Martian town.

But now I've got a plan. When Bobby gets back, we'll move in together, maybe get one of those rent houses on the south side of town. He'll get a job and I'll finish high school. Then I'll get a job too, and we'll save our money until we have enough to shake this town right off our backs.

I haven't told Bobby the plan yet, and all this waiting is wearing on my nerves. Wishing and hoping for too long can take a heavy toll. So, a couple days after the battle of Casa Crazy, when I get a glimpse of someone who looks a whole lot like Bobby, I have to wonder if I can trust my own eyes.

5

I'm at Corker Park with Brianna, sitting on a picnic table eating a snow cone, and on the street just to the east, Sophie Lowell rolls by in her red Toyota—Sophie's sister Mona and Bobby were real hot and heavy before he went into the army—and I swear, someone who looks just like him is riding in Sophie's passenger seat, wearing a red baseball cap and tipping a beer. I try to get Brianna to load up in her car and chase them, but she just tells me I'm imagining things.

"But it looked just like him," I tell her.

"No," she says, "you just want him back so bad, you think it looks like him."

Maybe she's right. Later, I tell my parents about it, and they laugh and say there's no way Bobby can be back yet. The army does things on a tight schedule, my dad says. My mom pats my cheek and tells me to be patient. "Besides," she says, "he would've called if he was coming home early."

They both grin ridiculously at me like I'm just their foolish girl and there's nothing easier than being patient about Bobby still being stuck out there in the bomb-infested world. But they must be right. It's probably just wishful thinking. If Bobby was back, he'd come straight to me before anything else. Still, I can't quit replaying, over and over, the memory of that car driving by. And each time I picture it, the passenger looks more like Bobby.

Saturday night, Tillman's sister Dani is having a party at her place, and the word is Sophie Lowell is supposed to be there. Nothing good ever happens at Dani's, but Tillman, Gillis, and Brianna are hot to party, and me, I don't care if people think I'm crazy—I'm determined to have a talk with Sophie about who she's been driving around with lately.

Besides, I have to admit it—I have a thing for Tillman Grant. I never told anybody but my girl Brianna, and she said I should let it go. But what can you do? Your heart's like a little kid. You can tell it to keep its hands to itself, but still it keeps reaching out for what it wants. That's how it is with Tillman—my heart won't stop reaching for him. It drives me crazy, those parts of myself I can't control.

Brianna says I'm being ridiculous—you can't fall in love at six years old—but I swear the first time I saw Tillman in Mrs. Gray's first-grade class, my stomach did a backflip. It didn't matter how big his Adam's apple was or that he was a little bit dense—he was dark and brown-eyed and hard-muscled as a Doberman pinscher. No one in our grade could take him in a fight. And tough as he was, something about his eyes made you want to take care of him, made you want to lean your head against his, stroke his hair, and say, "Everything's going to be all right, Tillman Grant."

Besides a lot of wrestling in the grass, nothing ever happened with Tillman till fourth grade. I couldn't help myself. We were stuck together in the classroom during recess—the teacher sentenced us to hard time because she overheard us cussing—and we started to get rambunctious as usual. I chased Tillman around and around the room, both of us jumping from one desk to the next, and finally one of the desks toppled over and he crashed to the floor. In the next second, I straddled his hips and without thinking at all, I leaned down and smacked a big, wet kiss right on his mouth.

This is the part I'll probably never forget till the end of recorded time—he reached up and wiped his mouth with the back of his hand. "Damn you, Ceejay," he said, all disgusted. "I don't want your ugly frogmouth on me."

That's what he said! It's not enough that I'm what I guess some people would say is a little stocky—just a little—but now I've got a frogmouth!

I know a lot of girls would've burst into tears at that, but not me. No. I punched him right in the eye and then rose up and sat at the back of the class with my arms folded across my chest. Didn't talk to him for the rest of the week.

But the bad thing is, still to this day, I'll look in the mirror at my mouth and see he was right. My mouth is too wide and my lips are too thin, just like an ugly frog. I try sucking in my cheeks and it works for a moment—I actually look almost pretty—but you can't hold them in forever. Lipstick doesn't help either. I'm a frogface, and kissing Tillman didn't turn me into any princess.

Anyway, his sister Dani lives in a trailer home south of town with her two-year-old boy, Ian, and whatever stupid boyfriend she's hooked up with at the time. Right now it just happens to be a weed dealer named Jace. Most of the people who hang out over there are the typical Knowles late-teens, early-twenties losers, and this night is no different. You know the type—they probably dropped out of high school and can't keep steady jobs. Most of them I see around town all the time, but there are also some out-of-towners who came in to buy weed and whatever else Jace has to sell. They're not the best types to hang around, but I'll take them over the goodie-goodies of this town any day.

When we get to Dani's, everyone is packed into the living room and kitchen, drinking beer and smoking weed. Plus, some idiot brought some OxyContin, which is like this extra-high-strength prescription painkiller, so half the gang gets to walking and talking like they just stepped out of a bad dream. Don't worry, I stay away from that kind of thing—I don't even like smoking weed—but Gillis, Tillman, and Brianna get a little more messed up than what they're used to. I'd drag them out of there, but Sophie still hasn't shown up.

At one point, Dani has little Ian asleep on the floor between a couple of chairs and Gillis accidentally steps on his head. Ian barely lets out a whimper, but Jace gets all pissed off and righteous and threatens to kick Gillis's ass. Like stepping on the kid's head is somehow so much worse than having him lying around in the middle of a cloud of cigarette and weed smoke. Nothing comes of the threat, though. As soon as Jace starts to get up, he loses his balance and falls back over his metal folding chair and lies there laughing so hard he forgets about Gillis completely.

Having had only a couple of beers, I see all this as very pathetic, but not as pathetic as what Brianna and Tillman get up to later. Brianna is a big girl, and I don't mean stocky like me. She's B-I-G. So she dyes her hair black, wears a nose ring and black, baggy clothes and black fingernail polish. You just have to know that's not the look her parents had in mind when they gazed down into the crib at their little pink baby and thought of a sweet name like Brianna. Me, I never went in for that look myself because it seems so obvious that you're trying to make people think you don't care about not being pretty. But whatever helps Brianna make it through the day is all right with me.

Still, there's nothing she wants more than a boyfriend, but this guy who starts hitting on her at the party is not what she needs. Not at all. For one thing, he must be thirty years old, and for another, he has this pockmarked, smooshed-in face that makes him look like a bank robber with panty hose over his head. To top it off, he's all proud about how he just came back from a year in jail for possession with intent.

None of that matters to Brianna, though. She's standing next to him at the kitchen counter, giggling and playing touchy-touchy and trading hits off a blunt. I try to get her to come outside so I can talk some sense into her, but she pushes me away and goes, "Just because Tillman's found himself a slut, don't start trying to ruin my time."

I don't know what hurts more—that Tillman really is hitting on some tramp or that Brianna went out of her way to say the meanest thing she could to me.

It's a fact, though. Tillman's latched on one of the out-of-towners. She looks like she's thirty too, but she's probably really only about twenty-four. She's just lived hard. Has a skeleton figure and gray teeth that you'd swear could fall out on the orange carpet any second. An absolute skank. It wouldn't surprise me if she worked part-time hooking at the truck stop by the interstate.

This is what I can't understand. What attracts a guy to one girl and not another? Why does he fumble around with someone he knows doesn't have any staying power when there's someone else right across the room who's mooned over him practically her whole life? No way is this girl even better-looking than me. Sure, she's thin, but as far as I'm concerned she's downright ugly, and I don't mean just physically. She has an ugly spirit too. You can see it in the droop of her eyelids and the slant of her mouth. Still, there Tillman is brushing her hair back and kissing her neck like she's the love of his life while his beer sloshes down his pants leg.

I go to the kitchen, get a beer, and stand there staring at this stupid wall hanging with all these corny sayings about how to be happy on it:

Dance in the moonlight

Blow on a dandelion

Kiss a kitten

Play with a baby

Bite the bottom out of an ice cream cone

Run in the purple clover

Say I love you

Not a single word anywhere about taking a handful of OxyContin and hitting the bong.

"Hey, Ceejay." It's Jace. He has a look on his face like he just came out of a coma. "What's going on?"

"Nothing. Just admiring the artwork."

He grins at me and narrows his eyes. He thinks he's a cocksman. "You know, there's something about you. You ever think about maybe wearing some makeup?"

"Why? Do you think I'm a clown or something?"

"What?" He's too much of a moron to get the joke.

"Nothing," I say. "I heard Sophie Lowell was supposed to be here."

"Sophie Lowell's a pain in the ass." He takes a drink of beer. "So, Dani tells me your brother's in Iraq."

"He was. He'll be coming home pretty soon."

He leans against the counter and runs his hand through his mop of thick brown hair. "Yeah," he said, "I thought about joining the marines, shipping over, and kicking some hajji ass."

"So why didn't you, then?"

"I don't like taking orders. I still might go over there, though. Recruit some of my buddies, get us some assault rifles, and do our own private commando deal. Shit, we'd take Baghdad in a day."

"I don't think they allow private commandos over there unless they're part of some big corporation."

"Hey, I'm not gonna ask for permission."

"Well, but I think the military would probably stop you before you got there."

"Screw the military. Bunch of meatheads. We'd have us a special chopper with rockets on it, machine guns. Black as metal-flake death. No one could stop us."

"So, what? You're gonna fight our military too?"

"We'll fight anyone who gets in our way."

I just shake my head. It's too stupid to even get offended by. "I gotta go," I say, and squeeze past him.

"Where you headed?"

32

"Outside. I feel a little sick to my stomach."

"Take a drag on the bong. That's the best thing for a sick stomach."

I don't even bother to respond to that. The whole party is too much for me—the drunk talk, the smoke, the baby on the floor, and especially Tillman's lips on that ugly girl's neck. But what did I expect? That he would get drunk and declare his undying love for me? Superpathetic.

If I had my own car, I'd hit the road, take a cruise in the country, but I don't, so I go out and sit in Gillis's, stare at the silhouettes moving across the closed curtains of the double-wide, and wait to see if Sophie will show up.

About five minutes later, the front door swings open and here comes Gillis walking across the yard to the car, his body leaning slightly to the side like someone walking in a high wind. Messed up again.

"What are you doing out here?" he asks, plopping down on the seat next to me. "The party's inside."

"I'm having my own party."

"Looks pretty boring." He puts his hand on my thigh. "But it doesn't have to be." He doesn't even look me in the eye. He just stares at my boobs, this goofy, loose-lipped, drunk smile scrawled on his face.

I yank his hand away and tell him to quit thinking with his penis because it's even stupider than he is. It's not like I'm surprised, though. Ever since about sixth grade, Gillis has had these periodic attacks of the raging hornies. If you're a girl—any girl—you don't want to be anywhere in the vicinity when it happens. It's not so great if you're a guy either because at the end of the evening, after all the girls have shut him down, he goes looking for a fight. How about that for gay?

"Come on, Ceejay." This time he puts his hand on my shoulder and looks me in the eyes. He almost seems tender for a change. "What are you holding out for? It's not natural."

I'm like, "How many times do I have to kick your butt before you learn it's never going to happen with us?"

"Hey, you gotta get some experience sometime. You might as well get it with someone you can trust."

"Trust to do what? Run the other direction if I get knocked up?"

"You're not gonna get knocked up. We'll be careful."

"Famous last words."

His hand slinks down toward my breast. I swat it away, and he moves it back to the headrest behind me. "We can just do oral if you want. That's not even really having sex."

"That's what you say. I say it's sex as soon as Mr. Trouser Snake takes the stage."

"Look." His hand slides down to the back of my neck. "It won't even be like it's me and you doing it. It'll be like two different people."

"How do you figure that?"

He leans forward like he's going to kiss me, but stops short. "Because I'll be pretending you're somebody else."

I have to laugh. "That makes me feel real romantic, asshole."

"Damn, Ceejay, is that what you're waiting for? Romance? Don't be stupid. You think any guy's going to go around buying roses and lighting candles for a girl like you? Forget it. I'm just trying to do you a favor so you don't have to go through life not knowing what sex feels like."

Oh my God—don't you know I slap the shit out of him then? And I don't hold back either. But it doesn't faze him for a second. Instead, he takes it for some kind of weird invitation to pounce on top of me and squeeze his hand between my thighs. It's superpathetic. The boy needs to be on some kind of medication—anti-Viagra. I could almost feel sorry for him, but I'm too pissed, so I haul off and head butt him as hard as I can. I mean, *wham!*

The secret to a good head butt is to drive the hard part of the top of your forehead right into the fleshy part of the guy's eyebrow. Not only will it daze him, but you're likely to draw a decent amount of blood, nothing serious, but enough to put a scare into him. And I'll tell you this—the head butt I put on Gillis is as good as it gets.

He rolls off onto the floorboard, and I'm out of the car before he can grab me again. I only look back once. Blood's trickling down beside his eye as he leans out of the car, propping himself up with one hand on the ground. "Goddamn you, Ceejay," he whines. "Goddamn you. You gave me a damn brain clot."

I just keep walking. "Shit," Gillis wails behind me. "Jesus Christ!" But I don't slow down.

About a half mile down the shoulder of the highway, I start to rethink my choice. Sure, someone I know is bound to drive by, either leaving the party or going to it—maybe Sophie will even stop for me—but at the same time, you never know what kind of creep might be loose on these little country highways—a serial killer, a rapist, the police. Too late, though. A pair of headlights pulls up behind me. They're so bright I can't even tell what kind of car they belong to. One thing for sure—if it is a serial killer, he'd better be ready for a fight.

6

The car turns out to be an ancient Volkswagen. The window rolls down and a voice calls, "Hey, do you want a ride or something?"

Suspiciously, I walk over, and what do you know?—it's Mr. White sitting behind the steering wheel. "What happened?" he asks. "Car break down?"

"Not exactly. Are you heading back to town?"

"Yeah," he says. "Hop in."

Mr. White's definitely not the rapist type, but he's strange enough you can't completely rule out serial killer. So what, though? I really need a ride, and if I can't handle myself against Mr. White, I deserve to end up sliced and diced and stacked up in his basement freezer. Besides, the mood I'm in, I don't really care what happens to me.

"So, what are you doing walking down the highway at night?" he asks as I slide into the hard seat next to him. But he doesn't ask the question like I must be some kind of moron. His voice is deep and mellow, which makes him sound confident and friendly at the same time. It's strange because it's so normal, yet it comes out of this guy who looks anything but normal. At least for around Knowles.

As we pull away, I explain how I got sick of the party with all the wasted people acting like idiots. No use in going into Gillis's antics or mentioning Tillman kissing a meth freak's neck. I'd just as soon forget all that.

"So why do you go to parties like that?"

"Hey, you have to do something around here if you don't want to get bored to death."

"I never get bored," he says. "I create my own realities without having to get wasted."

Creates his own realities? Who talks like that? Besides, it's not an easy idea to swallow coming from a guy who probably had to sit by himself in the cafeteria through the whole last year at school. I mean, if he created his own reality, you'd think he'd throw some friends besides Captain Crazy in there. But it's not worth arguing about.

"So," I say, "why do you always wear white? Is that part of your *reality?*"

He glances down at his T-shirt, then at me. "Actually it is," he says. "It's a statement. White is the opposite of black. Black is despair, so white's about hope. And when you make a statement like that, you can set a new reality in motion."

"You sound like a New Age hippie or something," I tell him, but he says I couldn't be further from the truth.

"In a way, I'm *Old Age*. Like about seven hundred years old."

"Are you reincarnated or something?"

37

He laughs. "You're hilarious," he says. "I like you. But no, I'm not reincarnated. I don't believe in that. It's just that I'm real into the Renaissance period. That's when things were really happening, huge things. People just like me and you changed the world in this gigantic, positive way."

But I'm not exactly in a positive mood right now because I'm like, "Really? Isn't that when Romeo and Juliet were hanging out? Look what happened to them."

He laughs again. It's a good laugh, not in any way at my expense, which is lucky for him. "I know what you're thinking," he says. "Suicide's kind of a downer. I liked your take on Romeo and Juliet in English class. That's how I knew you were cool, when you were all like, 'Juliet was stupid to off herself just because Romeo was dead. A girl doesn't need a guy to make her life worth living.' That was awesome."

How do you like that? The guy's been keeping tabs on me. That could be flattering or creepy. I decide to go for flattering for the time being. After all, looking at him more closely, I have to admit he's not exactly ugly. Sure, he's skinny with a long face, but he has good cheekbones and a strong nose. Not that I'm considering him for boyfriend material. After the way this night's gone, I figure I should just forget about that for the next decade or so.

"Well," I say, "I don't think too many other guys thought it was so awesome."

"The other guys are idiots," he says. "But you have to admit, Shakespeare changed the world. People are still reading him all over the place."

"So what are you going to do, change the world by wearing white and writing plays that bore high school kids out of their skulls? I really don't see anyone changing the world from a nothing town like Knowles."

He looks at me, then back at the road. "You make it sound like trying to change the world is unrealistic or something, but hey, it's better than not doing anything. Anyway, this town's just a speed bump on my way to where I'm going. I'm still trying to figure out exactly what I'm going to do, but one thing I know for sure is I'm going to get out of this town to do it."

Now that sounds more like it. I can get behind anyone who wants to blow off this dump town. My friends don't even bother thinking about their futures. Tillman and Gillis would be happy ending up like the rest of the losers at Dani's party.

I ask Mr. White where he plans on going when he gets out of here, and he's like, "There's only one place to go—New York City. That's where you have to go to get your ideas heard. Besides, it's hard to be a misfit there because that's where all the misfits flock to. Like ninety-eight percent of the population is made up of misfits. Maybe that's what I'll do. I'll start a misfit revolution."

A misfit revolution! Now that's an idea. Suddenly I forget about the crappy night I've been having. If there was ever anyone cut out for a revolution, it's me. "Well," I say, "you'll probably need a general if you're going to get anywhere. I mean, every revolution needs a general."

He looks at me, his gaze burning through his glasses. "You talking about yourself?"

"Why not? I'm as good a misfit as you. Besides, this town hasn't done me any favors. New York would be as good a place as any to go."

"Okay," he says. "You're hired."

From there, we start talking about what we'll do when we get to New York, how we'll hang out at cool coffee shops and see weird new bands in concert, and everywhere we go we'll round up converts for the misfit revolution. It's fun. I mean, I know we're just talking crap, but still, I'm starting to feel like it's really possible. As if I've got one foot out of town and away from my parents. For a while, I even forget Mr. White is buddies with the captain.

He's getting excited about the whole thing too, slapping the steering wheel with every new idea, his long hair dancing around his face. We talk about having misfit marches through New York City, thousands of misfits strong. Misfit festivals in Central Park. A misfit political party. A misfit president. Then we'll go international with it too.

I'm like, "We'll get my brother Bobby to go. If anyone can help us get it done, it's him. There's nothing he can't do." Of course, when Bobby gets back, I won't need any misfit revolution because I won't be a misfit with him around, but it's fun to think about us heading to New York together anyway.

Then Mr. White has to go and ruin the fantasy. "And we'll take Captain Crazy," he says. "He'll be like our grand spiritual advisor."

He looks at me, smiling as if he just came up with the best idea yet, but I'm like, "No way. I'm not getting in any revolution with that idiot."

His smile fractures. "Wait a minute. I know you got mad at the captain for talking out against the war, but if you really listen to what he has to say, you can't deny he's telling the truth."

"The truth! He was basically calling me and my brother—who fought in the war, by the way—cowards. If you think that's the truth, then you're as big an idiot as he is."

"He's not against your brother. He just happens to think the best way to support the troops is to get them home as soon as possible. The captain's on your brother's side a whole lot more than a bunch of phony patriots who don't know what they're talking about."

"Bullshit. I heard him. And on top of that, I was out at his place the other night, and you know what he told me? He told me I don't even know who I am. Me, he said that to. I guarantee you I know who I am better than anyone else in this town."

"So," Mr. White says. "It was you and your gang that paintballed his house."

"First of all, I don't have a *gang*, and second of all, I never said anything about paintballing anything. I just said I was out there."

"Right," Mr. White says, sarcastically. "Here's how much you know. That paint didn't hurt the captain at all. When I saw it, I told him I'd help him scrub it off, but he didn't want to. He thinks it's beautiful. And he's right—it is. He's also right about something else—you don't have the least idea who you really are."

Really! That's what he tells me! Just like that. And I thought he was going to be okay there for a little while. But I don't need some scraggly stick figure telling me I don't know who I am any more than I need to hear it from a crazoid hobo.

"You don't know the least thing about me," I say. "And you never will."

He starts trying to explain himself, but I'm like, "Turn left at the next stoplight, go down two blocks, make another left, and then I'll tell you where to go from there to my house."

That's pretty much it for the conversation. He asks me what I'm getting so bent out of shape about, but I just turn away and look out the side window until we get to my house.

"You won't stay mad at me," he says as I get out of the car. "Just wait and see."

"I'm not mad at you," I tell him. But, of course, I am. Doesn't matter. There's only one guy I need in my life right now, and that's Bobby.

7

Sunday afternoon the whacked-out drama that is my life continues. I'm in my room talking to Brianna on the phone. I'm hoping she might have some news about Sophie Lowell, but it turns out Brianna ditched the party not long after I did. Seems the smoosh-faced idiot who was hitting on her took off with another girl, an out-of-town skank who said she knew where to get some magic mushrooms. Poor Brianna. The only thing that halfway cheered her up was getting a look at the dent I put in Gillis's eyebrow before she left.

"Maybe you should talk to him about Sophie," she says. "He was still there when I left."

And I'm like, "Are you kidding? I wouldn't talk to him if he was the last leprechaun on earth."

Then, just as I get off the phone, my annoying little sister, Lacy, barges into my room with one of her stupid fashion catalogs, wanting to show me the latest cute sandals she has her eye on. She's such a wimpy girlie-girl. I'm like, "I don't want to see any of your prissy little sandals."

And she goes, "You just don't like sandals because you have beefy feet."

Beefy feet!

She thinks she's so cute. I've got news for her—maybe, unlike me, she has a nice petite figure, but let's face it—she definitely has the family round face and frogmouth.

So I go, "And you have a big, fat head."

"I do not!"

"It's like a pumpkin."

"Well, you have a square butt."

"You better shut up."

"Square butt, square butt."

I'm about two seconds away from wrestling her down on the carpet and giving her a Dutch rub when Dad shows up at the door.

"You two," he says, "knock it off and come downstairs. We're going to have a family meeting."

"It was her fault," Lacy whines, and Dad goes, "I don't care. Downstairs. Now."

He walks off and Lacy turns to me and goes, "See what you did."

But I know this isn't going to be about the two of us arguing. No, this is going to have something to do with Grandma Brinker. Mom got back from her weekly trip to Grandma's about thirty minutes ago, just enough time for her to fill Dad in on whatever this meeting is about. Not good. Family meetings usually end up with me having to do something I don't want to do. This time, I'm afraid it might mean they want the rest of us to go to Davenport to visit Grandma too.

It might seem strange that the whole family hasn't been going all along, but Grandma's never been too fond of having us visit. I would think, now that she's sick with cancer, she'd want us around even less. She definitely never liked me or Bobby. I remember her slapping him across the face one time for being "impertinent." Plus he busted her lawn gnome. Well, technically, I did, but she mainly got mad at him.

My theory is she thinks me and Bobby are too much like Dad when he was young. According to Uncle Jimmy, Grandma was totally against Mom marrying my dad in the first place. She thought he was riffraff or a juvenile delinquent or something. How ridiculous is that? My dad, a juvenile delinquent. He doesn't even cheat at bowling.

I'm sure Grandma thinks I'm hurtling straight to hell because I stopped going to church when I was fourteen. Sure, church people do some good things, like collect cans of beans and old shoes to give to the poor, but mostly it's just a bunch of *blah, blah, blah, don't do this, don't do that, throw some money in the collection plate*, all while you sit there struggling to keep from lapsing into a coma.

My mom and grandma are huge Christians, though. Dad says he is, but he doesn't actually go to church except on special occasions. He says he keeps the Sabbath in his own way, which means going fishing till noon. Of course, my sisters and little brother go, but Bobby gave it up at fourteen, just like me.

And sure, it was pretty open-minded of Mom to let us make our own decisions about going to church, but still, you'd think someone who believes in hell might try a little harder to keep us from roasting in the fiery furnace with pitchforks sticking

44

out of our butts like toothpicks in a Swedish meatball. Maybe she doesn't think we're worth saving.

Anyway, Lacy and I march downstairs to the living room, along with my little brother Drew, for the big family meeting. Dad sits in his favorite easy chair, but Mom keeps standing. She has her serious face on, which doesn't mean she's completely quit smiling. It's just turned down to about a three on the smile-o-meter.

"The first thing I want you to know," she says, "is that your grandmother is really making progress. I have complete faith that she's going to get better. But with her chemo treatments, she's feeling pretty worn out. That's normal. Sometimes, you have to put up with the hard days to get to the good. It's just that right now she can't do a lot of things she's used to doing and needs a little help. If I could take off work and stay with her while she gets through this, I would, but I'm lucky to get the days off I have been without losing my job."

Uh-oh. This is worse than I thought. I mean, if someone needs to stay with Grandma for a while and it's not Mom, who else in the room is it likely to be? It can't be Dad or Drew, and I don't see how it can be Lacy either. She has absolutely no sense of responsibility, unless you count babysitting jobs. And even then she let the Crowders' little girl get a peanut M&M stuck up her nose. She had to call them to come home and everything. They had to take the kid to the doctor to get it out.

So, no, I am definitely not expecting it when Mom says, "Your father and I have talked it over, and we've decided it would be a good idea if Lacy stays with Grandma, just until she recuperates a little more. I'll drive you over there after I get off work tomorrow."

Mom turns her smile up a couple of notches like this is the best idea since the invention of the curling iron. Dad stares at

45

the floor. You can tell he didn't have much input into this decision. And, of course, the first words out of Lacy's mouth are, "Me! Why me? Why doesn't Ceejay have to go?"

I admit I'm thinking the same thing. Not that I want to spend time with a grandmother who basically thinks I'm a thug, but it's hard not to feel like this is yet another way for the parents to let me know I'm not a real part of the family. After all, why else would they choose my weakly little fourteen-year-old sister over me? I'm definitely not going to argue about their choice, though.

Mom keeps her smile at a steady wattage. "Ceejay's going to work for your uncle this summer," she tells Lacy. "We've had that planned for a long time."

"But what about my plans?" Lacy whines. "What about all my friends?"

I'm thinking, *What plans?* Her and her friends lying around the public swimming pool all summer hoping some idiotic junior high boy will buy them a Coke?

"It's just a month or so," says Mom.

"A month or so!" Lacy whines. "I'll die if I can't be around my friends for a month."

Finally, Dad gets into the act—"I don't want to hear any more talk like that." His voice has a stern edge. Usually playing sergeant at arms isn't in Dad's nature, but he'll do it if he thinks he has to back up Mom. "Your grandma is part of this family and we don't turn our backs on family. We have to be there for each other."

Right, I'm thinking. Like how you didn't turn your backs on Bobby when the town assholes sent him into the army.

"But why does it have to be *me?*" Lacy's practically in tears now.

"Your mother already explained that," Dad tells her.

"Besides, it'll be good for you to think about someone besides yourself for a while."

At least someone finally had the sense to say that to her. I'm just surprised it was Dad. He usually treats Lacy like she's a shiny little princess who does no wrong.

She shuts up after that, but I know the look on her face. She's plotting something, probably some way to trick the parents into sending me to Grandma's instead. It's hopeless, though. Mom and Dad have their minds made up.

On our way upstairs after the family conference, I nudge Lacy's shoulder and tell her not to worry. There will probably be a whole fresh crop of boys she can drool over in Davenport.

"Why don't you go over there then," she fires back. "Maybe you'll meet a boy who likes you for a change."

"Hey, don't get smart-ass with me." I give her earlobe a hard flick. "I'm not the one making you go."

"But it wouldn't make any difference if you went," she says. "You'd be better off not hanging around with your stupid friends anyway."

I start to go for her ear again, but she cups her hand over it. "You're such a little bitch," I tell her. But I have to admit she's not altogether wrong, at least when it comes to Gillis.

8

In my room, I flop down on my bed and listen to the phone
ring. Without even checking, I know it's Gillis. He's afraid to
come over here and face me eye to eye, but he's called and
texted me so many times today it's not even funny.

This time, though, he leaves a message on my voicemail I'll
have to respond to. And if it turns out he's lying, that's the end
of us. For sure. Not only that, but I ought to crack his other eyebrow. Give him a fat lip. An Indian burn. A Dutch rub. Pink
belly. An atomic wedgie. I could tell him he's ugly too, but he
already knows that.

It's not like he's the greatest friend anyway. Actually, he's
the kind of person you hang out with not so much because you
like them as that they've just been around forever. What kind

of real friend tells you he has testicular cancer and he needs you to help him rub salve on it?

But I have to wonder about this message. Maybe it's just his way of making sure I finally call him back. Or maybe he's actually telling the truth. There just might be a chance I wasn't imagining things the other day when I thought I saw Bobby in Sophie Lowell's Toyota. Because that's what Gillis's message is about.

"I wanted to talk to you in person about this," he says, "but since you're so stupid and won't call me back, I have no choice but to talk to your voicemail. After you left the party, Sophie Lowell showed up, and I told her how you thought you saw her and Bobby." There's a pause. He probably thinks I'll go ahead and pick up, but since I don't, he goes, "And so Sophie's like, 'Maybe she did. Maybe I was driving him over to see my sister.'"

I almost drop the phone.

Now I *have* to call him back. The phone rings about six times. I know he's just letting it ring to get back at me. Eventually, he answers. "Oh, hey, Ceejay," he says casually. "What's up?"

"You know what's up, leprechaun. What's the story on Sophie?"

"Oh, that. Nothing much, except she told me Bobby might have called up her sister Mona a couple nights ago and said he was staying at Chuck Dunmire's place."

Chuck Dunmire! He was Bobby's best friend in high school. The two were thick. But still, it doesn't make sense. Why would Bobby come back and not tell his own family? Sure, he hasn't exactly been in close contact with us for a while now, but last time I talked to him he said he had to lie low for security reasons. Still, you'd think the military would let him call and tell us he's coming home early.

49

I go, "What's all this *maybe* and *might have* stuff? Did any of this happen or not?"

"I'm just telling you what Sophie told me," Gillis says.

"Well, you should've asked her more about it."

"She was plastered. There wasn't any getting any more out of her."

"You mean *you* were plastered."

"How about this, then," he says. "I'll take you over to Chuck Dunmire's and we'll see what's up for ourselves."

I pause for a moment. Gillis is not exactly who I want to hang out with today, but checking into this Bobby and Mona deal is the most important thing right now, so I tell him to come over as soon as he can. I'm not getting my hopes up, though. I've done so much hoping where Bobby's concerned, I don't hardly trust hope anymore.

When Gillis shows up at my front door, I have to admit it's pretty satisfying to get a good look at his face. His eyebrow's all swollen and yellow-purple around the edges from the head butt. He probably should've got stitches, but his parents are the type that won't send their kids to the doctor unless there's actually a bone poking out somewhere.

On the way to Chuck's, Gillis never says he's sorry for acting like such a jackass at the party. I guess he figures driving me around is as close to an apology as he wants to get. Even so, I know I'll end up forgiving him sooner or later like I always do, but I'm not going to make it easy. One- or two-word answers are about all he gets out of me the whole way over to Chuck's apartment.

Chuck was a real cool guy in high school, but now he's kind of a lowlife. Always stoned, can't hold down a job, knocked up Layla Evans but doesn't have anything to do with the kid. He used to be pretty good-looking, a real player with the ladies.

I even had a crush on him for about a year—but he's swelled up a little bit since high school. Now he lives in Truncheon Gardens, a flimsy stack of cardboard-boxlike apartments behind the Quick Stop.

When Gillis knocks on Chuck's door, we can hear the TV through the thin wall, but no one answers. Gillis knocks again, and I yell, "Hey, Chuck, it's me, Ceejay. Open up."

The door still doesn't open, so we keep knocking and yelling till finally Chuck calls out, "Hey, hold on, dammit, Ceejay, let me put some pants on."

Finally, he opens up, but he just stands there blocking the doorway, nothing on but his jeans. He has a beard now, and it's so thick you can hardly tell where it leaves off and his chest hair begins. Without bothering with any small talk, I come right out and ask him if he's heard anything from Bobby, and he's like, "Bobby? How would I hear anything from Bobby? He's still out on the east coast, right?"

"The east coast?" I say. "Last I heard he was in Germany."

So Chuck's like, "Yeah, right, that's what I meant—the east coast of Germany."

Something's weird. Germany doesn't even have an east coast, does it? Besides, Chuck seems antsy. I look around his shoulder into his apartment. Beer bottles clutter the coffee table, and right in the middle of them sits a single girl's shoe. A pair of panties lies next to the couch. No trace of Bobby, but obviously Chuck has some kind of action going on in there.

"Look," Gillis says. "We got it on pretty good authority Bobby came back to town early and he was staying over here."

"Who'd you get that from?" A surprised look passes across Chuck's face, but it seems exaggerated, like a bad soap-opera actor.

"Sophie Lowell," I say. "Mona told her."

Chuck shrugs. "Well, why don't you go talk to Mona, then. I don't know anything about it."

Just then, a voice calls out, "Are they gone yet?"

Chuck turns around, and that's when I see who he has in there with him—Amber Galen, one of the cupcake twins! I can't believe it. There she is at the end of the hall, nothing but a blanket draped around her. I know Chuck gets around quite a bit, but I never expected an uppity type like Amber to go for a guy like him.

When she sees me staring at her, she ducks back into the bedroom, and that's when I see the army-green duffel bag leaning against the wall at the back of the hall.

"What's that duffel bag back there?" I ask.

Chuck looks at it for a second like he's waiting for it to answer the question, then he goes, "That's just my laundry. That's all that is—laundry."

His whole attitude seems out of whack, but that might just be because he's in a hurry to get back to his cupcake. One thing for sure—we aren't going to get anywhere else with him right now.

"Come on," I tell Gillis. "Let's take Chuck's advice and go over to Mona's and find out just what's going on around here."

"I wouldn't go over there," Chuck warns.

"Why not?"

"Her husband's kind of paranoid. He's liable to freak if you start in asking questions about his wife's ex-boyfriend."

"Let him," I say. "Doesn't make any difference to me."

9

If Bobby's likely to look up anyone in town before his own family, it's Mona—even if she did go and get herself married while he was gone. She and Bobby dated all through his senior year. She was almost as wild as he was. One time he jackknifed into the Little River from the highest flimsy limb of this gargantuan oak tree on the bank, and she followed him right in. Hit the water so hard her bikini top came off. When Bobby used to climb out the window of one car into another while racing down the highway, she was one of the drivers. I was in the backseat when she came within two inches of sideswiping Brian Greer's Chevy. She just laughed and laughed.

Not that they didn't fall out every once in a while, but they were still tight when Bobby got sucked into the army. She cried on his shoulder the day he left and everything, said she'd wait on him for a million years. Three months later I saw her riding around town with Garrett Dillon. Guess they don't make a million years like they used to.

At nineteen, she moved in with Mark Schnabel. A year after that, she dumped Mark and married Rick Nichols. He's fifteen years older than her and has a beak like an owl, but he makes more money in a day from the construction business than poor Mark makes in a year driving a Coke truck.

Now she and Rick have a pretty fancy house in the Summer Gate addition. Obviously, she won't be able to say a whole lot if Rick's there, but I figure maybe I can get her out on the front porch. No way am I just going to call her. It's too easy to lie over the phone.

After a few punches on the bell, the door finally opens. It's Rick. He's not very tall but pretty wiry, the kind that thinks he's a tough guy, but I get the feeling, if it came down to it, he'd find a way to back out of a fight with a real badass.

"Is Mona here?" I ask him. He looks at us more like we're a couple of panhandlers stopping by to put the bite on him.

"Mona's not home," he says, and starts in quizzing me about what I want with his wife. I give him a made-up name and say I'm trying to find Sophie, that she's a friend of mine. That loosens him up, and he tells us Mona and Sophie took a trip into the city to shop, but we might be able to catch Sophie back at her place around eight o'clock or so.

"If you happen to see Mona over there," he says as we start to turn away, "tell her I'll be waiting up for her."

It's kind of creepy the way he says it. You get the idea he's trying to keep Mona on a short leash, but he can't get a good grip on it.

Sophie's a couple of years out of high school and lives in a duplex with Kara Jackson, which is quite a few steps down from the house Mona scored for herself. Sophie and Kara are sitting on the front porch steps smoking cigarettes when we get there. No Mona in sight.

"What's up, Ceejay?" Sophie says as we come up the sidewalk.

I'm like, "I don't know. Why don't you tell me? Gillis here says you've been going around telling people my brother's back in town."

"I'm sure Gillis says a lot of things." She glances at Kara, at the shrubs, at the porch step, but never makes eye contact with me.

"Come on," Gillis says. "You're not going to pretend you weren't at Dani Grant's party saying Bobby called Mona up, are you?"

She exhales a stream of smoke through her nostrils. "Oh, that. Turned out he wasn't actually in town after all. He was calling from New Jersey or somewhere."

I'm like, "New Jersey? Are you sure? He's supposed to be in Germany."

"Look." She stubs her cigarette out on the porch step. "Maybe he is in Germany. I'm not the one who talked to him."

"You're going to tell me I didn't see Bobby in your car driving by Corker Park?"

"Wasn't me," she says. "But I let Mona drive my car all the time."

Thinking back, I can't be sure Sophie actually was driving. I was paying too much attention to the passenger. "Well, where's Mona then? We went over to her house and her husband said she was shopping with you."

She's like, "Uh, yeah, right, we already went shopping."

She's about as convincing as a politician promising to cut taxes. So I tell her maybe me and Gillis will head back to Mona's house again.

She doesn't think that's such a good idea. Mona wouldn't be back yet, she tells us. She had some more shopping to do. "Don't mention it to Rick," she says. "She's looking for a gift to surprise him with."

"There's something you're not telling me," I say. She just shrugs, and I'm like, "Don't worry, I'm gonna find out what it is one way or another."

"Knock yourself out." She stands up. "I'm going in. My show's coming on."

Back in the car, Gillis is like, "You know she's lying out her ass, don't you?"

"No doubt. She's covering something up, but I just can't believe it's really about Bobby. He wouldn't come back without telling me. No, I'll bet Mona's running around on her husband, all right, but there's about six other guys I can think of off the top of my head she could be doing it with."

"I guess we go home now then, huh?"

"No way, leprechaun man. If Mona's got herself a boy toy, I know exactly where she'd take him."

10

When Bobby was in high school, I don't know how many times I walked into the house in the afternoon and caught him and Mona going at each other. And I didn't have to barge into his bedroom either. They did it all over the house, the living room couch, the kitchen, even on the washing machine—while it was running! Bobby told me later Mona liked how the vibrations felt.

Finally, I told him he better start going somewhere else before Mom or Dad caught him. Actually, Mom wouldn't be so bad since she'd probably just act like she didn't really see what was plain in front of her face, but Dad was likely to grab him by the ear and pull him out the front door by it. Give him a kick in the butt for good measure.

Bobby said maybe he'd just go downtown to the

Laundromat, screw on top of one of the professional washing machines—and I wouldn't have put it past him—but he ended up becoming a regular over at the rattiest motel in town. That became their place, and I'm sure Mona hasn't forgotten it.

"Okay, Detective McDermott," says Gillis, "where to now?"

"The Tip-Top Motel. And hurry it up, leprechaun."

The Tip-Top is a single-level motel next to the truck stop out by the highway. When we get there, Gillis asks how we're supposed to tell if they've checked in. The motel clerk isn't likely to give us any names, and we don't know what car to look for since Mona's known to drive a different car about every six months. I don't figure it'll be too hard to figure out, though. All we have to do is look for the most expensive car in the parking lot.

Sure enough, most of the cars at the Tip-Top are run-down rust buckets, but around the back, there it is—a brand-new gold Escalade. I couldn't be more sure it's Mona's if it had a personalized license plate saying GOLDDIGGER on it.

I guess I should be pleased with my detective work, but actually my heart sinks. I'm like, Could it be true? Could Bobby actually be in that room, just a crappy thin motel wall between us?

For a while Gillis and I sit there next to the Escalade playing stakeout, but that gets old pretty fast. Since there are no other cars within three parking spaces, we're pretty sure which room Mona must be in, so we decide to check it out. A narrow gap between the drapes is just wide enough to give us a peek inside. Not that I'm exactly crazy about going all Peeping Tom, but it's time to take action.

Gillis reaches the window first, and I have to elbow him out of the way. There's not much to see. The light's dim and the angle's bad, but I can make out a purse sitting on the table right in front of the window—an expensive Coach purse. Just the kind Mona's likely to spend Rick's money on.

"Come on," Gillis whispers as he nudges me out of the way. "Let me have a look."

"There's nothing to see," I tell him, and he's like, "Not even a little tittie?"

I grab his shirt and pull him away. "Jesus," I say. "You really do have a sickness, you know that? You need to go to the doctor and get a sedative for your hormones."

He just grins his leprechaun grin.

"Come on," I say. "Let's get in the car and wait. They can't stay in there all night. She has to get back to Rick and his platinum MasterCard sometime."

"Screw that," Gillis says, and walks over and pounds on the door. "Maintenance!" he yells. "We need to take a look at your air conditioner."

"What are you doing?" I can't believe that idiot. The last thing I want is to get caught spying.

"Just speeding this deal up," he says. "I don't want to scrunch down on the damn floorboard all night." He knocks again. "Maintenance! We think your wiring might be loose."

This time, I'm pretty sure the curtain moves. "Crap, Gillis," I say, grabbing his arm. "Get back in the car. You gave us away, you moron."

"We also have to restock your toilet paper," he hollers as I drag him away.

Back in the car, he's like, "I guess we'll have to give it up and go home. If they saw us, they'll never come out."

"We're not going home," I tell him. "Not on your life."

Instead, we park behind the truck stop next door, where we still have a view of Mona's Escalade and the motel room. Gillis goes in to get a burrito, and when he comes back, there's something too irritating about the way he wolfs his food. "So," I say, watching a chunk dribble onto his shirt. "You were a real asshole last night." Obviously, he could've gone forever without bringing it up, but I'm not going to let him off the hook so easy.

"What do you mean?" he says, putting on the dumb act. It's not much of a stretch for him.

"You know what I'm talking about. You try something like that again, and I'll bust you somewhere worse than your eyebrow. I mean it. I'll kick you so hard it'll hurt to even think about sex for the next ten years."

"Yeah, right, I'm scared."

"You better be. You better be one hundred percent scared."

"I don't know what you're whining about anyway. You ought to take it as a compliment."

"God, I hate you."

He just laughs. But the weird thing is I know he feels bad. He wouldn't have driven me around all day doing everything I told him to if he didn't. But can a guy just come out and admit it? Not in this lifetime.

We've been waiting behind the truck stop for twenty minutes before we get any action. First, the light brightens in the motel room, and then about five minutes later the door opens, but only one person steps out. It's Mona, all right. Her hair's cut different from the last time I saw her, but she still has the same bouncy walk from high school days.

"Damn," says Gillis. "I guess Rick's construction money can't buy everything."

Nobody walks out with her, though. I'm like, come on, dude, whoever you are, show yourself. My stomach twists into a knot. Mostly I don't want it to be Bobby, but in some ways I do. I mean, it'd be great to have him back, but at the same time,

I hate the idea that he's been hanging around town and not getting in touch with me. I could understand that he might not tell the parents, but me and him are thick.

Mona gets in the car, but still no one else comes out. Only after she pulls away does the door to that motel room finally close.

Gillis is like, "I guess her dude's going to stay and keep the bed warm."

"Looks like it."

"So, what do we do, follow her, wait to see what he does, or go home?"

There's no use in following her. She'd just head back to Rick Nichols and the big fancy house. For a second, I consider going over to the room and pounding on the door and yelling, "Hey, Bobby, it's Ceejay. It's Ceejay. Come on and open up. Let me in. I have to talk to you. I have to touch your face and prove you made it back in one piece." But that would just be pathetic. It has to be someone else behind that stupid locked door.

"Let's go," I say. "No way could that be Bobby in that room. No way." And I keep telling myself that all the way home.

11

That night, I'm lying in bed, but my mind is too busy to let me sleep. I roll over onto one side, then the other. Neither is any good so I switch to lying flat on my back, staring up into the dark. The evening replays in my head. At first, I feel stupid for running all over town searching for Bobby when it doesn't make sense that he could be anywhere but where he said he'd be—Germany. Then I feel frustrated, thinking I should have tried harder to see who was in that motel room with Mona.

Trying for something more positive, I remember this time when we went to the lake. I was eleven, but still Bobby let me and Brianna tag along with his group of friends. At one point, Bobby decided to swim out into the lake where one of his buddies was drifting in his parents' boat. Not wanting to be left behind, I tried to follow. I wasn't nearly as strong as Bobby, though, and pretty soon my arms started to give out, so I turned over on my back and just kicked with my legs. Then my legs got tired and I started floating, biding time till I got back some energy. But when I looked around, I realized I was headed out into the wide part of the lake instead of toward the boat. I totally lost my sense of direction.

I guess I panicked. I kicked my legs and splashed my arms, probably screamed like an idiot too. Then I felt it—Bobby's arm wrapping around me. I must have kept thrashing, because he pressed his head to mine and said, very calmly, "Be still, Ceejay. Be still. Be still."

I did what he said and clung onto him as he took me back to the shore, one arm around me and the other paddling. When we got to dry land, we sat on the bank, quiet until we got our breath back.

"Crap," I said. "I thought I was going under for sure."

He put his arm around my shoulder. "No way," he said. "Not while I'm around. I'll never let you go under."

Lying in bed, I close my eyes against the dark and listen to those words over and over in my head, hoping they'll lull me into a long, silent sleep. But instead of silence, a dream comes. It's not the lake but the ocean. And I'm not swimming. I'm walking along the ocean floor, feeling like I need to get somewhere but I don't know where. Then I see it—a huge pink octopus with a giant head and long tentacles waving up and down.

As I get closer, I see a couple of the tentacles have hold of something. It's Bobby! But he isn't panicked or anything. In fact, he looks kind of bored. I try talking to him, but no words come out, and he turns away, like I've interrupted him in the middle of something more important, and the octopus pulls him farther and farther away.

It's crazy. I feel like I'm supposed to save him, but how can that be? He's the one who's supposed to save me.

I start to yell at him, but just then I feel a hand on my shoulder. I turn around, and there stands Bobby, his face pale gray, like a drowned man. Then all of a sudden, I'm back in my room, lying in bed, staring up.

And this is the really, really, really strange thing. Bobby's face is still in front of me and his hand is still on my shoulder. He's right there—I swear—leaning over me, nothing but the small lamp on the dresser to light his face. I start to shout out his name, but he clamps his hand over my mouth.

"Shhh, Ceejay," he says. "Shhh. Don't wake up the others. Nobody else knows I'm here."

He takes his hand away from my mouth, and I hug him as tight as I can, making sure I'm not still dreaming. "Is it really you?" I ask, my heart in my throat.

"It's me." He peels my arms away and backs off, pulls the chair out from my desk and sits a few feet away.

"How can you be here?" I ask in a barely contained whisper. "Aren't you supposed to be in Germany?"

"Things changed." His voice sounds weary, old, but at the same time he's bigger now, muscled up, his neck nearly as thick as his head. His deep brown eyes look older too. No uniform, just jeans and a black T-shirt, but that doesn't matter. With his close-cropped hair and the way he carries himself, he still looks like a soldier. Or a hit man. I want to grab hold of him again anyway, but something about his attitude tells me to give him space.

"But how can you just show up like this?" I ask.

He glances around the room. It used to be his. "All my stuff's gone, huh?"

"It's in the garage, boxed up."

"The room looks smaller somehow. Everything looks smaller, the house, the town, everything but you. Look how big you are."

"It's been a while since the last time you came home on leave."

"Like a million years." He scans the walls, the floor, the curtains. "So much happened in this room. Now, it's like looking at an old friend who doesn't know me anymore."

I guess I know what he means. I remember this room when it was his—jeans and T-shirts draped over the chairs, posters of rockers and rappers on the wall, a pirate flag for a curtain. So many nights I used to come in here and talk. I'd tell about what was going on in school, and he would explain what to watch out for when I got into the higher grades. Like boys. He was the one who taught me how to do the perfect head butt.

He also told stories, made-up stories about a girl hero who traveled around to different galaxies and never took crap from anyone. Cirrilean Surreal was her name. She had her own kind of beauty. It was a magic beauty that only the most special people in the universe could see. I felt huge when I was with him in here. After he went into the army, I begged Mom and Dad to let me have his room. Now he's back in this weird way and the feeling is all mixed up.

"I don't understand," I tell him. "I can't believe you didn't at least call me to say you were coming home. How could you do that?"

"Listen." He looks down at the floor, then back at me. "I just came by because I know you were looking for me. I don't want you telling Mom and Dad I'm back yet. I'm not ready to be here."

"But you are here."

He shakes his head. "It just looks that way. But I don't want to talk about that. Just promise me you won't tell the parents."

I promise.

He walks over and touches my cheek. "You and me, we were always the most alike, weren't we?"

I nod. For some reason, it feels like tears are ready to burn into my eyes, but I can't let that happen, not in front of Bobby.

"You go back to sleep, Ceejay. Come see me tomorrow at Chuck's. Just you, nobody else."

"I can't go back to sleep. I have to talk to you. I have, like, a million questions."

"I know. But not now. We'd wake everyone up, and I just can't do that. You have to trust me. We'll have plenty of time to talk later."

"But is anything wrong? Are you in trouble or something?"

"Just come by Chuck's tomorrow and we'll talk then."

I chew on my bottom lip for a second, but there's nothing to do but agree. "I'll be there," I tell him. "Right after work."

"Work?"

"I'm working with Uncle Jimmy this summer. Tomorrow's my first day."

He smiles for the first time. "Uncle Jimmy," he says fondly, like the name by itself is some kind of private joke.

"I can skip work if you want me to."

"No," he says. "You can't let Uncle Jimmy down. Come by afterwards." He stands, and I expect him to lean down and wrap his big arms around me, but he doesn't. He just says, "See you tomorrow," then walks across the room and opens the door, careful to keep it from making a sound. Then he's gone without even looking back. No kisses, no hugs, just the shadow of the feeling of his hand on my shoulder.

What just happened? I ask myself. It's like I saw a ghost, only instead of fright, I'm filled with nothing but a burning whirl of confusion.

12

Work! I can't stand it. All I *want* to do that next morning is head straight to Chuck's apartment. What I *have* to do is start my new summer job working for Uncle Jimmy just like Bobby did back when he was in high school. Ace in the Hole Home Improvements is the name of his business. He paints houses, does carpentry work, builds decks, even mows lawns and plants trees if the price is right. The work isn't real steady during the winter, but I think Uncle Jimmy likes it that way. He's one adult who never completely lost that wild side of himself. Every once in a while, he'll still get in a bar fight if he has to. I guess he's my favorite uncle.

Up to now I've really been looking forward to working for him, even though I suspect the parents lined it up because they thought doing some manual labor would be good for me. The thing is, though, if I can save enough money for a down payment, Dad says he'll cosign on a car for me at the end of the summer. It'll be a long way from new, but at least I won't have to depend on my friends—or worse, my parents—to take me everywhere I want to go. Still, how can I think about that after Bobby's visit last night?

This whole morning, while getting ready for work, I can't quit thinking about him. What is he doing back so soon? You don't just get out of the army without a mile of red tape, do you? And why didn't he call so we could have a big party? I figured we'd have all our friends and relatives over for a humongous blowout, celebrating the return of our war hero. The main thing that eats at me, though, is why was Bobby so distant? Why didn't he pick me up and whirl me around and hug me till every ounce of worry I ever had about him squeezed out into the air?

Riding to work, I try to think of a way to bring up the situation without breaking my promise to Bobby, but it's not an easy subject to steer my way into while Uncle Jimmy's going on about his big weekend at Roadrunner's Roadhouse and how he wrestled Heath Pugh in the parking lot—again. Usually, I'd enjoy a story like this, but it's kind of annoying when I want to talk about something serious.

"You know what?" I tell him. "Maybe you should get married and slow down a little. You might live longer."

"Hell, Ceejay." He laughs. "Marriage wouldn't slow me down any. Take this situation at your house with Diane Simmons sniffing around in her low-cut blouses."

Diane Simmons is this church woman who's been bringing food by our house when Mom's out of town at Grandma's.

"I'll tell you what," he says. "If she pranced into my house while my wife's away, I'm afraid I'd be tempted to partake of more than just the potatoes and gravy."

"Really? Ms. Simmons?" Up to now, I haven't paid much attention to her, but come to think of it, she does wear her blouses pretty low-cut for a woman all the way up in her late thirties. "Don't you think she might be a little too churchy for you?"

"Are you kidding me? Some of those holy rollers come with the hottest fires burning down below."

"I guess you're about the only one who would notice something like that. I'm sure my dad doesn't see anything but the hot meals she brings by."

"Don't kid yourself, girl. Your old man might be married, but he's not dead."

I shake my head. "No, he's not dead, but he's asleep on the couch by nine o'clock every night." I'm not the least bit worried about my dad getting hot for some church woman's freckled cleavage. He's the most predictable person on earth. Anyway, it's Bobby who's still on my mind.

We stop in front of a big two-story house where Uncle Jimmy has a painting job lined up. The house looks pretty white to me, but I guess they want it whiter. Uncle Jimmy's hired man Jerry is already there, leaning against the side of his old clunker pickup. He's a skinny little guy with a lopsided mustache. Uncle Jimmy warned me he was kind of slow, but at least he's cheerful. A real morning person. Can't wait to get our equipment unloaded so we can get to work.

Painting, though, has never been my thing. I did paint the walls in my room, even the trim, but that's all. It's pretty boring, the same thing over and over, nothing artistic about it. I can see myself getting carpal tunnel by the end of the summer, but who cares? I just want the day to go by so I can do what I really want to do.

Finally, lunchtime rolls around. While we're scarfing our

burgers at Coby's Grill, Uncle Jimmy takes up the story of his weekend again. This time he goes into how he went home with a woman named Claire Fountain. She's recently divorced and moved in with her crabby old mother, so when they went back to her house, Uncle Jimmy had to crawl in through the bedroom window. Then, come morning, he had to climb right back out the same window. "Made me feel like a burglar," he says. "And she expects me to call her the next day? Ha!"

Jerry looks flustered over the idea of someone having sex in the back room while the woman's mother watches TV in the living room, but I think he admires Uncle Jimmy for it at the same time. Me, I love Uncle Jimmy, but stories like that just confirm my theory that, young or old, men are mostly dogs.

Finally, we get around to the topic of Bobby when Uncle Jimmy says he's going to hate having to turn Bobby's motorcycle back over to him when he gets home. He's been taking care of it ever since Bobby shipped out. Except, of course, when Bobby's come home on leave.

"The ladies love a man on a motorcycle," he says.

So here's my opening, the perfect excuse to pick Uncle Jimmy's brain about Bobby. I'm like, "Maybe you'll have to give it back to him sooner than you think. I hear sometimes they let soldiers come home early." I'm just throwing it out there like I haven't heard a thing about him really being back.

"I doubt that," Uncle Jimmy says. "Probably be lucky to get home next month like he thinks. I mean, I hope he does— don't think I don't—but they make it pretty hard to get out of the military these days. It's ridiculous. With that jackass Bush in the White House, you never know. He keeps sending troops back every time they think they're going home."

Then I guess he realizes that might sound harsh to me, so he reaches over, pats my knee, and says, "But don't you worry,

Ceejay, I'm sure he'll be back next month just like he said he would. You know Bobby. Nothing can get that boy down."

"But what if he showed up, like, tomorrow?"

"Don't get your hopes up about that, Ceejay. I mean, it would be great, but if he showed up tomorrow, I'd be worried that he was AWOL or something."

I don't say anything back. All of a sudden, I feel like the reality of the world is about three sizes too big. Bobby AWOL? I just can't believe that. Once we go back to the job, I try to put it out of my mind. Everything's going to be all right, I tell myself. The war's over now, at least where my brother's concerned.

13

Finally, we wrap up work for the day, and I can't wait any longer. Instead of going right home and asking Brianna or Gillis to come give me a ride, I coax Uncle Jimmy into dropping me off in front of Chuck's apartment complex, telling him a lie about having a friend who lives there. No shower. No change of clothes, just my paint-spattered jeans, T-shirt, and sneakers. I even have paint in my hair, but that's all right. If I put off seeing Bobby one more second, I'll explode.

Waiting on the porch after I ring the bell seems to take forever. I'm like, Why doesn't Bobby rip the door open? Isn't he as anxious to see me as I am to see him? Finally, the door swings back. It's only Chuck. He looks stoned.

"Uh, yeah, hi, Ceejay," he says, rubbing his beard. "I almost forgot you were coming."

I look around his shoulder to see if Bobby's behind him, but instead I see Amber Galen, the cupcake twin, standing by Chuck's CD tower looking for some music to play.

"Where's Bobby?" I ask.

"We have to go get him." He turns around and calls to Amber, "You coming with us?"

Her face twists into a sneer. "Are you kidding? You couldn't get me out there for a million dollars."

"Well, lock the door when you leave."

Walking down the stairs, I ask Chuck where we're headed, but he just goes, "Don't worry, nowhere too weird."

He doesn't give up much more information as we drive through town either. I ask if Bobby's with Mona again, but he changes the subject. He wants to know what I think of Amber. It's like he's a high school kid again, trying to pry out some top-secret scoop about his girlfriend. I tell him I don't know her all that well, but that it's pretty surprising to see her at his place.

"Why's that?" Chuck asks, lighting a cigarette.

"Because she's kind of a stuck-up bitch."

"So?"

"Well, stuck-up bitches usually don't hook up with guys like you."

"What kind of guy is that?"

"You know, Chuck—losers. No offense."

"That's all right." He exhales a puff of smoke. "None taken."

Pretty soon we're outside of town and heading down a familiar road. Again, I ask where we're going, but he just tells me to wait and see. There are only two places I know of out this way—Captain Crazy's and Tillman's sister's. We pass the spot where the captain's winged giraffe sticks up over the trees, so that just leaves Dani's place.

"What's Bobby doing out here?" I ask as we head up the gravel drive to the trailer.

"Nothing," Chuck says. "Just needed to pick up some product, that's all."

Dani comes to the door, and when we go inside, there Bobby is, scrunched down in the big orange easy chair. Facing him, on the other side of the coffee table, Dani's boyfriend, Jace, sits on the couch stuffing weed into the bowl of a wooden pipe. A gray-blue cloud of smoke hangs in the air above them.

Dani sits next to Jace, and Chuck squeezes in next to her. Now, I figure surely Bobby will bounce up from his chair and grab me, but he doesn't even say anything. He just points a finger like he's shooting me a hello. Like we haven't seen each other in about five minutes or something. Then he turns away and takes the pipe from Jace. He poises the lighter above the bowl, closes his eyes, and says, "God is great, God is good, thank you for this dope, amen."

It's too weird. So many times I've imagined him coming back and me running into his arms, but now all I can do is take a seat on the floor next to his chair while he sucks on the stem of that pipe. I feel like I've done something wrong somehow, like I'm being punished. Maybe he's mad because I took his room when he left. Or maybe he thinks I'm on the parents' side just because I still live with them. It's stupid to feel guilty when I haven't done anything, but I can't help it.

Jace goes back to telling a story that he must have started before we came into the room, something about how pythons have been introduced into the wild in Florida and are making their way across the rest of the country, living off raccoons and squirrels and family pets along the way. He heard a story about a two-hundred-pound python swallowing a bulldog right in front of the kids who owned it. They were traumatized.

He takes the pipe back from Bobby. "That's why I told Dani not to let little Ian sleep on the floor anymore. A python like that would slurp him up whole in a second."

"Jesus, Jace," Dani says, scowling. "Don't talk like that. Ian might hear you."

Jace waves that away. "He can't hear anything. He's sound asleep in the back room."

"You know what?" Chuck says. "Those pythons have been known to slither into cribs too. I saw an interview with one. All he said was, 'Mmm-mmm, that was some good baby.'"

"Shut your face," Dani tells him, firing him a nastier look than the one she shot Jace.

Bobby smiles, but not much. He looks kind of out of it, which isn't like him. Sure, in the old days, he smoked weed now and then but just enough to add to whatever fun he was already having. Now, the way he handles that pipe and the way he looks at it when the lighter flashes over the bowl, it's like nothing else matters in the whole universe.

The pipe keeps going around, and Dani keeps bringing out beers, but Bobby never talks much—no stories, no jokes, not a single one of those belly laughs of his that can make you feel like the whole world is funny. Even when Jace starts into this ridiculous BS about how he should be the star of his own TV reality show, Bobby just lets it go. I mean, how boring would that show be? Who wants to watch a part-time tow-truck driver sit around in his girlfriend's trailer house, smoking weed and talking about pythons eating bulldogs?

I'm like, "Hey, Bobby, why don't we get out of here, go get a Coke somewhere." But he just goes, "Coke's not really my thing right now, Ceejay."

My stomach feels like it's made of lead. I want to leave so bad, to get out of there and go someplace where we can talk—just us, nobody else—but he seems determined to melt into that orange chair while his eyelids droop farther and farther toward closing altogether. It's like he's ready to stay there all night, but finally Jace takes to the wrong subject.

He wants to hear war stories. Bobby says he doesn't want to talk about that, but Jace keeps after him, prodding with one question after the next. Is war like in the movies? (No.) Did Bobby have an assault rifle? (Yes.) What was it like to shoot one? (It's not like anything.) Did he ever get shot at? (I don't want to talk about it.) Did he shoot anyone? (I don't want to talk about it.)

Finally, when Jace asks if Bobby knew anyone who got killed, that's the end of the line.

"Look," Bobby says, standing up. "Come here, I'll tell you something about war."

Jace stands and walks over to Bobby. "Let's hear it, dude," he says.

Very casually, Bobby reaches up and clamps his big right hand around Jace's throat. "Here's the deal about war, asshole. I don't want to fucking talk about it. You got that?"

Red-faced, Jace tries to spit out an answer but can't.

"All right," Chuck says, slapping his knee. "Bobby! Awesome!"

Jace tries to claw Bobby's hand away, but Bobby grabs his throat with both hands, nearly lifting him off the ground. "Let's hear it," he says. "Answer me. Do you understand I don't want to talk about that shit?"

Jace sputters something but it's not a real word.

"Come on, Bobby," I say. "I think he's got the idea." I glance at Dani, expecting her to jump up from the couch and defend her man, but she just sits there grinning a loopy stoner grin.

I grab Bobby's arm. "That's enough," I plead. "Let him go. He didn't mean anything. He's just an idiot."

Finally, Bobby relaxes his grip, and coughing and almost purple, Jace eases down to sit on the coffee table. "Shit," he says, finding his voice. "What's wrong with you, dude?"

Bobby doesn't answer. He just picks his beer up and takes a long drink.

"I'll tell you this," Jace sputters. "I'm sure as hell not gonna get you that OxyContin tonight after this. You can just get the hell out of here. Christ, choking a dude in his own home."

"It's not your home," Chuck says, bright-eyed and happy over the whole situation. "It's Dani's."

"That's all right," Bobby says. "I've had enough of this company anyway." He starts for the door without even asking me to come with him.

Outside, he stops by the oak tree to take a pee. Right out in the open. From behind the fence, Dani's Rottweiler barks at him like crazy. "Hey, look out for that dog," Chuck calls from the porch. "You won't have anything to pee with if he takes a bite out of you."

We all three get into the truck, with me in the middle, but before we can pull away, Dani comes out and walks up to Bobby's window. He rolls it down and looks at her without asking what she wants.

"Sorry about Jace," she says, pulling her hair away from her face. She's dark and pretty, a female version of Tillman. At least, she's pretty when she's not sitting around with a look on her face like a stoned moron.

"It wasn't your fault," Bobby says.

She smiles. "Hey, I was thinking, if you still want to score some of that OxyContin, I could sell it to you some afternoon when Jace is at work."

"Don't you have to work?" Bobby asks.

"Yeah." Her smile takes on a flirty tilt. "But I'm off the day after tomorrow."

"Cool."

"I'll probably just be hanging around the house."

"Then it's a date."

"All right. It's a date."

As she walks away, an exaggerated swing to her hips, Chuck reaches past me to punch Bobby in the arm. "Bobby, my man," he says. "You still got it."

"Yeah," Bobby says. "At least I can fool 'em into thinking I do."

Chuck laughs. But it's not funny. Before today, Bobby hardly paid any attention to Dani, and now he's asking her on a date while he hardly even looks at me. No, there's nothing to laugh about at all.

14

Riding down the highway, Chuck's all fired up and laughing about the deal with Jace, but Bobby's quiet and cold. It's like sitting between a lit match and an ice cube. Back at the trailer, I thought as soon as we got out of there, I'd pour out all my thoughts and feelings, ask a million questions, lay out my plan about the two of us moving in together, but nothing pours out. I feel like I have some broken part of myself stuck in my throat, choking the words back into my stomach.

Chuck rambles off on the old days, stories about how he and Bobby used to tear this town up with their wild ways. Bobby barely pays attention, sitting there staring out the side window instead. Finally, Chuck pauses to take a pull on his beer and I jump in.

"So." I nudge Bobby with my shoulder. "When are you gonna call Mom and Dad and tell them you're back?"

"Sometime," he says, still staring out the window.

"He has to get his party on for a little while first," Chuck says.

But I'm like, "I don't understand. I thought you were supposed to be coming back next month, and then all of a sudden I hear this gossip that you're hanging out with Mona, and the next thing I know, you're sneaking into the house like you're on some kind of secret mission. What's that all about?"

"Look," he says. "It's not about anything. I'll call Mom and Dad in a couple of days. Don't worry."

Before I can say anything back, he twists in his seat to see out the window better and hollers, "Wow, what's that over there? Slow down, dude. I want to look at this."

We're passing Captain Crazy's place, so I figure Bobby's just now glimpsing the giraffe head—the captain wasn't a town fixture before Bobby's army days, and we sure never bothered to visit out here when he was home on leave—but now there's something more than just the giraffe rising above the trees.

"Damn," Bobby says. "It looks like some kind of giant silver bird."

Sure enough, it is a silver bird, but it's not flying. It's waving around on the end of a tall metal pole.

Chuck's like, "It's just some more Captain Craziness," but Bobby's all, "Pull over, pull over, I gotta see this!"

I'm like, "You don't want to mess around with Captain Crazy. He's an idiot. One hundred percent."

He doesn't care, though. As soon as Chuck pulls to the side

of the road, Bobby flings the door open and takes off running toward the woods.

"Bobby," I call after him, "don't go over there! We're dealing with a maniac here!" But he just keeps going.

I yell, "Stop him, Chuck," but Chuck's like, "Hey, this might be fun," and then he's out the door too.

What am I supposed to do now? I don't want to show up at the captain's after our commando raid on his place, but at the same time, I can't let Bobby slip away, so I bounce out of the truck and follow his trail through the trees and underbrush, heading for Casa Crazy.

Where the woods give way to the captain's front yard, I hang back while Chuck and Bobby forge ahead. The silver bird turns out to be part of a new sculpture the captain's trying to erect with the aid of—guess who? Mr. White. Decked out in his stupid costume of hope—white painter's overalls and cap, white T-shirt, and white sneakers.

"You need some help with that thing?" Bobby calls out, and the captain looks up from his work, his face beaming. "Hey, man!" he says. "A soldier of the light has appeared before us. Far out! Yeah, come on, come on. We need all the help we can get, man!"

Bobby hustles over and grabs a higher place on the pole while the captain and Mr. White work at fixing the bottom into the ground. Then Chuck joins in, and I swear they look like the dudes who raised that flag on Iwo Jima. Only instead of a flag, it's some kind of wild totem pole.

At the top there's the silver bird, an eagle, from the looks of it, and then, fixed to the pole below that, there are about seven flat sheets of tin, each one with a symbol painted on it, mostly animals—a wolf head, a running horse, a rabbit, and a chipmunk, things like that. The sun has dropped down about even with the treetops, and its light glints on the metal, flashing in different directions as the boys work the pole back and forth.

Mr. White says something about how they need to put braces on the thing, and Bobby hollers, "Hey, Ceejay, come here and help us out!"

I'm not exactly eager to get over there—I mean, after all, remnants of my paintball marks are still all over the house—but if Bobby wants my help, I'm bound to give it. When I grab the pole, the captain looks straight at me and smiles. That's all. He just smiles like he thinks this means I'm all of a sudden on his side. Of course, I do it because Bobby wants me to, but really, if it wasn't for that, I wouldn't care if the thing fell over and smashed to pieces.

So there we are, making sure the totem pole is straight and fixing wooden braces to it so it'll stay that way while the cement sets. At least that part feels good—working shoulder to shoulder with Bobby.

When we get everything in place, we stand back and look at the finished product. The sun has dropped below the trees now, its fading light adding a warm pinkish glow to the sheets of tin and the metal eagle.

"You see it now, don't you?" Captain Crazy says. He's looking straight at me, his eyes burning.

"See what?"

"You know."

I'm like, "Whatever." But it's kind of creepy. Like he thinks he knows what's going on inside of me.

He looks back at the totem pole and claps his hands. "Time to celebrate! Sacramental hot links! Hot links on a stick and blackberry wine!"

I'm like, "We don't need any wine. We have to be heading home."

But Bobby goes, "Are you kidding? Sure, we need wine. Bring it on."

"Hell yeah," adds Chuck. "Just what the doctor ordered."

Great, I think. All I want to do is leave as soon as possible, but fat chance. Until I can think of a way to get Bobby out of here, I'm stuck.

15

I'm sure not about to trust any homemade wine of Captain Crazy's, but I go ahead and try the hot links. We roast them over a little fire below the totem pole and eat them straight off the stick. Bobby and Chuck aren't so particular about the wine and drink it from jars the captain provides. Even Mr. White partakes, but only in small sips.

For some ungodly reason, Bobby takes to the captain right away and talks a lot more than he did at Dani's. He goes into how he likes the sculptures and even the way the paint splotches on the house and the lime-green truck look. He seems to think they're a part of the captain's artistic plan, and the captain doesn't tell him any different. Maybe I should appreciate the captain for that, but I'm not about to forget his fake Vietnam protest and how he basically called me a coward.

I keep quiet about it, though. At least for the time being. But if he starts any more of that nonsense, I'll show him who the coward really is.

Chuck asks the captain if it's true he used to make records, and the captain's face lights up.

"Sure did, man," he says. "Way back in the way-back times."

Bobby asks what that was like, and the captain says it was a *gas*, whatever that means. He tells us how one day he was doing his usual deal with the guitar and the conga drum on Sunset Strip in Los Angeles, and some big, psychedelic rock-god dude from the sixties happens by. "He was blown away," the captain says, real enthusiastic, like it's happening to him all over again. "He says, 'Man, we gotta get you in the studio,' and that's what happened. We went into the studio like a month later and laid down some tracks. That's when I did 'Sliced Penguins.'"

"That's off *Crash Landing on Pluto*," says Mr. White, and the captain's like, "Yeah, man. *Crash Landing on Pluto*. That was a gas."

"You know what I heard about that," says Chuck. "I heard you still got money coming in from that shit."

The captain grins at Mr. White. "Listen to this guy," he says. "He's all about the money, man. I don't worry about that. I'm not a banker. I don't work for the IRS, man. It's all about getting the word out."

"The song is a metaphor," Mr. White explains. "Penguins are like the world's most innocent animals. And that's what happens to innocence in this society. It gets all sliced up."

I'm thinking surely that will sound as ridiculous to Bobby as it does to me, but he nods like he understands perfectly.

"What about these sculptures?" he says, waving his hot-link-on-a-stick in their direction. "What's up with them? It's like they have some kind of meaning I can't quite put my finger on."

"Oh yeah, man, yeah," says the captain, his words coming in quick bursts, like he has to hurry before somebody or something tries to stop him. "They have a meaning, all right. Yeah, they do. No doubt you've met the Nogo Gatu."

"Nogo Gatu?" says Bobby. "No, I don't believe I have."

"Oh, sure you have," says Chuck facetiously. "You've met the Nogo Gatu. He was a year behind us in high school."

"I hear you, man," the captain says, looking at Chuck. "You don't believe in anything. But that's all right. That's all right. You just haven't opened up yet. Isn't that right, Padgett?"

Padgett is Mr. White. He nods.

"But he's young," the captain goes on. "He'll open up. He will. If you don't open up, if you don't see them and hear them and smell them, the Nogo Gatu will dance around you, man. They'll dance around you with the dark fire in their hands."

"I might have smelled them once," Chuck says, laughing.

"Shut up, dude," says Bobby. "I want to hear about this stuff."

Of course, I think it's pretty funny too, but I quit laughing. I don't want Bobby thinking I'm not on his side.

"So," Bobby says, turning to the captain, "what is it, this Nogo Gatu?"

He and the captain lock eyes, and the captain says, "You know who they are. I can tell that. You've been in the war, haven't you?"

Bobby's gaze turns toward the ground. "Yeah, I've been in the war."

Uh-oh, I think. Here it comes. The captain's going to stick his foot in it and start in with his protest baloney, but instead he goes, "I understand. You don't want to talk about the war. That's not something you can open up about just anywhere. That's cool. But I'm telling you that's where you saw the Nogo Gatu, and I don't mean the people. I'm not talking about the warriors. I'm talking about the frequency the world is on there. That's the Nogo Gatu frequency. It's dark and it tries to pull you in."

Bobby looks up at him again, and the captain goes, "See, man, that's why this'll be a good place for you here. The sculptures, they'll help you. Because the sculptures bring the Yimmies, and the Yimmies are what you need. You need their bright electroids. See him over there?" He points to the fat boy sculpture. "He was my first one. He told me to build all these others."

I'm thinking this is some pretty serious weirdness, but Bobby's like, "He told you? Like he talked to you out loud?"

"He probably called him on his cell phone," says Chuck, but the captain goes, "Look, man, I'm not saying the actual sculpture spoke out loud to me the way we're talking right now. I may be Captain Crazy, but I'm not that crazy. No, it was like the spirit of the sculpture vibrated his message directly into my inner ear drum."

"Well, yeah," I say, "when you put it that way, it doesn't sound crazy at all."

Chuck laughs, but Bobby shushes me. The captain seems used to sarcasm, though, and doesn't let it slow him down. "What I'm saying is there are all these different frequencies you can sense the truth on—two hundred and eleven of them—but most people only listen on one, the one we're talking on right now. But hey, man, I can tell you're opening up." He stares deep into Bobby's eyes. "You're opening up and starting to hear.

88

When you were young, you heard the Yimmies, but now you're hearing the Nogo Gatu. They're shrieking, man. But you can't listen to them too much. It's like listening to the rain. If you listen to the rain too much, you'll drown."

"What are the Yimmies?" Bobby asks.

The captain smiles. He has flecks of mustard in his scraggly beard, but his eyes sparkle like a little kid's. "They're the bright frequency, man, the good frequency. When they come, and you open up and they get inside you, you can do anything, man. Anything."

Bobby nods again, like he actually understands what the captain's talking about. "But this other thing—what is it, the Nogo Gatu?—what if you can't get away from it?"

I can't believe he's getting into this stuff. In the firelight his face looks so intense you'd think he's seen the stupid Nogo Gatu himself. He's never been the type to believe in crazy ideas. One time this weird girl from down the street was trying to tell us her mom was psychic, that she predicted the 9/11 attacks, and Bobby's like, "Then why didn't she call someone? Why didn't she try to stop it?" He picked that girl's whole story apart. Now he's buying into the captain's BS?

"But you *can* get away from the Nogo Gatu," says the captain, chewing on his hot link. "You have to call the Yimmies. See, man, that's why they told me to make the sculptures. They help hold off the Nogo Gatu. That's what I need to do. I need to hold them off until I get the aero-velocipede finished."

That's right—*aero-velocipede*. I'm like, Oh crap, another imaginary goblin from Captain Crazy's warped mind, but Bobby actually wants to know more about that too.

The captain glances at Mr. White, as if he needs his opinion on whether he should go ahead and explain. Mr. White nods.

"The aero-velocipede," says the captain. "It's the ultimate Yimmy sculpture because it can fly."

"It can *fly?*" Me and Bobby and Chuck say it all at the same time.

The captain's grin stretches out so far you'd think it might push his whiskers off his face. "Come on, I'll show it to you."

"That sounds good," Chuck says. "I've always wanted to see a flying sculpture. And maybe we can get some more of that wine while we're at it. I need a drink. Jesus."

"It's getting late," I say. "I don't think anyone needs more wine."

"No way," Bobby protests. "A little more wine never hurt anyone."

"All right," says the captain, grinning. He hops up, pretty spry for a crazy person in his sixties, and leads the way toward a dilapidated barn behind the house, Bobby walking at his side. It's beginning to look like I'm never going to have any time alone with him.

16

On the way to the barn, Mr. White grabs my arm and stops me. "What do you think now?" he says with a crafty little smile. "Are you beginning to see there's a whole lot more to the captain than you thought?"

I'm like, "If you mean, do I think he's even crazier than I thought before, then, yeah. Surely you don't believe some kind of dark-frequency monsters are dancing around out there, and these statues, or whatever they are, keep them away."

"Sure I do," he says, "in a way. Seems like your brother's getting into it too."

"Yeah, well, my brother's a good guy. He gives weird people a chance. He just hasn't seen the captain's true colors yet."

"Did you ever think maybe you're the one who hasn't seen his true colors? I mean, if you think about it, the Nogo Gatu and the Yimmies are no weirder than people believing in devils and angels. It's the same thing."

"Only what? It's just about being on a different *frequency?*"

"I'd call it a difference in brain chemistry. Devils/angels, dark/light, Nogo Gatu/Yimmy—it's all in the brain chemistry. In ancient societies, the captain would've been a shaman, a holy man. That's what true artists really are. Take his sculptures. The captain, he's our Michelangelo. He makes sculptures out of junk, turning it into something beautiful."

"Sorry to have to tell you this," I say. "But that is an actual load of crap. That guy's nothing but screwed up."

"Why do you think he's screwed up?" There's no anger in his voice, just a cool scientific tone. "What makes you think your reality is any more real than his? If you want to expand yourself, you don't have to drink or do drugs. Just try to see through someone else's eyes every now and then."

"You know, you may be even crazier than the captain is."

He smiles. "Thank you. I'll take that as a compliment."

I shake my head.

"You know," he says. "It was interesting watching you by the campfire, seeing the way you looked at your brother."

"Why's that?"

He looks me straight in the eye. "Because it's the first time I saw how really beautiful you are."

"What?"

He reaches out and gives me a little punch on the arm and then takes off walking toward the barn. "How about that for crazy?" he calls over his shoulder.

I just stand there and watch him for a second. It's hard to know what to think. I mean, surely he was making fun of me, but he didn't sound like it. And believe me, I've been made fun of enough I can recognize the sound of it in boys' voices pretty

92

much right away. They don't do it for very long. That's one hundred percent for sure.

But Mr. White didn't have a trace of teasing in his voice. He spoke in that same scientific tone, stating the word *beautiful* like it was just another fact. I guess most girls wouldn't want to hear it like that. They'd want something all romantic, with flowers and music playing, but that could just mean the guy wants to get in your pants. This is different. No hidden motive. It's just plain unbiased reporting.

And believe me, I don't get told I'm beautiful every day. I can't even remember my dad ever saying that to me. He's said it to my sisters but not me. But why does it have to come from a freaky dude like Mr. White? Why couldn't Tillman say it? Or even Chuck. Somebody I could really fall for. Still, I guess every girl wants to hear they're beautiful sometime, no matter who it comes from.

Inside the barn, Mr. White is already kneeling next to the captain. Bobby's squatting on the other side, and Chuck's standing behind them with one hand in his back pocket and the other holding a cup of blackberry wine. The only light comes from a mechanic's lamp hanging from a rafter. Me, I feel like I'm caught between two forces—wondering about this new development of Mr. White telling me I'm beautiful and then also wishing I could come up with something to say to get Bobby out of here.

They're all inspecting this thingamajig the captain calls his aero-velocipede. If he's going to try to fly this contraption, he won't get far—it doesn't have any wings. Right now, it just looks like a giant silver tricycle, only the seat's lower and has a high back and sparkly blue vinyl upholstery. The thing doesn't even have wheels.

Just about anyone who saw it would say it's just a big piece of crap, but for some reason Bobby has a different idea. He looks up at me and goes, "You can see it, can't you, Ceejay? Get some wings, some wheels, and an engine on this thing, and it'll be riding the sky with the eagles and crows."

He seems so happy about it, I can't bring myself to do anything but lie. "I can see it," I tell him. But all I can really see is disaster if someone tries to take this thing up in the air.

More cups of wine and more stories go around until finally the wine runs out. Bobby grabs his wallet. "Here, Chuck, I'll give you a few bucks. Run into town and get us some beer."

Of course, Chuck's totally up for it, but finally I have to put my foot down. Which isn't easy. It's not my place to tell Bobby what to do, but the last thing I want to see is him passed out on the ground in Captain Crazy's barn.

"No, you don't," I say, aiming the words at Chuck instead of Bobby. "It's late. I have to go home. And I sure don't want to get in your truck with you after you polish off a six-pack of beer on top of everything else."

"That's all right," Chuck says. "I'll drop you off when I go get the beer."

I'm like, "No way. I'm not going without Bobby."

Finally, Bobby looks up at me, smiling a drunk smile. "That's right, Ceejay. Don't you go anywhere without me. You're my best, best, best little sister. And if you're leaving, then I'm leaving too."

Sure, it took a few glasses of wine for Bobby to finally say something that sounds like him, but that's all right. It feels good, like cool water pouring down to the bottom of my stomach.

Unsteadily, he gets up and addresses the captain, "Captain, I'm glad to meet a man of your caliber. You've given me a lot to think about, sir." He shakes the captain's hand and starts to turn but thinks of one last thing to say. "I will be back. And you can bet, sooner or later, we will fly."

The captain grins and salutes him.

On the way to the truck, Bobby leans against me and I take his arm. He's more like his old self, happy and talkative, though more wasted than I'm used to. As we drive down the highway, he puts his arm around me. "I love you, Ceejay," he says. "You know that, don't you?"

"I know," I say. "I love you too."

"Thanks for being patient with me," he says. "I know I've been weird."

"No, you haven't," I tell him.

"Yeah, I have. It's just I'm not ready yet."

"Ready for what?"

"Anything."

"If you want," I say, "I can tell Mom and Dad you called while they were out and said you were coming back early. That way you don't have to make up something to tell them. I can say you're coming home this weekend or whenever you want."

He reaches over and strokes my cheek. "I'll leave that up to you, Ceejay. You're my girl. I know I can count on you to do what's best."

"That's right. You can count on me."

He scrunches down and leans his head against mine. "But I don't want to think about that stuff right now. All I want to do is ride."

"Okay," I tell him. "We'll just ride then." I still don't have answers to the million questions I want to ask him, but at least we're together and I'll settle for that right now.

17

My plan is simple—since I get off work before the parents do, I'll go home, get cleaned up, maybe go over to Gillis's for a while, and then come back just before dinner when I know Mom and Dad will both be there and spring my story on them. I'll make a big production of it, really build up the suspense, then—*bam!*—hit them with the phony news that Bobby called while they were at work and said he got an early furlough. He'll be home this weekend.

Should be easy, right?

Still, I go over my lines all afternoon while I'm painting with Uncle Jimmy. It's like I'm rehearsing for a play. I recite my little speech over and over in my head, thinking up answers to questions my parents might hurl at me and trying to visualize the facial expressions I'll need to make my delivery convincing.

I even pick out the outfit I'll wear. By the time Uncle Jimmy drops me off after work, I have everything well rehearsed.

"Did you hear me, Ceejay?" Uncle Jimmy says as I open the door to get out of the truck.

"What?"

"I said I'd be by to pick you up half an hour later tomorrow morning."

"Oh. Okay."

"Where's your head been today, girl? You seemed like you were off in another galaxy."

"Just daydreaming, I guess."

"Boys, huh?" He smiles slyly.

"What? No."

"Sure." He says it like he doesn't believe me. "Just do me a favor. If you meet up with a boy that's anything like I was when I was your age, run as fast as you can in the other direction."

I force a smile. "If I meet a boy like you, he'd better be the one to run."

I'm home a little later than I figured, so I hurry to get cleaned up and changed. I wanted my yellow top because yellow is a happy, good-news kind of color, but it's in the clothes hamper. White will have to do. Like Mr. White says, it's the color of hope, but it's also the color of innocence, and I may need both before I'm done.

When I go to Gillis's, he can tell right off that something's up, and I can't fool him like I can Uncle Jimmy. There's not much reason to keep Bobby a secret from him now anyway, but from the way he reacts, I wish I had.

Everything that comes out of his mouth is negative. Maybe Bobby's AWOL. Why else would he have to go sneaking around? Maybe the military police are searching for him right now, and if me or my family help hide him, then we could all go to jail. Or Guantánamo Bay. After all, it might be considered treason, this being wartime and all.

It's too much. "Why can't you just be happy for me?" I ask him, and I end up leaving earlier than I planned.

But now I'm not so sure I want to spring the news about Bobby coming back. I don't want to believe it, but I have to admit there is a slim possibility that Gillis might be right. Bobby could be AWOL. That would explain a lot.

The strange thing is my parents' cars are already parked in the driveway. They're never home this early. I'm like, *Red flag—something must be wrong.* As soon as I step inside, Mom bustles around the corner. She's still in her cheery office clothes. Even her makeup seems happy. "Ceejay! I'm so glad you're back. Come on in the living room."

Obviously Mom is in a good mood, but that's nothing new for her. She could discover a coupon for toothpaste in the newspaper and you'd think she hit the lottery.

She leads me into the living room, and there's Dad in the easy chair and my little brother Drew's on the couch looking like he's got somewhere more important he'd rather be.

"Sit down next to your brother," Mom tells me, her hands clutched together in front of her chest.

Dad smiles, his eyes glinting merrily the way they do just before he tells some awful joke.

I think I know what this must be about. Grandma Brinker. Her treatments have been a shining success. The cancer is gone, and the whole family will be going to visit her this weekend. And don't get me wrong—it's not like I'm hoping that's not true—but how am I supposed to tell them Bobby's coming home Saturday after they tell me something like that?

"I've got some really, really great news," Mom says as soon

as I sit down. She's so wired up it looks like her head might explode at any moment.

"I'm hungry," Drew says.

"We're going out to eat tonight," Dad tells him.

I'm waiting for the news—Grandma's cancer has been eradicated. But that's not what comes.

"Are you ready?" Mom is practically vibrating. "Your brother's back!"

"You mean Bobby?" says Drew. Like it could be anyone else. He isn't even excited. He was so young when Bobby went into the army that I guess he doesn't see him as anything more than some guy who shows up every once in a while on leave. Me, I'm dumbstruck.

"That's right," says Dad. He sounds as proud as if he'd arranged the whole thing himself. "He called this afternoon."

And I thought I was going to be the one to build up suspense and spring the surprise!

It turns out Bobby ran into Uncle Lee, Dad's other brother besides Jimmy, at the convenience store. Bobby tried to dodge him at first but no such luck. And really, it's a wonder something like this hadn't happened earlier. Bobby made Uncle Lee promise not to call anyone before he had a chance to. He said he wanted to walk into the house real casual like he was just back from a short road trip or something and see everyone's jaws drop. But I know what really must have happened—since Uncle Lee busted him, Bobby figured he might as well call to let the family know he's back before the gossip got around town.

For someone with as bad a hangover as Bobby was bound to have today, he was thinking pretty quick to come up with a story like that off the top of his head.

"So what do you think about that, Drew?" asks Dad. "You're going to have dinner with your big brother the war hero tonight. You can put off eating a little bit longer for that, can't you?"

"Yeah," says Drew. "I want a bacon cheeseburger."

"How about you, Ceejay?" says Mom. "Can you believe you're going to see your brother tonight after all this time?"

"Wow," I say, trying to come off like I'm thoroughly amazed. "I can't wait."

18

Chuck drops Bobby off in front of the house around 6:30. Through the living room window, I watch him walk toward the door. There's not exactly a spring in his step. He didn't even bring his duffel bag.

As soon as the door opens, the family flocks around him. My big sister Colleen is here now with her husband and little girl, but of course, Lacy's now stuck in Davenport helping take care of Grandma Brinker. Everyone takes turns hugging him, with Mom going first. As big as he is, you can tell she still thinks of him as her little boy. His hugs are stiff, though, awkward. It reminds me of the time at my grandpa's funeral when I had to dole out hugs to people I hardly knew.

When the squeezing is all done, Mom asks Bobby where his bags are, and he says he left them at Chuck's.

"Well," she says. "We'll go by and pick them up after dinner. You're staying at home tonight, young man."

"Okay," he says, but there's a little grimace that goes along with it, like he's already planning some way to get out of it.

"How come you didn't wear your uniform?" asks Dad. He loves to see Bobby decked out in his uniform.

"You know," Bobby says. "You get sick of that after a while."

"Where's your gun?" asks Drew.

"I didn't bring that either, little man. You'll just have to deal with me unarmed."

Drew looks disappointed. Later, while everyone's gathering their things to get ready to go to the restaurant, I pull him aside. "Listen," I say, "don't ask your brother a bunch of questions about war, okay? He's probably sick of talking about that."

Drew looks at me like I'm being foolish. "I don't have to ask him any questions about war," he says. "I'm a captain second grade at Halo."

At the restaurant, I start to see why Bobby might have wanted to postpone the family reunion ordeal. Before we ever get to our table, Dad's already pulled him over to three sets of diners to let them know his boy is back from Iraq. When the waitress comes with the menus, Dad has her shaking Bobby's hand. She's about Bobby's age and looks happy to get the chance to do a little handholding with such a good-looking guy. But his smile is stretched tight, like a suit you only wear once a year.

Luckily, he doesn't have to talk too much. Everybody's busy filling him in on what they've been doing since the last time they saw him. Colleen tells a million stories about how cute her little girl Reece is. Dad trots out his latest dumb jokes, and Colleen's husband Jason brags about his success in the insurance game. Me, I hold off. The things I want to talk with Bobby about are just between me and him. The rest of our Martian family wouldn't understand. Then Dad drops the bombshell.

After dessert, he pushes his plate aside and says, "Bobby, I hope this dinner was a little better than that army chow you've been putting away."

"It was good," Bobby says, scraping at the corner of his mouth with his napkin.

"Well, let me tell you, though, son. You ain't seen nothing yet. Saturday, we're going to have the biggest barbecue the McDermott household has ever put on. Everyone's going to be there, and you can ask anyone you want to come. We're going to do this homecoming up right."

You'd think a bone got lodged in Bobby's throat from the expression on his face. "You don't have to do that."

"The ball's already rolling," says Dad. "Your mom and me have been making calls all afternoon."

"And we're going to have a big German chocolate cake," says Mom. "Just like you like it."

Bobby stares at his empty dessert plate. He knows he's beat. Later, when Mom reminds him that we need to pick up his duffel bag from Chuck's, he doesn't even have the heart to argue.

19

That night, Bobby sleeps in my bed, and I take over Lacy's while she's away. He's still asleep when I head off for work in the morning, and he's nowhere around when I get home that afternoon. The parents were counting on him to be here for dinner, and I was counting on finally having some alone time with him before they got off work. But he didn't leave a note or anything, so I call Chuck on his cell phone to see if he knows what's up.

Turns out Chuck lent Bobby his pickup so he could go out to Dani's. I had completely forgotten about her offer to sell him some OxyContin. This doesn't sit well with me at all. It's bad enough he's standing up the family for someone like Dani, but the deal about the OxyContin bothers me even more. That was never the kind of thing Bobby was into. He never wanted to be sedated. Life was a celebration for him. He once told me that you had to look at every day like it was your birthday. "The day I forget that," he said, "you might as well shoot me."

Something's definitely wrong if Bobby's on the painkiller ride, and I'm determined to find out what it is. Brianna's only too happy to give me a ride to Dani's, doesn't even ask why I want to go. She's too excited about getting a call from Randy Pilcher, the smoosh-faced thirty-year-old idiot she cozied up to at Dani's party before he threw her over for someone with better drugs.

When I get in her car, that's all she wants to talk about. I don't mind. It's not like I really want to go into how Bobby's hooking up with Tillman's sister. But I'm not exactly ready to throw my support behind Randy—who spent a year in jail, remember—and how he wants to take Brianna out this weekend.

The date will have to be a secret, of course. Her parents would never let her go out with him. Or with anyone she thinks is cool, according to her. They don't understand her. They don't understand anything. They forget how it is to be young. Usually, I agree with her—my mom and dad are the same way—but when it comes to smoosh-face Randy, I can't help thinking parents might just be right every once in a while.

"So," I say when she stops for a breath. "Did you ask him why he left you at the party and took off with some other girl?" I'm not trying to be mean. I just want her to think the thing through.

"Oh, he explained the whole thing," she says. "That girl was his cousin and he had to go with her because he was afraid she'd get herself in trouble with this guy that sells shrooms."

"Really?" I say. "And you believe that?"

She glares at me. "Are you trying to be negative about this? You didn't talk to him. He's different than he looks. He's, like, real into music. We like a lot of the same bands. He's got every song Gore Squad ever recorded."

"I've got news for you—that group's old and they suck." All right, I am being pretty negative, but being supportive doesn't mean you have to side up with every stupid idea that plops out of your friends' mouths. "Look," I say, "I just think you need to step back for a second and get some perspective."

"I don't want to step back," she says. "I want to take a step forward. Otherwise, I'll end up like you."

"What's that supposed to mean?"

She looks at me, then back at the road. "You know what it means."

"No, really, tell me. What's supposed to be so terrible about me?"

She's quiet for a moment. "You're scared to death of guys."

"What are you talking about? I'm not scared of anything."

"Yeah, right. Ceejay McDermott, the baddest-ass girl in Knowles. Except when it comes to dudes."

"You're insane. I have more guy friends than girl friends."

"That's right—*friends*. But that's as close as you let yourself get. You're so afraid of getting hurt, you won't even try for any more than that."

"That's crap. How about that time I kissed Tillman?"

"When was that? Fourth grade? And ever since then, you go around mooning after him like he's the only one in the universe for you, but that's just your excuse so you don't have to put yourself out there to get hurt again by someone else."

That really twists in my stomach. I'm like, "Yeah? Well, you don't know what you're talking about. This isn't about me anyway. It's about you pretending some jailbird is a good guy when the reality is you're just desperate."

As soon as the word *desperate* flies out of my mouth, I know

it's pretty brutal. But I'm thinking, Hey, this girl has just se-
verely attacked my rep—*Ceejay the fearless.*

"Screw you," she says, which means she's done with the
subject. Except that the way she's strangling the steering wheel
with both hands pretty much means she wishes it was my neck
right now.

We ride on in silence. It's like a stranger sitting between us.
It's too weird. I mean, sure she started it, but life's too messed
up right now to have my best friend mad at me too. I have to
do something, shove that stranger out the car door. "Look," I
say, "there's something I haven't told you about why we're
going to Dani's."

"What? Tillman isn't there? I just assumed you wanted to
go out there so you could follow him around like a puppy."

"No, Tillman's not there. Bobby's there."

"Bobby? Your brother? I didn't even know he was back in
town."

"Yeah, neither did my parents. Until yesterday."

"What's he doing at Dani's?"

"What do you think?"

"Oh my God." She finally looks at me. "Are you serious?
He's hooking up with her?"

"Most likely."

"What about Jace?" she asks.

"Are you kidding me? Do you know anyone who wouldn't
choose Bobby over Jace if she had the chance?"

Brianna's like, "Yeah, but still. I mean, they're living together and all."

"Like that means anything these days."

"It might mean something to Jace. No telling what he'd do
if he caught them together."

"He can't do a damn thing," I say. "Not to Bobby." But in

107

the back of my mind I know Jace isn't exactly the type to square off and fight fair if he can get around it.

"So how does he look?" she asks. She always had a little crush on him but a lot of girls did.

"He looks fine," I tell her. "But he seems different."

"Different? Like how?"

"I don't know. Distant."

"I guess that makes sense. He's been a long ways away."

And just like that the stranger goes flying out the door and bouncing down the road behind us. We're Ceejay-and-Brianna again, friends to the end. That's what sharing a juicy secret can do.

We drive past the turnoff to Casa Crazy, but before getting to Dani's, we spy the captain's truck on the roadside, the nose pointing toward the shoulder, the back end poked deep into the high weeds. As we slow down, Mr. White appears from behind the truck and waves his arms at us.

Brianna rolls down the window. "Why don't you learn how to drive?"

He leans over with his hands on the roof of the car and peers in at me. "I think you better come over here and look at this." He sounds serious.

"Look at what?"

"It's your brother. He's had an accident."

"What? Jesus." Before Brianna can even park the car on the shoulder of the road, I'm out the door and running into the high weeds.

"Don't get in a panic," Mr. White says, following right behind me. "He's okay. He's just messed up."

"What are you talking about?" I don't bother looking back. "How can he be frigging okay if he's messed up?"

108

"I mean, he's not hurt bad physically, but he's either really drunk or on something."

Behind the truck, Captain Crazy is fixing one end of a rusty chain to the bumper. The rest of the chain leads to the bumper of Chuck's pickup. With the high weeds and the trees you couldn't even see it from the road.

"Hey, there," says the captain, sunny-eyed and smiling. "We'll get this big boy hauled out and back on the road in no time."

I'm not in the mood for smiles, though. "Where's Bobby?" I ask, heading for Chuck's pickup. "Bobby, Bobby, are you okay?"

Now I can see where the truck plowed through the weeds, missing several trees by inches before coming to a narrow ditch. The front end is lodged in the dirt on the far side of the ditch, and the back tires are slightly off the ground. The bumper and grille are crumpled but not too bad. "Bobby, Bobby, where are you?" I'm frantic.

"He's in the back of the truck passed out," Mr. White says. "I think he'll probably have a knot on his forehead, but other than that he's not hurt."

I peer over the truck's tailgate. Sure enough, Bobby's lying there on his side, fast asleep. He's breathing fine. He looks as peaceful as the days when I used to watch him sleep in his room at home.

I turn to Mr. White. "What the hell happened?"

"I don't know exactly." He brushes his long hair back from his face. "The captain and I were gathering blackberries for some wine when we heard this loud *wham!* When we got here, Bobby was already out of the truck stumbling around, looking all confused, yelling, 'There was an IED in the road. There was a goddamn IED in the road.'"

Behind me, Brianna's like, "An IED? What's an IED?"

Mr. White looks at her like she should know what it is. "An improvised explosive device. You know—a bomb like they make in Iraq to blow up military convoys?"

"A bomb?" Brianna says. "What would something like that be doing in the road here?"

"Nothing," Mr. White tells her. "There wasn't any IED. There wasn't anything but a branch sticking out in the road about two feet."

"God," Brianna says, "maybe Bobby got hold of some magic mushrooms or something and hallucinated it."

I'm like, "Oh, Jesus, Brianna, shut up. Bobby's not into that crap."

I climb into the bed of the pickup and kneel next to him. A knot is already rising on his forehead, but he isn't cut anywhere. I nudge his shoulder, trying to wake him, but he only rolls over on his side. He's like a wounded animal, which is just too weird. Bobby's the one who helps wounded types. He doesn't get wounded himself.

"This isn't good," I say, stroking his hair. "Maybe we should call an ambulance."

"Yeah, actually that's probably not a good idea," Mr. White says, leaning over the side of the truck. "You might get him busted. At the very least he'd get a DUI, but it might be worse than that. I didn't go through his pockets. No telling what he might have on him. Maybe he does have some mushrooms."

Looking back at Bobby, I can't help but think of the time he ran off the road into that golf-course water hazard. No way can I have the cops getting hold of him again. I check his pants pockets and sure enough there's a small pill bottle with nine or ten OxyContin tablets left in it. I'm like, "Crap, maybe he OD'd."

"No," Mr. White says in his matter-of-fact way. "He was messed up, but not that messed up. He just passed out while we went back to get the chain to haul him out of there. The best thing to do is get him to the captain's and pour some coffee in him. He'll be all right. He couldn't have been going too fast or the truck would be more busted up than it is."

I look him in the eye. The way he looks back at me, it's like he's got everything under control. I pat Bobby's head gently, and when I climb down from the truck, Mr. White helps me. For such a skinny guy, he's pretty strong, his grip on my arm warm and confident like his voice. It's as if he's passing that confidence on to me, making me feel like things aren't so bad.

For a while it looks as if we might not get the truck pulled from the ditch, but after a few more heave-hos, it finally pops out like a bad tooth. Bobby sits up and gazes over the tailgate. "What the hell?"

"Damn you, Bobby," I yell at him. "Don't you scare me like this anymore."

"Ceejay?" He stares at me like he can't quite focus. "What are you doing here?"

"I'm helping to get your sorry butt out of a ditch. That's what I'm doing."

He surveys the scene around him and scratches his head. "Wow," he says. "Freaky."

The pickup runs fine, so I drive it over to Casa Crazy with Bobby still in the back. That's about the last place I want to go, but we need the captain to pound the bumper and grille back into some kind of shape before Chuck gets a look at it. Plus, I don't want to drag Bobby back home where the parents can see what kind of shape he's in right now. It'll mean a lecture from Dad about missing dinner, but I figure I'll face up to that when it comes.

When we get to the captain's, he takes the truck around to the barn while Mr. White goes inside to whip up some instant coffee, leaving me, Bobby, and Brianna sitting on the wooden front porch. Right now, it's hard to pry much that makes sense out of Bobby, but from his slurred rambling, I gather he and Dani threw themselves a pretty serious private party at her place, which sounds like all kinds of trouble.

"Jace didn't come home while you were over there, did he?" I ask.

Bobby doesn't answer. Instead, he sits there staring at Brianna with one eyebrow cocked like he's an undercover cop and she's his prime suspect.

Finally, she's like, "What?" And he shakes his head and goes, "Who the hell are you?"

Her eyes go all disappointed. "What are you talking about? It's me, Brianna."

He stares a little longer. "Brianna Caster?"

"Yeah." A smile starts on her lips.

"Well, goddamn, Brianna," Bobby says. "Who the hell went and painted you all black?"

The smile turns into a big hurt zero.

"No one painted her black," I say. "That's just her look now." Brianna didn't have the Goth thing going last time Bobby was back on leave.

"Shit," he says. "You look like a bowling ball. I liked you better when you were just plain fat."

"Well," Brianna spits back, "I liked you better when you weren't such a drugged-up asshole."

She's trying to be tough, but I know she's hurt. "Don't pay any attention to him," I tell her. "He's too wasted to know what he's saying."

112

Bobby smiles, loose-lipped and droopy-eyed. "Wasted again!" he yells. "Hallelujah!"

The front door swings open, and out walks Mr. White with a cup of coffee.

Bobby's like, "Coffee? I've always been partial to beer," but he goes ahead and takes the cup and sips a little. "Instant, huh? That's some pretty bad stuff."

Mr. White sits next to me, and I ask him if the captain's really qualified to work on the pickup. He gestures toward the sculptures. "Anyone who can make those won't have any problem on a bent grille."

"Maybe he'll turn Chuck's grille into a sculpture," Bobby says, "like a dragon or something, swooping low across the road." He starts to take another sip of the coffee but just then a loud metallic pounding starts as the captain goes to work—*Bam! Bam! Bam!*—and the red tin cup drops from Bobby's hand and clanks onto the wooden porch.

His head whips around like he's expecting to see someone coming at him. His shoulders hunch up to his ears, and an expression I've never seen before twists across his face, a combination of rage and a sick kind of fright like his life is in danger.

"Goddammit," he cries, looking at the spilled coffee on his pants. "Where'd that noise come from?"

"It's all right," says Mr. White. "It's just the captain working on your buddy's truck. He'll have it fixed up better than new in no time." His voice is mellow and soothing, the way a doctor might talk to a patient. I'm not sure whether to appreciate that or find it annoying.

Brianna doesn't take the same tone, though. "Wow," she says. "Paranoid much? You'd think someone was shooting at you."

Bobby glares at her. The fright is gone from his face, but

some of the rage still boils in his eyes. "Don't talk about shoot-ing, goddammit." There's no kidding around in his voice. "You don't have the right to talk to me about that."

"God," she says. "When did you lose your sense of humor?"

He looks away. "Some things aren't funny."

"A little coffee stain never hurt anybody," Mr. White says as he kneels down to get the tin cup. "I'll fix you another one." He gives Bobby a gentle pat on the knee. "Then we'll go watch the captain work. The dude's a wizard with tools."

"Yeah," says Bobby, still simmering. "That's what we need—a wizard." He stares toward the tree line as if he thinks something might be hiding there, something that might come charging toward us at any moment.

20

When Mr. White gets back with more coffee, Bobby takes it and heads off toward the barn with Brianna right behind him. I start to follow, but Mr. White grabs my arm. "Why don't you stay here for a second," he says softly. "I want to talk to you alone."

Brianna looks over her shoulder. "Are you coming?"

"You go on," I tell her. "I'll be down in a minute."

"Well, hurry up," she says. "I don't want to be left alone with two crazy guys."

She and Bobby disappear around the side of the house, and it's just me and Mr. White, one on one. "So," I say, sitting back down on the edge of the porch, "what's so private that you need to talk to me alone?"

He sits next to me, almost touching me. "It's about your brother," he says.

And I'm like, "Look, don't lecture me about my brother. An accident like that can happen to anyone. He's just blowing off steam. He's been in a war, you know? Besides, he's probably just not used to driving anything that doesn't weigh a couple of tons and doesn't have a machine gun mounted on it."

"Don't worry," he tells me. "I'm not putting your brother down for anything. I'm thinking about him and the captain. The captain really likes him. He told me he did."

"Yeah, so?"

He pauses to adjust his glasses, like he needs them to focus on what he has to say.

"Well, I think it'd be good for the captain—and your brother too, actually—if they hung out some, worked on the aero-velocipede and all. And of course, you'd come with him."

"Are you kidding me?" I have to give him a long, hard look after that. "Why would my brother and I want to spend our summer hanging around a place like this?"

He tucks a stray strand of his long hair behind his ear. "Oh, I don't know. It could be the perfect place to launch the misfit revolution. After all, you're the only one I ever met who didn't act like that idea was too weird."

"Yeah, but that's only because I liked thinking about getting the hell out of this town and—I don't know—having a cause or something."

"Hey, revolutions have to start somewhere." He smiles, and then he does something really unexpected—he puts his hand on my knee. It's not like he's suddenly going all Gillis horny on me, but it's still strange. Not just because it's Mr. White's hand, but also because I don't really have all that many guys putting their hands on my knee.

He doesn't leave it there for long. He pulls it away and starts talking about how important Bobby and the captain will be for our revolution. "Of course, you'll be the general," he says, "but you'll have to admit—even if you don't like the captain—he's definitely a misfit."

"I can't argue against that," I say, but my mind is still going over the hand-on-the-knee thing. First, Mr. White tells me I'm beautiful, and then he sits here on the porch with me, practically shoulder to shoulder, and puts his hand on my knee. I'm starting to think all this talk about Bobby hanging around the captain is just a way of getting *me* to start coming out here. Maybe he even has a crush on me. How stupid would that be? I mean, me and Mr. White? It's ridiculous. If there was ever a bad boy's girl, it's me. Mr. White—he'd probably faint if someone challenged him to a real fight.

He goes on talking about how I'll probably start liking the captain sooner or later and how fun it is working on the sculptures and the aero-velocipede. I let him ramble. He's not really bad-looking once you get used to him, but he's so skinny. And the white overalls and painter's cap—no one dresses like that. I can just imagine the crap I'd catch from my friends if they saw me sitting around with Mr. White's hand on my knee.

This whole time the captain's hammering has kept up pretty consistently, but suddenly it stops, and Mr. White looks off in that direction. "They must be about done," he says. "Come on. Let's go over to the barn and see how they're doing."

He hops up and walks ahead while I follow a few steps behind. It's not like I want to show up at the barn—where Bobby and Brianna are—practically walking arm in arm with the likes of Mr. White. But watching him ahead of me, I'm shocked and almost disgusted with myself. I mean, who would've thought a skinny, stringy-haired dork could have a sexy walk?

21

Back by the barn, Brianna sits on the ground with a bored expression. Mr. White sits a few feet away from her, and I have to wonder if he's hoping maybe I'll plop down in between them. No way. Instead, I stand next to Bobby.

He sips at his coffee, all fascinated by the captain's skill with tools and his nonstop stories. He almost looks hypnotized. It reminds me of how we used to catch horny toads when we were kids and rub their stomachs. They'd get these satisfied little smiles on their faces and lie there all stretched out and stiff. My dad said that was their way of protecting themselves—playing dead.

I have to admit there's a big difference between the way Bobby acts out here with Mr. White and the captain and how he acts with the likes of Dani and Jace. It's like a peace comes across him. I'm just not sure why. Maybe it's the sound of the captain's voice, because I don't see how anyone can hardly follow the stories, the way they jump from topic to topic. At one point, he's telling us about hanging around with rock stars in L.A., and the next thing you know he's in a strip club.

"Never play in a strip club on acid," he says. "It's too freaky, man. It'll break your heart. No, man, strip joints are the saddest places on earth."

I don't hardly know what to make of it, but Bobby rocks back on his heels, smiles, his eyes nearly closed, and in almost a whisper, says, "Not quite the saddest, dude. Not quite the saddest."

Then the captain's off in a different direction. "You should've seen my brother at sixteen," he says. "He was pure. You ever been to the Rocky Mountains? No? Well, they have these streams up there, never been touched by a speck of pollution. That's how my brother Kyle was back when we were growing up right here in this town."

Bobby sits on the ground and leans back on his elbows. "I'd like to meet him. He sounds like a good dude."

"Yeah." The captain's voice goes soft. "I wish you could, man. I wish you could. I taught him how to play guitar, but he was the real musician. His fingers flew up and down the fret board. He knew almost all the Beatles' stuff. We were going to California together. I would've probably ended up backing him on bass. He would've been the front man, the singer. Sixteen years old and he had a voice like Howling Wolf. He read the Romantic poets and wrote lyrics no one could touch, except maybe Dylan."

"What happened?" Bobby asks. "Why didn't he keep playing?"

"He turned eighteen," the captain says. "That's what happened. He turned eighteen."

I'm like, "What's so bad about eighteen?"

The captain stops working and stares at the bumper of the truck. "The draft," he says, rubbing his fingers through his beard. "The goddamn draft—that's what's bad about turning eighteen."

"Vietnam?" asks Bobby.

"Yeah, Vietnam." The word seems to put a dark spell on the captain. "I tried to go down and tell them to take me instead, but they wouldn't do it. It was against their rules. So I said I'd sign up and that way they could put me and Kyle in the same unit together, but they wouldn't take me. My brain was too out of whack." He taps the side of his head. "Isn't that ridiculous? They'll drop you off crazy when they've got their good out of you, but they won't let you in that way."

"I hear that," Bobby says.

"Yeah." The captain nods. "And then I was home right here at this house the day those soldiers walked up to the front door in their perfect uniforms and brought the news that Kyle didn't make it. Sniper fire."

He goes quiet then, and we all sit there in silence, kind of like we're at a funeral. Mr. White looks at me like, See, I told you there was more to the captain than you thought. And I have to admit he's right. It's weird. Somehow I'd never thought of the captain having a kid brother he loved. I don't know what I would've done if Bobby hadn't come home from Iraq. Maybe I'd go crazy too.

When the silence has lasted long enough, the captain picks up his mallet to go back to work on the bumper. "And that's when I took off for California," he says. "No way I could stay around here anymore. But now I'm back and I see Kyle in everything, man, in the grass blades and the streams and the brick buildings downtown. He's everywhere." He looks at Bobby. "He's even in you."

Bobby nods. "Thanks. That's a real compliment."

As the captain works, it hits me he's working on more than just the truck. The same with the sculptures. It's like he's trying, over and over, to fix something that went wrong a long time ago.

By the time he gets the grille pounded into decent shape, Bobby is barely awake, even though it's still light out. The plan is for me to drive him back to Chuck's in the pickup—we both figure it's not a good idea for Mom and Dad to see him like this—and for Brianna to follow us, so she can drive me home to face the parental interrogation about where we've been and why we didn't come home for dinner.

I help Bobby up, but he's so unsteady on his feet, Mr. White has to help me get him to the truck. After he's safely tucked into the passenger side, I turn around and Mr. White is standing right in front of me, maybe a foot away. "So," he says, "you see what I mean about the captain? He loved his brother just like you love yours."

"Yeah, maybe he's not completely bad. He's still a lunatic, though."

Mr. White scratches his cheek. He seems a little nervous. "I was thinking, maybe I should give you my phone number in case you want to talk sometime, you know, about your brother and everything."

"Your phone number?"

"Yeah, you know? The number for those little things people hold in their hands and use to talk to each other?"

I don't have much—or any—practice with guys wanting to give me their phone numbers, so it's not like I have an excuse prepared for turning him down. I'm just like, "Sure, yeah, okay." What else am I going to say—"No, you're too frigging weird"?

The awkwardness continues. Neither one of us has a pen, so I have to dig one out of Chuck's glove compartment. But now there's nothing to write on, so Mr. White goes, "Hold out your arm."

"What?"

"Hold out your arm."

He grips my wrist with one hand and writes his number on my forearm with the other. I look past him to make sure Brianna isn't watching. Luckily, she isn't.

"You can call me anytime," he says.

"Uh, yeah, sure," I tell him, and walk around and climb into the pickup. I tell myself that when we get Bobby to Chuck's apartment, I'll wash it off, but for some reason I don't. And the funny thing is, as I'm riding home with Brianna, I keep my arm turned so she can't see it, but I can feel it there on my skin, practically like it's glowing.

22

Almost as soon as I open the front door, the parents are all over me.

"Where were you?"

"Why didn't you call?"

"Where's Bobby?"

You know the drill. It's like they expect you to think of what they want every second of the day. So I lay out this story about how Bobby wanted to get together with some of his old friends from around town, and we just lost track of time. Of course, Dad doesn't think losing track of time is a good excuse, but he buys the story. After all, it's pretty much true. I just left out some of the details.

Mom's all deflated because Bobby's spending the night at Chuck's. She's worried he's going to get sidetracked with his friends and not make it to the big barbecue party on Saturday, but I tell her not to worry. "He wouldn't miss that for anything," I tell her. "That's practically all he could talk about—how great it's going to be."

That calms them down, so they let me off with a warning about how I'm sixteen now and need to be more responsible. I'm tempted to come back with a wisecrack about how responsible they were to let their son get shipped off to a war, but I figure it's best to leave that alone for a while and just head to my room, where I can put the earbuds in and crank something loud.

Of course, the truth is Bobby never said he was charged up about the barbecue, but I can't help thinking it might actually be good for him, get him around normal people instead of Captain Crazy. It'll also give him a chance to see how much respect everyone has for him and what he's done for our country, even if the judge and lawyers and all the other dickheads gave him a bad deal by sending him over. He's a hero and everybody knows it. Well, almost everybody.

I can't believe it the next day when Mom tells me Lacy won't be coming back from Grandma's for Bobby's homecoming. I'm like, God, what a self-centered little creep. I call her and lay right into her before she can even get *hello* all the way out of her mouth. I'm all about how much Bobby's meant to our family, to us kids, to our town, and to the whole country. "I'm sure you met some pimple-faced boy over there in Davenport you think you can't live without," I tell her, "but you need to start thinking about someone else besides yourself for a change and get down here and support your big brother."

But she has her argument ready. "It's not any boy, Ceejay. It's Grandma. She needs help around the house."

Right. I'm not buying that, not with Mom always going around advertising how great Grandma's doing with her treatments. "Are you telling me Grandma can't get by one weekend without you? I mean, what do you do for her anyway? I have to do your chores for you half the time."

She comes back with how she does a lot, that Grandma even taught her how to cook, which makes me laugh. "Sure," I tell her. "What do you do, make toast? Besides, what's Grandma ever done for us in the past but treat us like stray cats. I'm talking about you being here for your brother's homecoming from the war. The *war*, Lacy. Can you get your little peanut brain around that? Bobby was always here for us back when he lived at home. One hundred percent. Grandma sure wasn't."

"He was there for *you*." Her voice sounds small.

"What?"

"He was there for you, Ceejay. You were his pet. He hardly even talked to me, acted like I was too little to bother with. I mean, I love him and all, but you two were the ones who were close. It was like you had your own club and the rest of us weren't invited to join."

How about that? Mommy and Daddy's little princess trying to act like *she* was the outsider around the house. Ridiculous. I'm like, "Hey, we tried to include you a lot more than Grandma ever did. Remember that time we played Storm the Castle at her house? Bobby was Sir Lancelot and I was Joan of Arc and—"

Lacy cuts in. "And I was your servant, Little Miss Puddin' Head."

I can't help but laugh. You have to admit it's a funny name, but I guess it wasn't so funny to her at the time.

"The point is," I say, "how many fifteen-year-old boys are going to go out of their way to play games just to entertain their little sisters. And what happens? Grandma has to go and ruin the whole thing by throwing a fit all over us."

"You stole her lawn gnome and tossed it off the Twelfth Street bridge."

"Well, that's the kind of thing that happens to people who treat you like crap."

Just for the record, here's what happened with the lawn gnome incident. We were on one of our rare visits to Grandma's—I was about nine—and Grandma confiscated my skates from me for skating in her kitchen. Took them and said she wasn't giving them back till I left the next day. This was back when I thought I wanted to be in the roller derby, so those skates meant a lot to me.

Anyway, I got the idea to kidnap her lawn gnome and hold him hostage. Of course, Bobby thought this was hilarious and volunteered to help me carry him across the Twelfth Street bridge, where we could stash him behind the grade school. Then we'd lay out the deal to Grandma—she'd get the gnome if I got the skates.

But on the way, Bobby had the idea it would be funny to set the gnome on the bridge railing and pretend he was about to commit suicide.

"Don't jump, little fella," Bobby said, standing back like he was afraid to make any sudden moves. "You've got your whole life ahead of you!"

"Don't worry. I'll save him," I cried, and lunged for the gnome. Only instead of pulling him back to safety, I accidentally pushed him over the edge. *Crash!* There he was in a million little gnome pieces on the concrete below. I guess we were lucky a car wasn't driving under the bridge at the time.

At that point, I was all for running away, but Bobby said we had to stay and clean the thing up, then take the shattered corpse back to Grandma and tell her we'd pay for a new one. I didn't like the sound of that, but I always did what Bobby said.

The problem was Lacy found out what happened and went running off to squeal to Grandma before we could explain things for ourselves. Of course, Grandma didn't believe it was a mistake. She accused Bobby of killing her stupid gnome on purpose. And he didn't even do it—I did!

He took the full blame, though, said I didn't have anything to do with it, but Grandma didn't want to hear any explanations. She told us we were just nothing but mean kids and that she shouldn't be surprised with the way our father raised us. That didn't sit well with Bobby.

"You're the one who's mean," he said. "Taking a little girl's skates away for no good reason. You're just a mean, dried-up old woman."

That's when Grandma called him *impertinent* and slapped him. *Pow!* Right across the mouth.

"Go ahead and hit me again," he said, staring her down. "Hit me as much as you want. But don't badmouth my sister and my father."

Grandma's hand trembled, her lips quivered, her eye twitched, but she didn't hit him again. She never told our parents about the situation either. I don't know why. But after that, Bobby and I made every excuse we could to avoid going back to her house.

"And you know what?" I tell Lacy over the phone. "There never would've been a big problem if you hadn't squealed on us to Grandma."

"Well," she says, "the only reason I told on you was because you wouldn't let me go to the bridge with you."

I had forgotten that part, but it was true. She had begged us to let her go on our gnome adventure.

"Well," I tell her, "how could we let you go? You were crying like a baby. We didn't want some little baby going with us."

"I cried because I wanted to hang out with you. That's all I wanted when I was little—to hang out with my big sister. But I gave up. You didn't want me, so I just gave up."

"And you're giving up on Bobby now too. Is that it?"

"I'm not giving up, Ceejay. I just can't come home right now. I just can't. Bobby will still be there in a month when Grandma's better, but right now she needs me and Bobby doesn't."

I sit quiet for a moment, staring at the wall. What a sister. Her whole life the parents played her as the favorite, and now she's trying to act like she's the one nobody wants. Well, if that's the way she wants it, that's the way she'll get it. "You're right," I tell her. "He doesn't need you around. And neither do I."

Before she can cough out a response, I hang up on her. Usually I'd say that makes me the winner, but somehow, this time, I don't really feel like I won much of anything.

128

23

On the big day, even though there are a lot of preparations to take care of before the party kicks off, Bobby heads out somewhere with Chuck, saying he'll be back in plenty of time. Mom acts like that's okay. She says she wouldn't dream of putting him to work. After all, the party is for him. But as the time for the party gets closer, I catch her glancing at the clock, her usual perky smile still on her face but worry in her eyes. Finally, with about ten minutes to spare, Bobby and Chuck reappear. They've been taking care of their own preparations—making sure they have an enormous blue ice chest fully stocked with beer.

Pretty soon people start packing into the house and backyard. They're everywhere. Our place really isn't big enough for a crowd like this—uncles, aunts, cousins, church people,

Grandma and Grandpa McDermott. My parents have all their friends there, and so do my big sister Colleen, her husband, and Drew. Tillman, Gillis, and Brianna all show up together. But out of everyone there, Chuck is the only one Bobby asked to come.

Before Iraq, a party like this wouldn't have fazed Bobby. He would've had his whole rowdy bunch here with him. Probably would've pulled some crazy stunt just to see the looks on the church people's faces. Like the time he and his buddies painted themselves red and ran through the middle of a church picnic wearing only their underwear. Now, as one person after the next comes at him with their fat smiles and handshakes, he just stands there like a dazed boxer soaking up punches.

Me, I don't get much of a chance to talk to him, so I'm glad to have my close circle with me. Otherwise it'd be easy to feel very, very purple in an all-yellow world. Of course, I'm always glad to see Uncle Jimmy. He's having a great time. Bobby and Chuck have been generous in sharing their beer with him. He sidles up to me by the backyard flowerbed and nudges my arm. "So," he says, "I guess your little sister is still in Davenport taking care of your Grandma Brinker, huh?"

I tell him that she is, and he goes, "That's good. That way your mom can stay down here and keep your dad away from Diane Simmons."

This is the second time Uncle Jimmy has hinted that Diane Simmons, the church lady who comes by with food while Mom visits Grandma, has her sights set on Dad. And this is the second time I tell him he's crazy for thinking that.

"Really?" he says. "Well, check that out." He nods toward where my dad is standing. Ms. Simmons is about two inches away from him, waving her boobs around. Dad says something

130

and she laughs and touches his arm. I look around for Mom. She must be in the house.

"I tried a little flirting with her myself a while ago," Uncle Jimmy says. "And I've been known to work a lot of magic in that department over the years, but not this time. I'm thinking your dad's already put a spell on her."

"I can't see my dad having anything to do with any spells."

"You didn't know him back in the day."

"Yeah, but I know him now. She can flash her cleavage all she wants, and he's probably not thinking of anything but the next joke he's planning to tell."

"You're probably right," Uncle Jimmy says, but you can tell he doesn't mean it.

Across the lawn, Ms. Simmons laughs again. Dad's smiling like he's running for office. "Of course I'm right," I say, but I'm not so convinced this time.

As the afternoon unwinds, I'm surprised Bobby's hands don't turn blue from frostbite after reaching into the ice chest for so many beers. Drinking doesn't seem to do him a whole lot of good, though, not like it does for Chuck, who is practically glowing. You'd think this party is for him. He's flirting with the middle-aged ladies, talking football with the middle-aged men, making children giggle, and he still has time to wrap his arm around Bobby's neck every once in a while and say how glad he is to have his old buddy back in town.

I can see why girls fall for him. He may be the most irresponsible guy on the planet, but responsibility is beside the point when you're around him. There's nothing in the world to worry about. Life is shiny. It's as weightless as an astronaut. No wonder Bobby chose to stay with him instead of here at home.

Finally, Bobby has all he can take of the cheery faces,

nagging questions, and happy backslaps. He disappears. Mom asks me to go see if he's upstairs and get him to come back down. "I'm sure he's pretty tired," she says. *Tired* being her way of saying *drunk*. "But it's almost time to put the food on. He'll feel better with a little something in his stomach."

Upstairs, I find him lying on my bed listening to one of his old CDs. I've kept it on the shelf while he was away and played it every once in a while to remember him by. He opens his eyes and, seeing it's only me, he smiles. "Ceejay," he says. "My super-stupendous best sister. Have you come to rescue me from myself?"

"Mom sent me." I sit on the side of the bed. "She wants you to come back down. It's almost time to eat."

"Okay," he says. "I knew I couldn't get away with hiding for long, but it's so damn weird down there. Just let me listen to this next song."

The song he's talking about is called "Emerald Soul." It's loud, the kind of song that scrapes all the negative feelings out of your shoulder blades. He listens to it with his eyes closed and his hands folded across his stomach. When it winds down, he sits up and looks at me.

"That's my favorite song," he says. "I remember one time Mona and I were walking down the street, and we heard that song playing out of someone's open window. It was perfect—like the soundtrack for how bright the sun was and the sound of the breeze shaking in the leaves. It was playing just for me. I was in the exact right place at the right time." He looks toward the window as if maybe he could see that moment again if he tried hard enough. "Man," he says, looking back at the floor. "Where did moments like that go? They're gone. You can't get them back. Now it's like I'm always in the wrong place at the wrong time, and there isn't any right place to be anyway."

"You'll get them back," I tell him.

"I just want to turn off the radar. I just want to drown it out."

"The radar?"

"That's what it feels like over there. Like you've always got to have your radar on. You have to watch everything every second. You have to listen for it. You have to feel it with your whole body. If you don't, the fucking universe will cave in on you. Even with the people here you feel like you have to look at every face, every movement. I just want to turn it off."

I put my hand on his arm. "There won't be stupid parties like this every weekend. Just wait. You'll get settled in and then everything will go back to normal. Maybe you could get your own little rent house and I could come and live with you."

"Maybe." He smiles at me, but it's the smile an old man might give a little kid for saying something sweet and naive. "Okay," he says, clapping his hands, "time to stop my sorry bullshit and go back down to work the coal mine."

Once we're in the backyard again, he seems almost rejuvenated, even manages a smile here and there. Mom comes over, clasps his arm and leans her head onto his shoulder. She's beaming. Uncle Jimmy takes a picture of them with his cellphone camera, and at the last second Chuck jumps in and kisses my mom on the cheek. She swats him on the arm, but you can tell she loves him if for no other reason than that she knows he loves Bobby.

Finally, the time comes to fire up the backyard grill. This is really Dad's chance to play the star. His red cap says COOKOUT KING across the front and his apron reads HOT DOG! The grill is a stainless steel Weber with all sorts of accessories. Top of the line. Dad takes a couple of spatulas and a set of tongs and juggles them before he starts slapping the food on. There's trays of meat next to him—burger patties, hot links, chicken breasts. I guarantee none of the men will touch the chicken.

Mom's in the kitchen working on side dishes, so who do you think decides to play assistant chef? Ms. Simmons. I'm starting to believe Uncle Jimmy isn't crazy after all. Not that I think Dad's up to anything with those giant boobs of hers, but it's all too obvious she's ready to serve them up whenever he's ready.

I'm standing in my little group with Bobby, Brianna, Gillis, and Tillman, who's made it clear he's bent out of shape because we had to cancel our paintball game for the party.

"Look at old Ms. Simmons flashing her girls at Dad," I say. "Think she's horny much?"

Gillis stares at her. "I don't care how old she is," he says. "I'd stick my face down in the middle of those things and not come up for air for a week."

"You're sick," says Brianna.

A worried expression crosses Bobby's face, but it doesn't have anything to do with Ms. Simmons' boobs. "Jesus," he says. "What is that?"

"What?" I say.

"That smell. What's that goddamn smell?"

I'm like, "I don't know. You mean the burgers grilling?"

"Get me out of here," he says. It's not worry on his face now. It's that same mix of panic and rage he had that night the captain's hammer pounding startled him.

"Turn that smell off," he cries. "Turn it off. I think I'm gonna puke."

He heads toward the house, shoving guests out of the way as he goes. "Turn that smell off!"

I'm chasing after him and everyone's staring like we're both

134

crazy. He has trouble getting the patio door open and when he finally does, he lunges inside, and then it's like his legs melt and he collapses onto his knees.

I'm at his side. "What's wrong, Bobby?"

"Shut the door," he says, his face pale and his lips sagging like he really might puke. "Shut the fucking door, so I don't have to smell that."

Everyone inside is gaping at him. Someone mutters, "Looks like he drank a little bit too much."

I pull on his arm. "Let me help you up. We'll get you upstairs."

His arm trembles as I help him upstairs and he gulps for air. "I want to lie down," he says. "I want to lock the goddamn door."

I no sooner get him into my room than Mom and Dad follow us in.

"What's wrong?" Mom asks. "What happened?"

"Nothing," I say, helping Bobby sit on the bed. "He's just worn out."

"Too many beers," Dad says. He looks Bobby over like he's sizing up some kind of repair job he's getting ready to work on. "We'll get a burger into him and he'll be all right. Ceejay, go get some aspirin."

I look at Bobby to see if that's what he wants, but he's like, "I don't need any aspirin. And I sure as hell don't need any of that burning meat."

Mom says, "Maybe a chicken breast would be better." And Bobby goes, "No, I don't want a chicken breast either. I don't even want to get near anything off that grill."

"Hey," says Dad, "that grill's practically new."

Mom's like, "Just a nice chicken breast and maybe some cold fruit."

I can't believe it—the parents can be so dense. They have no idea they should just let me and Bobby alone right now.

"Aren't you listening?" Bobby pleads. And then he says something really strange. "I don't want any of that stuff. It smells like you're burning human flesh down there."

Dad laughs. He actually laughs. "Don't worry," he says, his eyes crinkling at the corners. "Those burger patties are from good old American cows. We're not cooking any humans around here."

Bobby stares at Dad for a moment, his face drained of color. "You don't get it," he says. "You haven't smelled burning human flesh before, but I have. It gets in you. It smokes your lungs and your brain and you can cough and cough and you can't get the ashes out."

That's something I've never thought of—the way a burning person would smell. It's almost enough to make you sick just thinking about it.

Mom sits on the bed next to him and pats his back. "All right, honey," she says. "You don't have to go back outside. Just come down to the kitchen and we'll fix you up a cold-cut sandwich."

"No, we won't," Dad says. He's all serious and take-command now, trying too hard at being a big tough-love dad. "Listen, son, I know you've been through some bad things, but there's a lot of people who have come to see you down there. Now, I didn't say anything when you started putting beers away one after the next—I liked my beer when I was a young man too—but I'm not going to let you disappoint your family and friends because of the way something smells. So get off your butt and come back down there and be the hometown hero these folks came to see."

"Hometown hero, huh?" Bobby glares at Dad. "Is that what

136

I'm supposed to be? Well, let me tell you what kind of hometown hero I am."

He stands and looks Dad in the eye. There's something in Bobby's face, something in his voice, that makes me dread what he's going to say.

"You want to know why I'm home early?" he asks without waiting for an answer. "It's because the army kicked me out, that's why. They don't want me, don't want a single thing to do with me. That's how much of a hero I am."

My legs suddenly go weak. Bobby kicked out of the army? How could that be? Something has to be wrong. Somebody has to have made a mistake. I mean, look at him—his shoulders are so broad, his arms so big around. No one in their right mind could kick him out of the army.

"What are you talking about?" Dad asks, his look of command starting to crack.

"I'm talking about the army throwing me out on my ass, Dad, that's what I'm talking about." Bobby looks at Mom, who is still sitting on the bed. "I'm sorry I'm not a hero, but that's the way it is."

"But you got an honorable discharge, right?" asks Dad.

Bobby shakes his head. "Of course it wasn't honorable. Do I look honorable? It was a general discharge—no benefits, no GI Bill, no VA hospital, no nothing. I don't exist to them anymore."

"You can't be serious," says Dad. "How could they give you a general discharge?"

"It's not that hard," Bobby says. "All you have to do is get caught by the German police with a couple hundred dollars' worth of hash on you."

Dad looks stunned, but in a way I'm relieved. Bobby was just being Bobby, I tell myself, out for a wild time, and the uptight military types couldn't understand that was just part of what makes him the baddest soldier to ever come out of Knowles. Of course, Mom doesn't see it that way.

"Hash?" she says, wide-eyed, like hash is something that comes straight from Satan.

"Yeah," Bobby says. "Hashish. It's a kind of drug. You smoke it."

"I know what it is," Mom says. "I just don't know why you'd want to have it. I thought you put all that kind of thing behind you when you went in the army."

"I didn't *want* to have it. I *had* to have it."

That, I'm not sure I understand. It just doesn't sound like Bobby.

Dad acts like it's a total lie. "That's a load of crap and you know it. You don't *have* to have drugs. You choose to."

"Yeah, well," Bobby says, "there isn't much choosing about it when the alternative is bad enough."

"A son of mine." Dad shakes his head. "Thrown out of the army."

"Not too pretty, is it?" Bobby says. "I'm sure you won't blame me for not hanging around pretending I'm some kind of hero in front of your friends."

He waits a moment for Dad to say something, but no response comes, so he turns to Mom. "I'm sorry. I should've told you before you got everyone over here. Or maybe I should've just stayed away."

"Don't say that," Mom tells him, her voice cracking.

"What are you going to do, feel sorry for yourself now?" Dad says, and I want to yell at him to shut up. I want to order him and Mom both out of the room because they aren't doing anything to help, just like they didn't help the last time Bobby got in trouble and they sent him off to the war.

Bobby just smiles a heartless smile, his mouth like a cold, twisted strand of wire. "No. What I'm going to do is get the hell out of here. This isn't where I belong. Not anymore." He dodges around Dad and heads for the hall, bumping his shoulder against the doorframe on the way out.

"Bobby," Mom cries, but Dad just says, "Let him go."

Let him go. That's all.

For a moment I stare at Dad, expecting him to change his mind and go hurrying after Bobby. I want to hear him say, "Come back, son. We don't care anything about any general discharge. Getting caught with drugs doesn't change what you did in the war. You're still a hero to us." But he doesn't say that. He just stands there.

"God." I look from Dad to Mom and back. "I can't believe you two. Can't you see this is all your fault? All this talk about being a hero and you were such big cowards you wouldn't stand up for him when he needed it most. Well, if you're not going after him, I will."

I burst out of the room, but when I get to the top of the stairs, Bobby's already halfway down and doesn't turn around when I call after him. Chuck is standing at the bottom of the stairs, but Bobby doesn't even seem to recognize him. He just tears open the front door and leaves it hanging open behind him.

Outside, about halfway down the block, I finally catch up to him. "Hey," I say. "Do you think a stupid general discharge means anything to me? Who cares? It doesn't even sound bad. So, you had some hash on you—a soldier has to unwind after being in battle. We'll get a lawyer and fight it."

"Go home, Ceejay."

"You don't even have to go to the lawyer's office. Just give me the discharge, and I'll take it over there Monday morning."

"You think I saved the paperwork? It's not like I thought someone was going to want to hang it on the refrigerator."

"But it's stupid. They just can't do that to someone like you."

He stops and glares at me. "Someone like me? What do you think I'm like, Ceejay? You think I'm still that same guy I was in high school? You think I'm the tough dude who protected you, who stuck up for little dudes against bullies? Well, I'm not. That guy got killed in the war."

He stares at me for a moment, and it's like someone else is looking through his eyes.

Chuck pulls up to the curb in his truck. "I figured you might need a ride," he says through the open window. Bobby looks off down the street. "Do me a favor, Ceejay. Go back to the house and pack my stuff up in my duffel bag. I'll come get it tomorrow."

"You mean you're not going to stay at home?"

He opens the door to the pickup. "I don't even know what home means anymore." He gets in the truck and I stand there and watch it get smaller as it heads down the road.

This isn't right, I tell myself. This isn't right. Nothing is right in this whole frigging world.

24

Standing on the front porch, Mom looks like someone slapped her, while Dad looks more like he's ready to slap someone, anyone. "Good job, Dad," I say as I walk up to the porch. "You really handled that well."

He just glares at me. Mom reaches her hand toward my shoulder. "Ceejay," she says, but I just brush by. Inside, people stare at me like I'm some bank robber's sidekick, but who cares? They're not my friends. I don't have anything to say to them. Instead, I go out to the backyard where Gillis, Tillman, and Brianna are still hanging around scarfing burgers. "What the hell happened?" asks Gillis with his mouth full.

"Nothing," I tell him. "Come on. Let's get out of here."

We pack into Brianna's car and drive by Chuck's, but no

one's there, so we drive around looking for Bobby. Up and down the streets we go, but no luck.

"He probably doesn't want to be found," Brianna suggests.

"I wouldn't if I was him," Tillman says.

I whip around and look at him in the backseat. "What's that supposed to mean?"

"Nothing. I just don't think I'd want to go back to the party after freaking out big-time like he did."

"He doesn't give a damn about that," I shoot back.

"Then what is it?" Brianna asks.

I don't really want to tell them about Bobby getting kicked out of the army, but they'll find out sooner or later. No need to sugarcoat it either. I tell them about the hash and everything.

"But that doesn't mean Bobby has anything to be embarrassed about," I say. "The ones who gave him that stupid discharge should be embarrassed. They should be ashamed. Squeezing everything they can out of a soldier, then throwing him over for one mistake."

"You can't really be shocked, though," Gillis says. "I never could see the military lifestyle mixing too well with a dude like Bobby. Too many rules."

"Shit," adds Tillman. "I wouldn't last six months in the army myself."

"Just think," says Brianna, "now you don't have to worry about him going back to Iraq anymore."

They're just trying to help, I guess, but I still feel all tangled up. Driving hopelessly around Knowles doesn't do any good either, so after about an hour, I have Brianna drop me off at home.

The party's over, of course. I'm sure Mom and Dad didn't come out and explain Bobby's exact situation, but everybody was bound to know something weird was up. I can just imagine how it must have gone. Mom putting on her smiley face. Dad taking his station at the grill, trying to crack bad jokes. People probably hung around for a while just to be polite—it'd be rude to let the food go to waste. I'm sure they even tried to look like they were having fun. But after tossing their paper plates and plastic forks in the trash, one by one, two by two, three by three, they made their excuses to leave. And that's out of politeness too. Only bad guests would keep their hosts smiling fake smiles any longer than they have to.

When I walk through the door, the parents are in the backyard cleaning up. Usually I'd help but not right now. I don't want to see my parents. Don't even want to hear their voices.

In my room, I crank up "Emerald Soul" and blast it loud and heavy. I have this feeling I need to be somewhere else, like another dimension or something, but I don't know how to get there. And yes, I'll admit it, the tears come flooding out. That's okay, though. Nobody's around so it doesn't really count.

When the song ends, I dry my stupid eyes and pick up my phone. I have to talk to someone, but who? Definitely not my sisters. They always take our parents' side against me. Chuck wouldn't be bad, but he wasn't home when we went by. For a long time, I lie there just holding the phone. It's smooth and warm in my hand. Finally, I dial every digit in Mr. White's phone number but one. Then I take a deep breath and press the last one too.

"Hello?"

"Padgett?" Using Mr. White's real name for a change sounds funny coming out of my mouth.

"Ceejay?"

I ask him if he has time to talk and he says he does. Only Mr. White wouldn't have anything else to do on Saturday night. At first, I mumble around, not sure of where to start, but then he says, "It's about Bobby, isn't it?" and I tell him yes, and everything busts out from there.

I tell him about the restaurant the other night and all the beers Bobby had today, how he talked about the song "Emerald Soul" like it was a magic spell that somehow got drained of its power, and how he freaked out thinking the burgers smelled like burned human flesh. And how he finally admitted the army booted him out for possession of hash.

Luckily, Mr. White listens without coming back with a single theory about why Bobby did what he did. I slide off the bed and sit on the floor and pour out my memories of Bobby before the war and how we were the only ones in our family who were the same and what I thought and felt the whole time he was away. I ramble and ramble, and all Mr. White says is *yes*, *mmm-hmm*, and *I see what you mean*, and that's exactly what I need.

I talk for over an hour. My mouth is dry and my throat is sore, but I can't hang up. Even when the words stop coming, I can't hang up. After a stretch of silence, Mr. White says the best thing he can right now, "I could come get you and we could go riding around if you want."

"That'd be good," I say. "I'll be standing in the driveway."

Once he picks me up, we go driving in no particular direction, neither one of us saying a word. He must sense how hollow the town seems to me right now, so he heads into the country, onto the narrow highways and fire roads. Finally, he parks beside a field that's clotted with old oil-patch equipment.

We get out and climb the fence, and he leads me over to an oil drum lying on its side, and we sit there and look across the field. "I love the way this stuff looks in the moonlight," he says. "It's like modern sculpture."

"Looks like the rust and the weeds are taking it over."

"They're not taking it over," he says. "They're taking it back. It's beautiful."

He picks up a pebble and tosses it in the direction of the rusted remains of a pump jack. You have to like the way he looks right now. I'm not going to try to kid anybody and say he's handsome, but his face has character. You know, like Abraham Lincoln or somebody.

"Have you ever thought about what it'd be like if you died?" he asks.

"You mean like would I go to heaven or hell?"

"Yeah. Or anything. It doesn't have to be heaven or hell necessarily. I mean, who wants to go to heaven with a bunch of jerks who didn't understand you while you were here? No, if I died I'd want to have my ashes spread out in a field just like this. That way it'd rain and the sun would shine down, and I'd end up part of a stalk of grass or a weed, even. That'd be good, I think."

"You might end up being part of a worm."

"That's all right. Worms aren't so bad." He smiles at me and I have to laugh. An hour ago, I wouldn't have thought I'd ever laugh again.

"So, does that mean you don't believe in God?"

"I didn't say that. But maybe God's not sitting on some throne up in heaven, moving everyone around like a bunch of chess pieces. Maybe God's everywhere. You know?" He waves a hand toward the field. "That's how I look at it. God could be like this pure energy. For all I know God could be the Yimmies like the captain's always talking about."

"Yeah, sure," I say. "You're going to have a hard time convincing me God's hanging around here."

He studies me for a second. "I'm sorry," he says. "Here I am, rattling on about some theory while you're worried about your brother."

"That's all right. I guess I just need to have hope, huh?"

He's quiet for a moment, his face somber.

"What's wrong?" I ask.

"Nothing," he says. His voice sounds odd. The confidence has cracked. Suddenly, it occurs to me that maybe he has some things he needs to talk about too.

"You know, it's weird," I tell him. "You talk about what you're going to do in the future when you get out of this town and all, but you never talk about your past life, like why you moved from the city to a dumpy little town like Knowles in the first place."

"You don't want to hear about that."

"What are you talking about? Of course I want to hear about it. You've listened to me whine all evening. I'd be pretty crappy if I couldn't return the favor."

He picks at the back of his hand like he's trying to remove a scab. "Okay, but it's the same old story you hear a million times—boy thinks everything's fine at home, or at least not too screwed up, and then *bang*, his parents split up." He pauses. "My mom and dad were both social workers—you'd think they'd get along great, having so much in common and all—but I guess she was having an affair with their boss, this older dude with a big, fat head. Apparently Dad had no idea. Then this department supervisor dude got some bigger job out of state, so Mom comes in and tells Dad she's leaving him."

"Jesus, that's pretty ugly."

"Yeah. She gave me the whole tired cliché about how just because she and Dad fell out of love, that didn't mean she quit loving me. Then she moved away and I haven't seen her since. So much for her still loving me, huh?"

146

"I don't know. People do weird things."

"Dad pretty much lost it, started drinking, missing work. Got fired from his job and ended up working at a Big Buy store, wearing one of those blue vests and a name tag. He hated it. Then he got fired from there too. Next thing I know it's like I'm the parent, trying to save him from himself."

He pauses for a moment before going on. "Finally, he had this bad car wreck with me in the car. He was drunk and blew through a stoplight. This little Toyota rammed right into his door. He was the only one who got hurt—broken leg—but he ended up in rehab. I guess he was lucky he didn't get tossed in jail. So, anyway, I moved over here to stay with my aunt. He's back home now, but he's not exactly in shape to take care of anybody but himself for a while. Maybe that's why I want to save the world—because I couldn't save my family."

"Maybe," I say, not really wanting to get into the psychology business right now. "So why didn't you move in with your mom?"

He stares across the pasture for a moment. "I talked to her about it, but she said it wasn't a good time. Something about how she was trying to put her life together with her new dude. Maybe later, she said."

I'm like, "Wow." I mean, what else can you say?

"Yeah," he says. "And then I was supposed to go down and visit her next weekend, but she called the other day and cancelled. She just found out she's pregnant. Forty years old and pregnant again, starting a whole new family. So it looks like there's never going to be a right time for me and her."

"That sucks," I say. Suddenly I feel very close to him. It's weird how bad things can draw people together. "But I'm glad you're here."

"You are?"

"Yeah."

"I'm glad I'm here too."

"You know what?" I bump my shoulder against his. "I used to think you were really a weird kid."

"And now you don't?"

"No, I still think you're weird, but it's a good kind of weird."

"Thanks." He chuckles. "That's about the best compliment I've ever had. It's even better coming from you."

I look away, smiling. "You know, there's something I've been wondering about. Why didn't you ever talk in English class? That would've been fun. I'd love to have seen Mrs. Halber's face when she heard you coming with your misfit revolution stuff."

"Yeah," he says. "Teachers don't like it when you're too smart. And guys want to beat you up."

"I wouldn't have let that happen."

"You wouldn't, huh?"

"I promise you."

He laughs. "You know, you're the only one in this town I had any interest in getting to know."

"Me?"

"Of course. I mean, look at you. You have this incredible energy about you. I saw it the first time you walked into English class, like you owned the room. I thought, Look at that girl. She doesn't let what people think of her change one little thing she does. It was pretty magnificent."

"Yeah?" I say. "So that time you gave me a ride home, why did you say I didn't have any idea who I really am?"

"Because you don't. How could you? You're so much more than you could ever think you are. Thoughts aren't even big enough for it."

"Oh."

We meet each other's gaze for a second, then both look away. I wish I knew some perfect thing to say back to him, but I don't.

Across the field, the moonlight washes across the broken machinery, the high grass, and the sunflower stalks. Glancing down at Mr. White's hand, I wonder if he'll put it on my knee again. He doesn't, though. We just sit there side by side until it's time to go, and that's just fine.

25

At home, the parents are lying in wait. No sooner am I in the door than Dad pops out of the shadows and orders me into the kitchen for a talk. Mom's already in there. She sets a slice of pie on the table in front of me, like she can buy me off with that.

Dad sits across from me, his hands folded on the tabletop. Mom sits to my right. "Where have you been?" Dad says. He sounds like an FBI agent interrogating a terrorist suspect.

"Out with a friend," I say.

Dad wants to know who this friend is. Mom's probably already called all the usual suspects, so I tell the truth. "Padgett Locke," I say. "You wouldn't know him. He's new in town."

"You didn't see Bobby?" Mom asks.

"No. He's probably in deep hiding after the way you guys treated him."

"Don't try to lay the blame on us," Dad says.

"We just want what's best for him," Mom adds.

I can't look at them. Everything about them seems annoying right now. My dad's built like a cement mixer with a Bassmaster T-shirt on. Even my mother's hair annoys me. It's so perfect. How can it be so perfect when everything else is so messed up?

"This is a serious thing," Dad says. "It can affect your brother's whole future, getting discharged that way—without honor."

"Bobby's not the one without honor," I say, staring at the limp slice of pie. "He did his part."

"Ceejay," Mom says, "we don't love Bobby any less. We want to help him, get him back on the right path."

Dad follows up with, "Your brother needs to know—and so do you—that the choices you make matter. They have consequences. You can't go around being a wild kid all your life. You have to take that long step into responsibility land. I know. I had to do it."

Finally I look up at him. "So what kind of choice did you make today, Dad? You ran Bobby out of the house. You wouldn't even let him tell his whole story. And Mom, you didn't even make Lacy come back here for her own brother's homecoming from the war. Those are some real great choices."

Dad stares at me, and I try to match him but have to turn away before the tears start.

"Ceejay, your sister is doing what she has to do right now," Mom says. "I talked about it with her. It's not like she didn't want to come. It's just a hard time with your grandmother right now."

"The world doesn't revolve around your brother or you," Dad says. "Your grandma has cancer. Do you understand that? Cancer."

I nod.

Dad goes on, "I don't know what's wrong with your brother. Maybe some army buddy of his got him on that hashish, but that's a weak man's way to go, and that's not how I raised your brother or you."

"Bobby's not weak," I say, my eyes and face burning.

"If he's not," Dad says, "then he'll come back here and face up to us. He'll face up to us and to himself. And then he'll get his butt in gear and face up to his responsibilities as a man. If he gets in touch with you, you tell him that."

"And tell him we love him," Mom adds.

I shove the untouched plate of pie away. "Is that all?"

Dad leans back in the chair and folds his arms across his chest. "For now," he says.

26

Of course, Bobby doesn't have any intention of facing the parental firing squad. He doesn't even come back for his duffel bag. He sends Chuck over Sunday afternoon instead. Mom's sweet to him about it, but even she can't hide how crushed she is that her son wouldn't come get it himself. Dad doesn't say a thing. That's his strategy. He thinks all Bobby needs is to do a little growing up, as if he's just going through a phase like a junior high boy whose voice is changing or a girl getting her boobs.

Everybody has some kind of opinion about Bobby. Mom acts like he's a little boy with a bruised knee, and if he'd just come home and let her put something on it, everything would be all right. Brianna thinks he lost the big fun side of himself in the war. Gillis says he can't be too worried about Bobby if he's

153

still nailing some sweet ass off Mona, and Tillman thinks Bobby hasn't really changed all that much. He says Bobby was always crazy, but it's just not funny now that he's out of high school.

I don't pay too much attention to Tillman's opinion, though. He's nursed a grudge against Bobby ever since fifth grade when Bobby came down hard on him for playing keep-away with skinny little Ronald Farquar's glasses. "You think Ronald's pathetic?" Bobby told him. "Well, from where I'm standing, you're the one who's pathetic, taking a little dude's glasses away from him like that. Now, why don't you and your giant Adam's apple give 'em back before I go jackass wild all over your frame."

Before that, Tillman had always looked up to Bobby, which just made it worse. Especially the Adam's apple part. I guess that's how it is, though—you don't want to think you're wrong, so you have to think the other person is.

At work, Uncle Jimmy tells me not to worry too much about Bobby. It's just the wild life of the army he's still living. Uncle Jimmy's had buddies who came back from being stationed in places like Taiwan and Malaysia and they knew how to get their party on better than anyone he'd ever met. Even Jerry throws in his two cents. To him, Bobby sounds like Batman, a superhero with a dark side that he's bound to overcome. Of course, I wouldn't be surprised if Jerry thought most people were superheroes compared to his goofy little self. Probably thinks I'm Wonder Woman.

The only person that doesn't really have an opinion is Chuck. He just says Bobby is Bobby. That's Chuck for you. He looks at things for what they are. Then one day, I call his apartment, and he drops an absolute bomb on me—Bobby isn't staying with him anymore. He moved in with Dani.

Don't you know my heart just about caves in through the

rickety floor of my stomach when I hear that? How am I ever going to talk him into moving into a little rent house with me if he's shacking up with some girl?

I'm like, "Dani! You have to be kidding. I thought he was still all hot for Mona."

"Maybe he is, but what's he going to do—move into her attic or something? I don't think her husband would like that too much."

"What about Jace?"

"Dani gave him the boot. Packed up all his stuff and told him never to come back. Can't blame her, can you? That guy's a tool."

This sounds like a completely terrible idea, and not just because I was hoping me and Bobby would get our place together. Dani is just not a good match. Sure, she's Tillman's sister and everything, but there's something a little diabolical about her. She gravitates toward trouble. Mistakes ugly drama for passion.

Later, when I talk to Tillman, he's not too happy about it either, though for the opposite reason. He claims he actually likes Jace. Thinks Jace is great with Dani's little boy. "I don't want to say anything bad about Bobby," he tells me, "but he's semi-psychotic."

I'm like, "Screw you. He is not."

"Well, all I can say is he better treat my sister right."

"What's that supposed to mean?"

"You know what it means."

Nevertheless, he ends up agreeing to call his sister and get us invited out there. I want to see just how permanent this situation appears, and Tillman says it'll give him a chance to see how Bobby is with his sister and her son, Ian. "I want to see for myself how Bobby stacks up next to Jace," he says. "I have an idea that'll be real interesting."

I don't like the sound of his voice. It's almost like he's plotting something. Sometimes Tillman can be a little sinister, just like his sister, but I figure he's not smart enough to pull off anything too evil.

So the next evening rolls around and it's me, Tillman, Brianna, and Gillis heading to Dani's trailer. As we pull away from Brianna's, I casually drop the suggestion that maybe we should see if Padgett can come with us, and Brianna's like, "Padgett? You're calling Mr. White *Padgett* now?"

"Yeah," says Gillis. "What's the deal? Are you going romantic for this idiot or something?"

I'm like, "What are you talking about? It's just that he's been good with Bobby. That's all."

"Forget it," says Tillman. "We're not taking that pussy over to my sister's house."

I start to argue but decide against it. What can I say? I'm not even too sure why I want to bring him along.

As we pull onto the winding gravel drive that leads to Dani's trailer, Bobby's motorcycle comes into view—he must have gone by and picked it up from Uncle Jimmy—and then so does Captain Crazy's lime-green pickup truck. I'm not exactly happy to see that, but Tillman is completely pissed.

"Are you kidding me?" he says. "Your brother's bringing Captain Crazy over here? I knew Dani taking him in was a bad idea."

"Just shut up," I tell him. That's the only argument I can come up with. It's not like I want to put out a lot of energy defending the captain as appropriate company for Dani's two-year-old.

Dani meets us at the door and takes us inside. Bobby's sitting at the kitchen table with little Ian, in his booster seat, on one side and the captain on the other. He looks a little too much at home for my taste.

The captain shoots a big, bright smile our way. He has a napkin tucked into his collar for a bib, but it looks like his beard's doing the real work as far as catching crumbs. They're finishing a heat-up pizza and Ian has tomato sauce smeared across his face. He looks like one of those little bitty clowns that come piling out of a miniature car at the circus.

Dani tells us to get ourselves some pizza and beer and have a seat in the living room. She also has some ice cream and strawberries for after the pizza's gone. It's weird—she seems to be trying to come off as some kind of grown-uppy party hostess like you see on TV, but you can't really take her seriously. I mean, Martha Stewart probably threw dinner parties for more upscale groups than us even when she was in prison.

It's like I've stepped into the middle of some demented freak-show family, and Bobby's the head of the household.

Once everyone's finished with their ice cream, we're left in the living room staring at each other. Tillman gets up and heads back to the bathroom. I glimpse him pulling his phone out of his pocket and have to wonder who he's calling. Just about everybody who will put up with him is already here.

Sitting on the couch, the captain is beaming. It's like he can't believe his luck to be invited to such a gathering. "Well," he says, giving his knees a hearty slap. "We've got 'em on the run today, don't we?"

"Got who on the run?" Gillis asks.

The captain just smiles and winks at him. Ian toddles across the room, stops in front of the captain and stares at him. Dani tells him to come back over to her, but the captain's like,

157

"Let him stare. I don't mind. Not a bit. Children are attracted to the Yimmies. You can't blame them."

Dani's like, "The what?" and the captain goes, "The Yimmies, man. They're here today. Very much beautifully so."

Dani looks at Bobby for an explanation, but he just says, "The Yimmies. Dude. That's what I'm after." He studies the captain and Ian with a satisfied expression on his face, like the captain and him have been friends for decades.

"Ian," says the captain, "would you like to see an aero-velocipede?"

Ian nods and the captain sits on the floor, pretending to pull levers, push pedals, and guide a steering wheel, all while making a sputtering engine noise with his tongue sticking out of his mouth. Ian claps his hands and squeals with glee. Then the captain hops up and runs around the room with his arms jutting out like wings until he knocks over a lamp and pretends to crash down onto the orange carpet. The way Ian stamps his feet and laughs, you'd think his favorite cartoon character just walked into the room.

Bobby glances at Dani and jabs his thumb in the direction of the captain as if to say, "See, that's why I invited him to come over in the first place."

The captain sits there grinning. "Come here, Ceejay," he says. "I'll teach you how to fly."

"That's all right," I tell him. "Maybe later."

He cocks his head to the side. "Okay, but you have to learn sometime."

Of course, Ian is more than ready to take flying lessons, so the captain gathers him up and runs around the room making his engine-sputter sound.

"Goddamn," Tillman says to Dani. "You're gonna let Captain Crazoid play with your kid?"

"He's harmless," she says, but from the look in her eyes, I'm not sure she one hundred percent believes it.

"You know what?" says Bobby. "When the captain gets the Yimmies, there isn't anyone better to have around a kid. He's like a whole bookful of fairy tales come to life."

Tillman ignores that. "What happened with Jace?" he asks Dani. "I thought you guys were doing pretty good together."

Most people wouldn't ask a question like that right in front of a girl's new boyfriend, but Tillman never was too great with manners.

Dani scrunches up her nose as if he just let off a stink bomb. "Jace wasn't going anywhere," she says. "He had a bunch of talk, but it wasn't anything but noise."

"Yeah," Tillman says, "well, how about you, Bobby? You got a job lined up?"

"I'm not in any hurry," Bobby says. "I have some money saved. Besides, what am I going to do, skulk around Wal-Mart wearing an apron? Give me a break."

I mention that Uncle Jimmy has a lot of work lined up this summer and could probably use another hand, but Bobby just takes a pull on his beer and says, "Yeah? I'll think about it."

The captain stops in the middle of the room, little Ian still tucked under his arm. "Me and Bobby already have some work to do this summer, don't we, Bobby?"

"That's right," Bobby agrees. "We have the aero-velocipede to finish."

"And miles to fly when it's done," says the captain, the light in his eyes dancing.

This is scary to me. I'd hate to see Bobby pouring his savings into the captain's stupid aero-velocipede, but worse, I'd hate to see him try to fly it.

Tillman isn't exactly impressed with that project either.

He looks at his sister and shakes his head. "I don't know what you're thinking, Dani. Jace was doing pretty good selling weed, and then he had the part-time tow-truck deal on top of that."

"Yeah," she says, "like selling weed is a real great occupation."

"Well," Tillman says, "you sure don't mind smoking it."

Bobby's not even paying attention to any of this. Instead, he makes funny faces at Ian while the captain holds the boy up by the armpits.

Tillman goes on, "And Jace never brought any escapees from the nuthouse over either. He had fun parties with cool people."

"Right," Dani says. "Cool jailbirds and meth freaks."

"Wait a minute," says Brianna. "If, by jailbirds, you're talking about Randy Pilcher, he's a good guy. You can't condemn someone because they went to jail once."

Randy Pilcher is the smoosh-faced knucklehead that Brianna's been fooling herself into thinking she has a crush on. He's been calling her, but they only went out once since she met him at the party. He took her to the sprint-car races and then back to his place, which is a garage apartment behind his mother's house.

"Randy's a fun guy," says Tillman. "He's got some good stories."

But Dani's like, "You hang around with him then. I don't want anything to do with that crowd. They don't respect me anyway."

"Maybe that's not their fault," Tillman says.

"What's that supposed to mean?"

"Think about it," Tillman says, glancing at his watch. It's weird—I've noticed him checking his watch several times now.

160

"You got somewhere to go?" I ask him. "You keep looking at your watch."

"I'm just bored," he says, but a couple minutes later, he checks it again, and just after that, I hear the sound of a car pulling up the gravel drive. Tillman smiles, but it's not a happy kind of smile.

Car doors slam and then a drunken voice hollers, "Hey, soldier boy, I want to have a word with you out here."

It's Jace.

"Oh gawd," says Dani.

I'm like, "What's going on?" and Tillman says, "Who knows?" but from his expression, you can tell he does know something.

"Soldier boy," Jace yells again. "Come on out!"

A weary look crosses Bobby's face. "I guess that's your ex, huh?" he asks Dani.

"Don't pay any attention to him," she says. "He's too scared to actually come in here."

Jace is persistent, though. "Unless you want your motorcycle busted up and scattered around the yard, you better get your ass out here."

I'm like, God, this is just the kind of thing I was afraid of.

"Looks like I better go on out," Bobby says, rising slowly from the couch. "He's just gonna keep annoying us if I don't."

"He'll go away," says Dani, but Bobby's like, "No, he won't. The only way to keep a guy like that away is to give him one good ass-kicking."

There's nothing to do but follow him outside. Dani even brings Ian with her. We stand in a line in front of the trailer. On the far side of the big front yard, Jace stands with three of his buddies, including smoosh-face Randy Pilcher. Jace holds a baseball bat in his right hand.

161

"You got a problem?" Bobby says. His fists are balled at his sides, ready to go.

"Yeah," says Jace. "I got a problem with a military reject snaking my girl out from under me."

Bobby's like, "You can't keep your girlfriend, that's your fault. But if you got the idea you want to use that bat on somebody, here I am."

"I don't know," Jace says. "That's quite an army you got there with you. You even got a spaz and a two-year-old on your side. We're quaking and shaking."

"Yeah, well, we outnumber you," I holler at him. Then, looking down our lineup, I'm like, "Isn't that right?"

Tillman's the first to take a step back. "Hey, this isn't my fight," he says.

I look Gillis in the eyes, but he's like, "I don't know, Ceejay."

The captain scratches his beard, then breaks ranks and trots to his truck. I can't say I'm shocked at that.

"Whoa," calls Jace. "Looks like your army's deserting you."

"Come on, Brianna," yells smoosh-face Randy. "You know you're on my side, girl."

Brianna stares at the ground.

"Don't worry," I tell her. "Me and Bobby'll handle this ourselves," but Bobby goes, "No, we won't, Ceejay. This is my fight. You stay out of it."

"You know me better than that," I tell him.

Jace smacks the barrel of the bat against his palm. "Well now, let's get it on."

Brianna's still staring at the ground. Tillman leans back against the wall of the trailer, his arms crossed. Gillis stares at me, a confused leprechaun. The captain fires up the engine of his pickup, and Dani stands on the porch with Ian clutched against her. The thought hits me that this is how you know who people really are.

"Why don't you put down that bat," Bobby says.

Jace snickers. "Because I don't want to."

"You're gonna wish you did," Bobby says, and as soon as the *did* drops out of his mouth, he takes off running across the yard. A few feet in front of Jace, he pulls up and slings back his right fist like he's ready to throw a titanic punch. Jace takes a batter's stance, but just as he swings, Bobby does what I've seen him do before. He ducks his head and flies shoulder first into Jace's waist as the bat whooshes around clipping nothing but air.

As soon as they both hit the dirt—Bobby on top—Jace's buddies run to help, and I make my own charge. I'm almost there when I realize Gillis is right at my shoulder. We pull smoosh-face Randy off the pile, but there's still this guy Dean on Bobby's back, and this fat tub of crap named Steve is trying to kick Bobby from the side.

Randy hops up, ready to dive back into the fray, but he has something else to deal with instead—the big, old lime-green crazymobile is heading straight at him, the captain inside screaming with pure Yimmy glee.

Randy tries to dodge behind Jace's car, but it's too late—the captain's barreling down on him. At the last second, Randy has to jump as high as he can so he goes rolling off the hood instead of taking the grille up his butt.

From there, the whole thing is hilarious. Gillis and I gang up on Steve, and as soon as we toss him aside, the captain zooms in. Now he has Steve and Randy both on the run. All we have to do is rip Dean off Bobby's back and keep him off, which isn't too hard, because all of a sudden Brianna's mixing it up with us. She must have gone inside to get a weapon, but all she found was a flyswatter, and she's chasing Dean around, swatting him like crazy on the back of the head as me and Gillis get our punches and kicks in.

That Brianna. She's my girl. One hundred percent.

This is better than playing paintball in the woods. We could keep at it for a week, but finally, we chase all three of Jace's buddies up on top of his car, the crazymobile growling like a junkyard dog beneath them.

"Keep that crazy asshole's truck away from us," smoosh-face Randy hollers desperately.

The answer to that is three gunshots. It's Dani. She's holding a pistol in the air with one hand while clutching Ian against her chest with the other. She has this conceited expression on her face like she's the queen of everything she sees. I'll bet a million dollars she got the idea to fire off the gun from some TV show and has been waiting years for just the right moment to use it.

"Now everybody who came with Jace, get the hell out of here," she shouts, her voice hard and triumphant. "And you might as well go with them, Tillman."

He shrugs. "I was just staying neutral," he says. "It's not my fault everyone went wild."

"Yeah, right," she says. "I wouldn't be surprised if you didn't set the whole thing up."

"It's true, isn't it?" I say. "That's why you were checking your watch. You told those guys Bobby was going to be here."

Before he can answer, Randy cries out from behind me, "Good God, look what that bastard did!"

I turn around and see Bobby, the baseball bat in his hand, walking away from where Jace lies splayed out like so much trash dumped in the yard. In all the excitement, nobody bothered to keep tabs on what was going on in their pile.

Randy jumps down from the car roof to get a better look. "You practically killed him, you son of a bitch. I mean, look at his face, what's left of it."

Jace lies still on the ground. His face looks like it got caught under a lawnmower.

"He wanted to know what war's like," Bobby says without bothering to turn around. "Well, there you go."

Randy stares at Dani as if he's begging her to do something, but she just goes, "You better scrape him up and take him to the emergency room." Then she kisses Ian on the forehead and walks into the trailer with Bobby.

As Jace's buddies gather him up, Tillman comes over and stops right in front of me. "I hope you're real proud of your brother now," he says. He doesn't wait for me to answer. He just turns and walks over to the enemy side.

I want to yell something at him, but what would I yell? I loved you, you traitor? I've spent my life daydreaming about you? I wanted you like I never wanted anything else?

No. There's nothing to say.

27

Turns out Jace wasn't killed. His buddies didn't even take him to the emergency room, though they probably should have. He had so many different kinds of drugs in him he was afraid the hospital would call the cops, and they'd arrest him right there in his little backless hospital gown. It didn't take much convincing. The other guys were pretty wasted themselves, and they didn't want to get busted either. A couple days later Jace did go in to have his broken nose ratcheted back into place.

All this I hear about from Gillis. Tillman told him about it. Gillis still talks to Tillman, but you better believe I don't. Who needs him? I found out who my true friends are. When it came right down to it, Gillis was clutch. He didn't leave me hanging. And I can't say enough about Brianna and her flyswatter. She's my girl right down to the ground. Not only because she defied smoosh-face Randy, but because I know how scared that girl gets. And she took my back anyway.

Then there's the captain. I never in a million years would have expected it, but he really came through in that lime-green truck. Who knows how the battle might have turned out if he hadn't come chugging along. He and Bobby don't think the fight was as funny as I do, though. Bobby says fighting isn't a laughing matter, and the captain says something about how the Nogo Gatu come cloaked in violence. That's all right. I have to give the captain a break for that nonsense after the battle at Dani's trailer.

I'm still not convinced his aero-velocipede is a good idea, though. Actually, it worries the crap out of me, but Bobby's got it in his mind he wants to help fix the thing up and fly it. He won't listen to anything I have to say about how dangerous it is, so the next best thing I can do is to make sure I'm there anytime he goes to the captain's to work on it. Besides, I figure it won't take too long for him to get sick of Dani's drama, and I'll be around when he does.

Of course, the parents aren't exactly happy about me hanging out at the captain's, but as far as I'm concerned that's pretty hypocritical. After all, they've always stuck up for the captain, told me and Lacy and Drew we shouldn't make fun of him. I've even caught Dad standing around on the street corner outside the drugstore gabbing with the captain like they're old high school buddies. But somehow it's supposed to be different for me to hang around Casa Crazy in the evenings. Dad doesn't order me to stay away, though. He knows I'm with Bobby, and right now, I'm the only connection the family has to him.

They do come up with another way to keep me from going there, though, at least for a little while. Actually, I knew it had to happen sooner or later—the family trip to Davenport to visit

Grandma Brinker. Mom has been going over there every week-end, and Lacy's been there practically the whole summer, but this will be the first time the rest of us have visited since she got diagnosed. It's going to be awkward, to say the least.

Like I say, we've always been at odds with Grandma Brinker, and not just because of things like the gnome incident either. She never wanted Mom to hook up with Dad in the first place. And then after Grandpa died, she married that mean old moneygrubber Davis Brinker, and he didn't like any of us. He finally died last year, and I felt like the biggest hypocrite in the world sitting at his funeral.

Dad assigns me the job of telling Bobby about the trip, but I'm like, "Why should I tell him? He's not going to want to go any more than I do."

Dad scowls. "This is about family. Your brother needs to stop feeling sorry for himself and think about others for a change."

"Feeling sorry for himself?" I can't believe how wrong Dad can be about his own son. "If you think that's what he's doing, then you should go over and tell him that yourself. You know where he is."

"He's the one who stormed out," Dad says, folding his arms across his chest. "He should be the one who comes over here first."

I look at Mom for support, but she doesn't say anything. She just stands there looking like she's about to choke on her little half-smile.

Of course, when I tell Bobby about the trip, he flat out says he's not going. Grandma never wanted him around when she was healthy, so why should she want him around now? It makes sense, but I know I can't use that or any other excuse to get out of going to Davenport. Neither can my little brother Drew, though he mopes around the house like an innocent man on death row for three days straight. He thinks it's really unfair that we have to go on Thursday, and Dad's not coming until Saturday. Mom explains that Dad has to work, but Drew's like, "Hey, I have a life too, you know."

"That's right," Mom says. "And your life is going to be with us in Davenport this weekend."

"No one ever listens to me!" he wails, and stomps upstairs to his Xbox.

Me, I understand Dad has to work, but I don't like the idea of Ms. Simmons the church floozy bringing him dinner—and her cleavage—Thursday and Friday night while we're gone. Ever since Uncle Jimmy tipped me off to her game, I've been watching her pretty close. She's shameless, scuttling around our house in her low-cut blouses, laughing like a nitwit at Dad's corny jokes, even reaching over and touching him on the arm or the knee while they sit at the kitchen table.

What's she doing staying for dinner anyway? She should just drop off the food and get lost. That's what a real Christian would do. But does Dad tell her that? No. He actually enjoys having her there—my own dad, a victim of mammary hypnosis. You can see how I don't like the idea of him alone in the house with that woman for two nights in a row.

Needless to say, I'm not in the greatest mood in the world as we drive over to Davenport, and when we finally get there, I don't feel any better. It's not as big a town as Knowles. They don't even have a movie theater. But Grandma lives in a pretty nice two-story house on a street with trees that are so big and bushy they look like they've been there since before the American Revolution. Mom gets all bubbly and smiley as we pull into the driveway and she spots my little sister Lacy mowing the lawn. Myself, I'm stunned. Lacy mowing a lawn? The girl whines if she has to take the trash out.

169

She's happy as a puppy to see us, though, even me. Of course she's happy to see the others—she probably thinks they're here to rescue her from Grandma—but after the last time I talked to her on the phone, I figured she wouldn't want to have anything to do with me. Not true, though. It's like she doesn't even remember that phone call. Unlike me—I still can't forgive her for not showing up for Bobby's homecoming.

She even wraps me up in a big, sweaty hug, which is also new—she never sweats. And her clothes are nothing like her usual girly fashion, not a stitch of pink anywhere on her, just a gray Mickey Mouse T-shirt, a pair of denim shorts, and old grass-stained sneakers with no laces. "Wow," I say. "Who are you and where's my little sister?"

She laughs. "Isn't this a great makeover? And it didn't cost a cent."

Inside, Grandma's lying back in the recliner in her house-coat, slippers, and a curly gold wig that doesn't even come close to looking natural. I know her hair fell out from taking chemo and everything, but this thing looks like something she stole off a mannequin at a department store. On top of that, she's lost weight. Not that she couldn't stand to. She was always a little plump, but this doesn't look natural either. It's beginning to dawn on me that Mom's been sugarcoating things even more than usual.

Everybody tells Grandma not to get up, but she does anyway, and it's more hugs all around. I feel like I'm being engulfed in old-lady perfume, but Grandma seems to really mean it this time. At least she acts like it. Usually, she just doles out a quick squeeze and a peck on the cheek that makes you feel like something coming down an assembly line and she's just doing her job.

While Lacy finishes mowing the lawn, the rest of us sit in

the living room with Grandma. Mom and my big sister Colleen drum up some conversation for a while, but Grandma's tired and seems more than happy to let them do most of the talking. It gets boring pretty quick. Drew focuses on his Game Boy, and even Colleen can't pretend to be part of the conversation for very long.

Finally, Lacy finishes up with the lawn and asks me if I want to walk downtown with her after she gets cleaned up. There's not likely to be much excitement in downtown Davenport, but I figure it has to be better than sitting around listening to my mom talk about what the ladies at the hair salon have been up to lately.

As Lacy and I walk along the tree-lined street, she gives me the rundown on Grandma's condition. Yes, she's lost hair and weight and can't keep her food down, but she still has a lot of spirit. Lacy has a hard time convincing her to rest instead of doing housework. Grandma's always trying to wrestle around with the vacuum or the dust mop. Lacy has started getting up at six in the morning just so she can beat Grandma to doing the chores. But she's not complaining. She actually laughs about it. She admires Grandma's spunk.

"I don't know," I say. "It looks like Grandma's a lot worse off than what Mom's been telling us."

"Well, that chemo's hard stuff," Lacy says. "There's no getting around that. It's a battle. But I don't care how little or skinny she looks right now, Grandma's a real fighter."

"I'm sure she is," I say. "Maybe she thinks she can slap cancer across the face like she did Bobby."

Lacy looks hurt. "Come on, Ceejay. That's not fair. That was a long time ago, and Grandma's changed."

"We'll see."

As we get to Main Street, she tells me the real reason she

wanted to come down here. Turns out she's involved in a program at the library where she reads books to little kids. She's decided she loves little kids and wouldn't mind working with them someday as a career. Apparently, she hasn't really had a chance to hang out much with anyone her own age, which is odd because back in Knowles her friends were her life. We're talking about Little Miss Social here. Not to mention boy-crazy.

No, I figure one of these little library rug rats must have a cute older brother Lacy's dying to worm her way into meeting. So I ask her, very casually, if she's come across any interesting boys since she's been in town, but she's like, "Oh, there's a couple of nice boys at church, but I haven't got time for that right now."

No time for boys? She has to be kidding. This is the same Lacy who practically burned out her little pink phone from rattling on and on to her friends about which boy had the best hair, the prettiest eyes, or the cutest butt.

She's not lying about the kids at the library, though. A whole pack of them are gathered in a space in front of the kiddie book section. They actually cheer when they see her. Even the librarian claps. Lacy smiles and waves like she's a celebrity strutting down the red carpet. Walking behind her, I can't keep from feeling out of place. If Lacy is the star, then I'm the party crasher. I wouldn't be surprised if somebody asked to see my library card and then kicked me out for not having one.

The kids all fall silent as she reads them a book about crocodiles and then another one about a six-year-old astronaut. They're sitting there gazing up at her, their faces beaming like little mirrors turned toward the sun. Afterward, they gather round her chair, leaning into her, touching her arm, her shoulder, her hair. She knows all their names and exactly how to make them giggle. Then she introduces me to them, and the shocker is they take to me right off. Apparently, Lacy has already told them about me, so they're like, Wow, this is great— the legendary Ceejay McDermott all the way from Knowles.

"And now," Lacy announces, "we have an extra-special surprise. Ceejay's going to read you a story!"

The kids all clap and squeal but I'm shaking my head like, No way. Too late, though. Lacy shoves a picture book at me, and the kids all plop down on the floor again and gaze up at me like I'm Santa Claus or something. There's nothing to do but sit in the chair and give it a go. The story is really stupid, all about a dog who learns how to drive a train, but the kids love it. They even want me to do a special voice for the dog part, which is definitely out of my comfort zone, but what can you do when you have a bunch of kids gazing up at you like that?

When I finish, they cry out for me to read it again, but luckily the librarian comes to my rescue, telling them that's all the stories for today. Lacy puts her arm around me and goes, "See why I want to work with kids now?"

"I guess it wasn't completely awful," I tell her, but the truth is I really did get kind of a charge out of it.

When we finally leave the library, I'm ready to snag some French fries and a Coke, anything to just hang and relax, but Lacy's like, "No, we have to go by the drugstore to pick up some things for Grandma. And besides, it'll be dinnertime in a little while."

I'm like, "Surely Grandma's not going to do the cooking," and Lacy goes, "Oh no. I'm fixing dinner. Grandma taught me how to make her famous meat loaf."

The weirdness continues. I mean, Lacy *cooking*? I have to ask myself what is going on here. Is it possible the goody-goody thing can be for real?

28

Okay, I admit it—the meat loaf turns out to be semi-awesome. Even Drew puts down his Game Boy to rave about it. We're all sitting around the dining room table, and Grandma starts bragging on Lacy and going on about how glad she is the rest of us have come to visit and even says she can't wait till Dad gets here. Of course, she's always hated Dad, but if she's being fake nice now, she sure is doing a professional job of it.

Everything's not sunshine and rainbows, though. Just as Lacy's about to trot out the chocolate pie, Grandma's face goes pale, and she picks up this little plastic bucket she's kept at her side ever since we got there. I've been wondering what it's for—now I know. She leans over and vomits into it. Not a violent heave like when you're a kid and you throw up and it sprays halfway across the room, but more of a slow gray leak.

No one says anything, not even Drew, who's sitting there watching her, bug-eyed. When Grandma's done, Lacy takes the bucket from her as if it's nothing but a dirty dish. From the dinner table we have a full view of her in the kitchen as she empties the bucket into the garbage disposal and starts cleaning it without a single hint of disgust.

Grandma wipes her mouth with her napkin, and goes, "Darn my luck, I'm so sorry. I hoped I could make it through dinner without this. I probably ruined everybody's appetite."

"Don't you worry about that," Mom says. "I've had to clean up after every one of these kids when they've thrown up, and you had to clean up after me when I did. It's just part of life."

That's Mom for you, putting a positive spin on the topic of puke.

"Oh, Grandma's always trying to apologize to me too," chirps Lacy as she scrubs the bucket. "I just tell her I don't even notice it anymore."

I guess Lacy has witnessed quite a bit of puking since she's been here. But the way she handles it—jeez—I can't hardly see how she could be faking about how much she cares for Grandma. I mean, later that evening, she even helps her take a bath. That's dedication. Of course, Grandma never took her skates away or slapped her across the face either.

But the thing is, Grandma's just as much of a surprise. Aside from the puking, she tries her best to stay upbeat and pleasant. Used to be, she was always cranky with us—didn't like us underfoot, yelled at us for sitting on her car, wouldn't let us play with the water hose—but now she can't tell us enough how glad she is we're here. Even me. She also says she's concerned about Bobby, but she doesn't complain about him not coming. She just says she'd love to see those big brown eyes of his again. I'm surprised she even knows what color his eyes are.

The real test comes on Saturday when Dad shows up. For as long as I can remember, every time she says Dad's name, which is Don, it sounds like she's talking about something gross she found sticking to the bottom of her shoe. Then half the time, when he says something to her, she doesn't bother to answer, acts like she can't hear him. I always figured since her second husband owned three restaurants in three different towns, she thought she was on such a high social level that Dad's voice couldn't even reach her.

Just before lunch, Dad comes into the house with a watermelon tucked under each arm for a present. We're sitting in the kitchen, and I expect Grandma to make some snide remark about the size or color of the melons, but she doesn't. "Would you look at that," she says. "I've been craving watermelon all week long. You must have read my mind, Don."

And what do you know? She genuinely seems to appreciate it, even says *Don* like it's just a regular name. When Dad sits down to talk, there's nothing uppity about Grandma. In fact, she comes off kind of humble, a little embarrassed, even. Some people might see this as an opportunity to get back at Grandma for years of abuse, but not Dad. No. He turns on the old smile and charm as easy as flicking a light switch. And sure, that's good of him, but I'd rather see him do that with Bobby instead of getting all self-righteous about the discharge fiasco.

Later that evening, I find out what the embarrassment in Grandma's voice is about. The whole family—except Drew, who went inside to watch TV—is sitting on the deck in the backyard finishing off the watermelon, and she reaches over and touches Dad on the arm. "Don, I just want to thank you again for this wonderful watermelon. I think it's the best I ever had."

Dad acts like there's nothing different about her at all, like she's been this nice the whole time he's known her. "They're pretty good, all right," he says. "Got them at that roadside fruit stand on the edge of town."

"Well, I just want you to know I appreciate it," she says. "And I appreciate how good you've been to my daughter and grandkids. I don't guess I've let you know that before."

I'm thinking, *That's right. You sure haven't,* but Dad's all, "Oh, you don't need to say anything. I'm just getting by the best way I know how."

"No," Grandma says. "I do need to say it—and I need to say it in front of everyone sitting here—because they all know I haven't shown my appreciation like I should have."

Dad chuckles. "Don't you worry about that. I didn't take any offense. After all, it couldn't have been easy having some uncouth, hot-tempered teenager like me sneak in and steal your prize possession from you." He winks at Mom.

"You didn't steal a thing," she says. "I think my little girl had a good head on her shoulders, and she saw what she wanted."

"And she's regretted it every day since," says Dad, and Mom just laughs along with him.

"No, she hasn't," says Grandma. "But I'm afraid you might have regretted having me as your mother-in-law a few times."

"A man doesn't complain about winning the lottery," says Dad. "And that's what happened the day I got married. Don't you know my temper would've got me in all sorts of trouble if it wasn't for your daughter? She straightened me right out."

When the parents get on a lovey-dovey trip like this, it usually makes me want to gag, but not this time. After hearing about Ms. Big Tits, it's actually kind of welcome. I mean, it'd be just too weird if the parents split up. Even if I do find a way to move in with Bobby, I'd probably have to go visit them separately on holidays.

Grandma's got something she wants to say, though, and she's determined to get it out in front of the whole audience. "It's just that we got off on the wrong foot, and I guess I was too proud to change my ways for too many years. Looking back, I can see the things I couldn't see when you two first started dating. I'd just lost my husband. One day we were as happy as a husband and wife have a right to be, and the next thing you know, a senseless traffic accident took him away from me."

"That had to be hard," says Dad, patting Grandma's arm.

"I was lost," she says, her voice trembling. "I was lost. But that's not any good reason to take things out on you. You're a good man, Don McDermott, and I'm blessed to have this family of yours around me."

By now, Mom's crying, and everyone else but me has tears welling in their eyes. It's not like I'm hard-hearted about it—I mean, this is pretty heavy stuff to lay out in front of the whole family—but still I'm like, Really? Can you pretend you're going to make up for about an eon of treating someone like crap in one evening? Sure, it'd be hard to lose your husband and everything, but you don't have to take it out on everyone else.

Dad's sympathetic about it, though. He leans over and kisses Grandma on the cheek and says, "I appreciate that. It means the world to me."

For a while everyone sits there in awkward silence, but Dad's not one to let things get too serious. "Say, have you all heard the one about . . . ," he says, and goes on to tell one of his usual awful jokes. This time it's just what the moment calls for.

Later, it's just me and him straightening things up on the deck after everyone else has gone in, and he tells me to sit down next to him. So there we are sitting on the deck with our legs dangling over the edge, and I figure he's going to start in on how I need to soften up toward Grandma.

"You know," he says, "I'm really proud of the way Lacy's sacrificed so much to help your grandma."

"Yeah, she's done a lot more than I gave her credit for," I tell him. Of course, I'm not surprised he's proud of her—he's never made a secret of that—but I hope he doesn't expect me to start giving Grandma baths or something.

That's not what he's getting at, though. "I want you to know I'm proud of you too," he says. He even wraps his arm around my shoulder. "I always have been, but I'm especially proud of how you're sticking by Bobby. I guess I haven't known how to act with him, but you seem to, and I think that's as important as anything."

This is about the last thing I expected. I'm like, What? He's actually admitting he could've done better by Bobby? Maybe he thinks he can get me to be all nicey-nice like everyone else is pretending to be, but I'm not ready to let him off the hook as easy as he did Grandma.

"Well," I say, "it's not so hard to know how to act around someone if you love them."

"You know I love your brother." He tries to look me in the eyes, but I turn away.

"Yeah, right. If you loved him, how could you send him off to the army in the first place?"

He takes his arm away from my shoulder and folds his hands between his legs. "I didn't send him off. You know that. We had a tough choice to make. Sometimes that's how life is—you have to choose between two bad things. I sure couldn't see him going to jail."

"You could've fought harder for him." I don't yell or even raise my voice. I just state it like a fact on the news.

"Maybe so. Maybe I could've fired our lawyer and got a different one. But none of us thought the war would be like it has

179

been. We've talked about this whole thing before, Ceejay. You know as well as I do we all thought our troops would just go in and get out and it'd all be over. It was supposed to be finished by the time Bobby even got out of boot camp."

"Well, you were wrong about that, weren't you?"

"Yes, I was. You're right. I trusted the wrong people. But I always wanted the best for Bobby, just like I want the best for you. And I admire how you're standing by him. Sometimes that's about the best you can do. But, you know, standing by someone doesn't mean you have to go along with everything they do."

"Yeah? But it sure doesn't mean telling Bobby you're ashamed of him either."

He winces at that, and I halfway expect him to tell me to quit back-talking him, but he doesn't. For a moment, he stares across the yard, then he goes, "I wish I'd said something different to him that day, you know, when he told us how he left the army. If I could take it back and change it, I would. Because, the thing is, a soldier does our country's hardest work for us. That's the truth. There's nothing harder. And I don't care anything about what happened with him in Germany. He did a soldier's job and I respect him."

"Don't tell me. Tell him."

"I want to." He studies his hands for a moment. "You know, Ceejay, there's a lot of things I probably need to tell people that I haven't. Your grandma got me to thinking. It took a lot for her to say what she did tonight. That's the way it is. The things you need to say the most are the hardest to get out. And the truth is, I'm afraid I haven't let Bobby or you, either one, know just how much you mean to me as much as I could."

Oh God, I say to myself, here it comes—he's going to hand

me a load of sentimental crap that can't make up for a single thing.

"You see," he goes on, "it's just that you two were always closer to each other than you were to the others, and I felt like you were the ones who were the most like me."

He catches the look of disbelief on my face.

"I'm sure you think that's foolish," he says. "You probably can't see how you're anything like your old, fat dad, but you sure are. And I guess I never wanted to let on about that for fear the others might think I was playing favorites with Bobby and you."

Of all the weirdness to hit me this weekend, that might just be the weirdest. I have no idea how to respond, so I look around at the stuff left out on the patio table. "So," I say, "I guess we better take the rest of these dishes into the kitchen."

"I guess we should," he says. "But you think about what I said, Ceejay. And you tell Bobby, the next time you see him, the whole family stands behind him. We want him to come back home."

"Sure," I say. That's all. I gather up the dishes and head into the house, thinking of how desperate I am to get back to my real life. Bobby will probably have a good laugh over Dad trying to pretend he's like us. Or maybe he won't. I'm not so sure about anything anymore.

29

The next evening, when we get home, I head straight to my room and shut the door. I can't wait to call Bobby and see what he has to say about the bizarre stuff that went down this weekend, especially the conversation with Dad. Dani answers but she tells me—and I guess I shouldn't be surprised—Bobby's at the captain's. She sounds a little ticked off, and I know how she feels. Okay, so the captain did a great job of taking our backs when Jace showed up with his baseball bat, but does that mean Bobby has to make him his new best friend? I'm sure Dani wants some one-on-one time with Bobby just like I do.

I have to coax Brianna into driving me to the captain's, but when we get there, she's not real gung ho about hanging around, so I tell her to go on home. I can always catch a ride home on the back of Bobby's motorcycle.

"Well," she says, "if for some reason he can't give you a ride, just call me."

I know what she's thinking—Bobby may be too wasted to drive me home. "Don't worry," I tell her. "I'm sure it'll be cool."

In the barn, it's only Bobby and the captain. I have to admit I'm a little disappointed Mr. White isn't around. According to the captain, he got a part-time job at the bowling alley and has to work tonight. Anyway, they've made progress on the aero-velocipede since I've been gone. Seems Bobby ordered wheels online using Dani's computer, and now that they've attached them to the frame, the thing looks more like it really could get somewhere. On the ground, at least. They still don't have wings or a motor.

But the captain and Bobby aren't satisfied to just make it look like the pictures they have hanging up all around the barn. Since it's supposed to be a flying sculpture, their next step is to cut the shapes of stars and crescent moons and suns out of tin and weld them to the frame. It's going to be time-consuming, Bobby explains, but when it's done, it'll be the coolest flying sculpture anyone ever made. I feel like asking just how many flying sculptures there are in the universe, but I can't get sarcastic with Bobby the way I do with my friends.

"We're naming her Angelica," he says. "Because, you know, she's like a mechanized angel." His eyes are bright, but he's not drunk, maybe just a tad high. That's okay—at least he's happy for a change.

The fact that they still don't have a motor is more than all right by me. I'd just as soon they never really tried to fly it. For me, the fun thing is listening to Bobby once he starts talking. Sure, it's a pain that he wants to hang around with the captain so much, but at least he's starting to open up more.

Tonight, the captain is quieter than usual, giving Bobby a

183

chance to talk about the army, which is something he hasn't done much of since he's been back. But still he doesn't say a whole lot about what went down in the actual war. The one time he mentions confronting hajji on the street, he sounds like he's reading a military report. Not an ounce of emotion in his voice. He might as well be telling about something that happened to someone else.

Mostly, he talks about the wild things he and his army buddies did. He especially likes telling about his favorite buddy, a Texas dude named Covell. He used to tell me about him on the phone and in e-mails, but hasn't talked about him for quite a while. Covell was the funniest guy Bobby ever met, had a real bona fide comedy routine about all his brothers and sisters and cousins. His jokes weren't like anyone else's. They were really more like funny stories than jokes. Covell was raised on a ranch, but he'd watched enough TV to know how to go about polishing a stand-up act. That was his dream. Once he got out of the army, he was heading straight to New York City to make it big in the clubs. He was going to be groundbreaking.

I suggest Bobby ought to write Covell and get him to come visit, but he's like, "Yeah, well, no, that's not going to happen."

"Why not?" I say. "He sounds like a fun guy to hang around."

"Maybe you're right," he says. "Maybe that's what I need to do—hang with Covell."

"Sure," I say. "I'd like to meet him." Not that I want to share Bobby with someone else necessarily, but Covell sounds like a healthier buddy than the captain.

For some reason, though, Bobby's enthusiasm trails off, and he goes quiet on me. I feel like somehow I said something wrong and that I need to cheer him up again.

"So," I say, "here's something funny you'll get a kick out of." And I go on to tell about my conversation with Dad at

184

Grandma's, how Dad said he thought he was so much like the two of us. "Can you believe that? As if he went to our high school we'd even hang out with him."

"I don't know." Bobby stares at the tin moon he's been working on. "From what Uncle Jimmy told me, Dad was pretty wild back in his high school days."

"Well, he's a long way from his high school days now."

"Maybe so," he says, standing up. "But I'm a long way from mine too."

He starts toward the door of the barn, and I ask him where he's headed.

"I'm going to run out and get me some beer," he says. "About a case ought to do."

"Wait a minute. I'll come with you."

"No, you go on and stay here. Can't fit you and the beer both on the seat. It won't take but fifteen minutes."

So he rumbles off on his motorcycle, and it's just me and the captain in the barn. The captain shoots me a sheepish smile, like he knows it's weird for me to be left alone with him. For about the next thirty minutes, as he works with his sheet of tin, he rambles on about how Leonardo da Vinci and all these other guys designed flying machines, leading right up to the Wright brothers making the first flight at Kitty Hawk. After a while, I'm not really listening anymore.

"I wonder what's taking Bobby so long," I say, cutting into the captain's lecture. "He should've been back by now."

The captain puts the tin sheet down. "I don't think he's coming back," he says, looking at me sympathetically.

"What do you mean? Why wouldn't he come back? You don't think he had a wreck, do you?"

"No, I just think he needs to be alone for a while. That's how it is sometimes when the dark thoughts hit."

185

"Dark thoughts? What dark thoughts? Did I say something wrong? He seemed like he was in such a good mood. Then all of a sudden, things changed."

"That's how it is," the captain says, and picks up the tin sheet and goes back to work. "He'll be back tomorrow or the next day. He can't stay away from Angelica for too long."

"Well, I can't wait till tomorrow or the next day. I need a ride home tonight."

The captain grins. "Is that all? I have the truck right out there."

"That's okay. I'll wait a little while longer."

Another half hour of listening to the captain ramble about the history of flight, and still no Bobby. Finally, I break down and call Brianna. She doesn't ask any questions. She just says, "I'll be right over."

When she gets there, we drive by Dani's to see if Bobby's motorcycle is parked outside. It's not, so we cruise slowly down the highway looking for signs of a wreck. Luckily, we don't see any. Then an idea strikes me—the Tip-Top Motel. And sure enough, when we pull up in the parking lot, there's Bobby's motorcycle parked right next to Mona's Escalade.

"Don't you dare tell anyone about this," I order Brianna.

"Don't worry," she says. "I don't want to see someone get killed any more than you do."

30

I never say anything about the Tip-Top Motel situation. Sure, cheating on Dani is creepy, not to mention dangerous, but I can't help hoping this means Bobby might be ready to move out of the trailer. Of course, he needs a real job if we're going to get our rent house. He can't keep spending all his energy working on Angelica, but somehow he can't seem to stay away from her. Which means I can't either.

We go in the evenings when it's cool. Mr. White's over there most of the time, except when he has to work late at the bowling alley. Actually, I'm glad when he's there. He gets my jokes and has some good ones of his own. Half the time I end up talking to him more than my own brother.

Gillis doesn't like the idea of hanging at the captain's, so he's hardly ever there. The thing is, though, I'm not sure if he has a problem with the captain so much as he does with Mr. White. What Gillis really has against him, I couldn't say. He just seems to have a bug up his ass, says he's got better things to do. Maybe being around Mr. White makes him feel stupid. I wouldn't be surprised. It's hard for one guy to admire another guy for being smart.

Brianna comes over every once in a while, but it's not her favorite thing to do. She just comes because I'm her best friend. Dani's not so supportive of Bobby. After showing up a couple of times and even bringing little Ian, she decides she'd rather stay home, smoke weed, and watch reality shows on TV. She'd be smart to be more concerned about what Bobby's up to, but as the days pass, I don't see any more signs of him sneaking off to be with Mona. Good thing. Dani's not someone to get cross-ways with.

So mainly it's just the captain and Bobby working on Angelica while Mr. White and I listen to them talk. Sometimes I wonder if Bobby would even miss me if I didn't show up. For so long I ached to have him home, and now it's like he's still not all the way here. I don't want to be mad at him, but every once in a while I can't help it. I feel like jerking him away from that stupid Angelica and telling him to quit acting like such a—I don't know what—a ghost? Of course, I don't do it, though. No, I just sit there like a do-nothing lump, watching him work. Around my friends, I've always been the take-charge girl. If something needed doing, I did it. But now I'm stuck, frozen, waiting around for something to happen that will make everything go back to the way it used to be between Bobby and me.

When I can't take the sitting and watching anymore, Mr. White and I get out of the barn and go around to sit on the front porch, look off at the moonlight washing across the sculptures, and talk about our own stuff. Something about him soothes me down, makes me feel less frustrated about the way the summer's going. It's come to the point where he's not even Mr. White anymore. I've started thinking of him as Padgett instead. Strange as he is, he's becoming a real friend, and you don't call your real friends something like Mr. White.

There's a lot I can talk about with him that I can't talk about with Brianna or Gillis or even Bobby because they already know all my stories about myself. I bet I could tell him about more than just biographical things too. When you're the badass chick, no one expects you to go around talking about your emotions, but maybe I could with Padgett. The problem is I don't. I don't know why—there's so much trying to get out of my throat, but something holds it back.

He's holding back too. Sure, he'll go on and on about one theory after another and analyze what makes everyone else tick, but he doesn't say much about his own feelings. When I ask him if he has a girlfriend waiting for him back in the city, he changes the topic and goes into how his aunt basically got jilted at the altar when she was seventeen and never got over it. He makes the story interesting, but I was hoping to hear something a little more personal.

One night, after the motor for Angelica finally comes in, the captain and Bobby are having a hard time trying to get it to fit Angelica's frame. It's kind of freaking the captain out—and Bobby's not so pleasant to be around either—so Padgett and I leave them to it and hang out in the Casa Crazy living room, listening to some old vinyl records and talking about something besides mechanized angels.

Now, I'm sure when people drive out to look at the sculptures in the front yard, they think it's pretty bizarre, but let me tell you—they don't know bizarre unless they've seen the inside of the house. For one thing, there's all these splintery crates of records stacked everywhere, next to the overstuffed couch, the tattered chairs, the bookcase. He must have a couple thousand albums from the fifties through the seventies. Not a single CD anywhere. He wouldn't even know what an MP3 was. On the walls, he has paintings and wood carvings and huge sheaths of butcher paper covered in cartoon drawings—all his own work. Nothing is normal.

The wood carvings are all heads, bald heads with dark, polished faces that either grin in complete glee or frown in despair. The cartoons are probably supposed to tell some kind of story, but even Padgett doesn't know what it is—bug-eyed, bearded men carrying huge apples or loaves of bread, women with big boobs and short skirts, pelicans, reindeer, and penguins cut into sections. Padgett says he knows the penguins stand for innocence, but the rest of it's a mystery, even to him. He'll figure it out one day, though, he tells me.

Mostly, we talk about one of my favorite subjects—life in the city. He tells me about movies and music that no one around here has even heard of. He's been to plays and art museums and concerts. I want to know about all that stuff. You may not expect me to be a big art-museum type of girl, but actually I can draw pretty well. Tigers, eagles, bulldogs. That kind of thing. Lions too, a lot of lions. I filled a notebook full of animal heads during social studies class.

So I can see myself walking around in a museum or going to the amphitheater to watch cool bands that would never even pass through a town like Knowles on their way to play someplace else. I picture going to stores and water parks, restaurants, coffee shops, and outdoor cafes. The idea of the rent house on the south side of town fades. Instead, I picture me and Bobby walking up the stairs to a cool apartment with a balcony that looks out on the city. It would be good for him there, far away from the crap around here. I'd get a job and go to night school, and Padgett would be there, so I'd already have someone else I know to hang around with too.

Don't get me wrong, though. It's not like I'm imagining some kind of future romance between me and Padgett. I mean, no girl wants a boyfriend she can beat up. It's just that, in the city, I could be a different Ceejay McDermott, one nobody else but Padgett even suspects could exist.

That doesn't mean he might not have a little bit of a crush on *me*, though. He's always talking about how he wants to show me these cool places, how he wants us to see everything together. He puts on this old sixties rock record of the captain's—the words are something about "hold on baby, baby, I won't let you go"—and starts talking about how he's pretty sure he's going to get to move back to the city come fall.

He's like, "I don't want to do all this stuff by myself, you know. A guy needs a partner in crime, a partner in the misfit revolution."

I'm thinking, Oh my God, is he going to ask me to be his girlfriend?

"I know we both have another year of high school to go," he says. "But the way I see it—"

A knock at the screen door cuts him off. It's Richard, the captain's older brother. I feel like he just snapped some kind of spell. Up to this moment, we've been lost in our own universe, far away from adults and everything that goes with them. But the thing is, I don't know whether to feel relieved or disappointed that Padgett didn't get to finish what he was starting to say. I mean, how could I respond without ruining everything?

31

Richard opens the screen door and pokes his head in. "Excuse me, Padgett. I'm here to see my brother."

Obviously, Padgett's been out here so often, Richard knows him pretty well and doesn't think it's weird he's sitting around in the captain's living room.

"Uh, yeah," Padgett says. "He's around here somewhere."

"Down at the barn, I suspect," says Richard, starting to turn away.

"Uh, hold on, I'll go with you," Padgett tells him. "Come on, Ceejay."

From the way he's acting, I get the idea he doesn't especially want Richard to go to the barn, but I don't know why. Since Richard's always bailing the captain out of trouble,

I thought the two of them must get along pretty well, but as we walk to the barn I gather that's not exactly the case.

Richard's a tall, thin old dude with wispy gray hair, and a stiff, careful way of walking as if everything around him is covered with radioactive germs that might jump onto his skin if he doesn't watch out. His comments and the expression that spreads across his face as he looks around at what the captain's made of the farm remind me of our high school principal, Mr. Thornton. If it wasn't for his job, Mr. Thornton would probably stay as far away from teenagers as he possibly could, and it looks like that's the way it is with Richard too. If he didn't feel responsible for his brother, he'd never set foot on this place.

Before we get to the barn, Padgett shouts for the captain and Bobby to come out to talk to Richard, so here they come, the captain with this sheepish look on his face, like a little boy who's been caught doing something he wasn't supposed to.

Richard seems to like Padgett all right, but he's a little wary of the likes of me and Bobby hanging around. As we stand there, about thirty yards from the barn, he quizzes us about what we're doing out here, as if he thinks maybe we're out to scam the captain. What he thinks we would be after, I don't know. It's not like the captain is rolling in money or anything.

Just trying to clear things up, Bobby mentions that we're helping the captain with the aero-velocipede. Big mistake. Padgett and the captain both grit their teeth when he says it, and Richard's like, "You mean you're still working on that contraption? I told you I didn't want you fooling around with that anymore. You need to get rid of that thing, and I don't mean maybe."

"Wait a minute," Bobby says. "There's nothing wrong with

Angelica, man. We've put our sweat into her. The whole thing's one hundred percent by the book. All we need to do is get the engine harnessed in there, and she'll be good to go."

The captain nods hopefully, but Richard isn't going for it. "You aren't harnessing any engine," he tells his brother. "In fact, you need to tear that mess down to scrap. Make it into one of your sculptures if you want, but if I come back out here and you're still building it, I'm going to get a truck and haul it off to the dump myself."

The captain looks at the ground, his shoulders slumping.

"Aren't you even going to come look at it?" Bobby asks. "You can't make a judgment without seeing what we've done. This thing is spruce. You'd be amazed."

Richard looks at Bobby. His expression isn't totally unsympathetic. "I know who you are, and I know your dad. I'm sure you mean well. But you don't understand the whole situation here. It's just too dangerous."

Bobby starts to argue some more, but Padgett cuts in. "It was just supposed to be a sculpture in the first place. We don't even care if it flies. We'll just set it out by the fat boy. It'll look good there. I'll make sure everything's all right, Mr. Monroe."

Richard studies Padgett for a moment. "Okay. I don't care if you put it in the yard, but I don't want to see any engine hooked up to it. You understand me?"

Padgett nods. "I understand."

After Richard leaves, Bobby turns to Padgett. "Goddamn, man, why did you say we weren't going to try to fly? Because I can guarantee I don't care what anyone says—I'm going to take that thing up as soon as we get it finished."

Padgett tosses him a sly expression. "I never said we wouldn't try to fly it. I just said it was supposed to be a sculpture. Which it is. This way we buy ourselves a little time."

Bobby smiles. "You're a good man. I'm glad you're on my team."

The captain isn't too happy, though. "This is bad," he mutters nervously. "Bad, bad, bad."

Richard's visit has definitely short-circuited something in him, but he's been fidgety for the last couple of days, ever since the engine came in from whatever Web site they ordered it off of. They can't get it mounted right. It seems too big for the frame, and when we go into the barn to work on it tonight, he gets more and more upset as they wrestle with it. He's like, "If there's something wrong with one part, then there's something wrong with the whole. The process is coming undone, man." His hands shake. He paces around the barn, bumping his head on the mechanic's lamp, causing weird shadows to bounce around the walls.

Bobby says everything's going to be all right, but he doesn't look like he believes that himself.

"They're out there, man," the captain says, gazing through the barn door at the darkness. "The Nogo Gatu is in the woods. They're surrounding us."

"But the sculptures," Bobby says. "They'll get rid of them, won't they?"

"Not tonight."

"What's wrong?" I ask Padgett. "What's he talking about?"

"It's like this sometimes," Padgett says. "He's held it off this time longer than usual."

The captain wrings his hands. The twinkly happiness that usually plays in his eyes when he works on something disappears, replaced by this god-awful worry that borders on terror.

"We need to get out of town," he mutters. "We need to get out of town. We need to get out of this whole decade, this century, this millennium. Do you have my keys? Who has my keys?"

195

"Your keys are in the house," Bobby says. "You don't need them. We don't need to go anywhere." He tries to put his arm around the captain's shoulder, but the captain shrugs it away and goes, "I've got to go in and get my keys. We have to make a run for it, man. We have to make a run for it."

He takes off for the house, but it's not so much running as a herky-jerky race walk. "Stay away from me," he yells at the darkness. "I told you, man, I don't have anything to do with you. I don't have what you want."

On his front porch, he struggles for a moment with the doorknob, then bursts inside, the three of us right behind him. He paces around the living room, checking out one window, then the next.

"Settle down," Bobby says. "Have some wine."

The captain looks at him. "Are you infected? Are any of you infected? I have to know. I can't let infections in here."

"You know us," Padgett says. "You know we're not infected. We're on your side."

But the captain's like, "I don't know about that, man. You may not be who you say you are."

There's a scratching sound at the door, and the captain's eyes flare wilder. "That's them. They're going to get in through the cracks."

The scratches are followed by a bark. It's Dobie, the captain's dog.

Padgett explains this but the captain's like, "How do you know? It could be a trick."

"No, look," says Padgett, "I'm going to open the door and let him in. It'll be fine."

"I smell carbon monoxide," the captain says, cowering in the corner. "That's what they smell like."

196

The door opens and Dobie comes trotting in all happy and ready for company, but when he sees the captain, it's like he knows something's wrong. His tail stops wagging and his ears lie back. Cautiously, he approaches the captain, stopping a couple of feet away. It's amazing—there's so much concern in his brown eyes. He's been through this before.

"Dobie," the captain says. "Oh God, it's you. It's you, boy." He kneels down and the dog licks his beard sympathetically.

I'm like, "Wow, the dog knows what's going on."

"Dogs are good at that kind of thing," says Padgett.

Bobby walks over, squats next to Dobie, and pets his neck. "Why don't you take Dobie in the bedroom with you and try to get some rest? We'll stand guard out here."

The captain searches Bobby's eyes, I guess to see if he's really who he's supposed to be. "Okay, man," he says, satisfied for the moment that Bobby's really Bobby. "Right. I can trust you. You know what's what. It's the Nogo Gatu, isn't it? They're out there."

Bobby nods. "It's them, all right."

"Maybe we can hold them off." A little speck of hope cracks through the thick fear in the captain's eyes.

"We'll try our hardest."

Bobby helps the captain into the bedroom, Dobie following close behind. It takes some persuading, but finally the captain lies down on top of his bedcovers, fully dressed. Dobie hops up and lies down too, the captain's arm wrapped around him. For about ten minutes, we all stand guard around the bed as the captain mutters softly to himself. I can't make out the words, but it sounds like a prayer or a spell.

He doesn't go to sleep, but he seems calm enough now that we leave him there and walk out to sit on the front porch.

197

Bobby stares toward the woods. From the drained look in his eyes, you'd think he halfway believes the Nogo Gatu might really be gathering out there, planning their attack.

I'm like, "That was weird. I've never seen him freak out like that. And all because a couple of parts on the aero-velocipede wouldn't fit together."

"That's not all it is," Bobby says. "It's more than that."

"It's been coming on for a while," Padgett says. "I could tell. He goes through cycles. They're not completely regular, but I've seen it before. He goes through these periods where he gets higher and higher, and then you know pretty soon it's going to bottom out. He held it off this time longer than usual, probably because of Bobby. I mean, it's just a theory, but I think it's because Bobby reminds him of his little brother."

"You mean the one who died in Vietnam?" I ask.

Padgett nods and Bobby goes, "His brother was lucky. He didn't have to drag that war back here with him."

"I don't know," Padgett says. "The philosopher Friedrich Nietzsche said that whatever doesn't kill you will only make you stronger."

"Yeah, well." Bobby stares into the distance. "Some things just take a longer time to kill you."

The way he says it gives me a chill.

"But look at the captain," Padgett says. "He didn't let what happened to his brother kill him. He doesn't let the Nogo Gatu kill him either."

"Don't be so sure about that," Bobby says. "What do you think he's building Angelica for? All she needs to do is get up in the air, and after that it doesn't matter if she keeps flying or not. If she flies, she flies. If she crashes, she crashes. Like a Russian roulette machine. The only thing the captain doesn't know is I'm taking her up first, and I don't care if she crashes either."

I can't believe what I'm hearing. This can't be Bobby. I would say he's just drunk or stoned on OxyContin, but I know he's not. Maybe he's bummed about the captain and thinking about the war again. I don't know. But I can't believe he'd really crash that stupid flying machine on purpose.

"You're not going to get the chance to see if it'll crash," I tell him. "I won't let you go anywhere in that thing. I'll take a sledge hammer and bust it to pieces first."

He looks down at his hands. "You might as well bust me to pieces instead."

"Screw you, Bobby." I'm on my feet and looking down on him now. "You can't say that crap to someone who loves you. You just can't say it."

"Listen to you. You think you love me, huh? I told you— you don't even know me anymore. How could you. Small-town Ceejay, living amongst the green fields and the rolling hills. What could you know about how it is to be stuck in some desert where it's a million degrees outside? You suspect every hajji you see and wish you had an extra set of eyes because everywhere you go it feels like there's a rifle trained on the back of your skull. Cars are burning on the side of the road, and you don't want to look in them because you might see a fried kid in there. No, you don't know me, Ceejay."

I lean in and stare into his eyes. "But you aren't there anymore. You're here with me. Right here. And I do know you. I know you one hundred percent. And I'm not going to let you start talking about giving up. That isn't you, Bobby. I know it's not."

He stares back at me for a long time without saying

anything. His brown eyes—they used to be so deep, but now they're as thin as pennies. Then a sad smile edges across his face. "Okay," he says. "Okay. Have it your way. That was just stupid talk on my part anyway. I mean, who would crash an aero-velocipede they helped make with their own hands? Nobody. I'm just an idiot blathering about nothing. It doesn't mean anything."

"It better not."

"Of course it doesn't." He grabs my hand and I sit next to him. He puts his arm around me and squeezes me tighter than any time since he's been back. "You're my girl," he says. "You know that, right? You're the guardian angel of my messed-up soul."

32

The next evening, Bobby's slated to take Dani and little Ian to a movie, so he won't be at the captain's. Which is good as far as I'm concerned. It's one thing to hang out with the happy-Yimmies captain, but obviously the seriously weird Nogo Gatu–infected captain is no good for Bobby at all. Still, even though the captain calmed down by the time I left last night, I can see why Padgett thinks it's important to go out and check on him.

I'm on lunch break with Uncle Jimmy when Padgett calls. Besides wanting to go to the captain's tonight—the first time that it would be just me and him without Bobby—he also wants me to stop by the bowling alley before he gets off. Says he has something important he wants to talk to me about. For the rest of the afternoon, as I'm slathering paint back and forth on the job, I keep rolling that over in my mind. Just what is this important something he needs to talk to me about?

Of course, I still haven't found out what he was about to say right before Richard barged in on us last night, so maybe he's figuring to finally get that off his chest. And from the way he was going on, I suspect I might just know what it is—he's going to ask me if I want to be more than just friends. Maybe he's even got it in his mind that I should move to the city with him. Either one would be crazy, but somehow I can't help being a little excited about the notion. Not that I'd say yes, but it would sure be nice to have someone ask for once.

After work, I head to Gillis's to see if he'll give me a ride to the bowling alley. Padgett doesn't get off till nine, so I figure I'll hang around with him there and then we'll drive out to the captain's. Should be easy, right? Gillis, he's been the same guy my whole life. He may be obnoxious sometimes, but you can count on him. Or so I thought.

He steps out on his front porch in just his jeans, no T-shirt or shoes. It's not the most attractive sight in the world, but I'm used to it. I ask him about giving me a ride to the bowling alley, and he starts quizzing me about why I want to go. I explain everything except the part about what I think Padgett might have on his mind about me and him.

Gillis stands there with a little sneer on his face like I just asked him to drop me off at the sewage treatment plant. "What do you see in that dude?"

"Padgett? He's a good guy once you get to know him." I even suggest that if Gillis talked to him a few times, they might become buddies, though actually I doubt that.

"Is that all he is to you?" Gillis says. "A buddy?"

"What are you talking about?"

"I've seen the way that dude looks at you. He doesn't think he's just your buddy."

"I don't know about that."

"I do. I'm a dude. I can tell."

"Well, so what if he does have a crush on me. What does that matter?"

"I knew it—he does have a thing for you. A wimp like that."

"He's not a wimp," I say. "He's just smart, which is more than I can say for most of the guys around here."

"Jesus, you've got a thing for him too."

"Don't be ridiculous."

"Well, don't expect me to drive you over there. According to you, I'd probably be too stupid to find the way."

"So you're not going to drive me?"

"No."

"I don't get it. What's it to you if he likes me anyway?"

He waves his hand as if he could flick the question out of the air. "It's nothing to me. Nothing at all. Get Brianna to drive you. I'm busy."

He walks back into the house, slamming the door behind him, and I'm left standing on the porch thinking, *What the hell?*

Twenty minutes later, Brianna's driving me to the bowling alley and I tell her the story. "Can you believe that?" I say.

"Of course I can believe it," she says. "Don't you know what it means?"

"That he's been snorting crank?"

"No, stupid, it means Gillis has a thing for you."

"No way."

She looks at me like I'm a child. "Why else would he get mad because he thinks somebody else is interested in you? He's in love with you. He's always been in love with you."

I'm like, "That's stupid. He's never said anything close to romantic to me. Most of the time he treats me like a guy, except when he gets drunk. Then he treats me like I'm a slut he picked up at the truck stop."

"Come on, Ceejay. What do you expect? Guys don't know how to act around you. You're like this badass chick. What do you think they're going to do, buy you a box of chocolates? Talk French to you? Make you a mix CD of love songs? No, they're not going to do any of that. Gillis is probably just being the kind of guy he thinks you want."

"Well, he's wrong about that."

"Yeah, but how's he supposed to know any better when you're always going around with your armor on?"

"If a guy wants to look hard enough, he'll see past that."

"Really? Like who are you talking about—Mr. White?"

"His name's Padgett. And if you really want to know—yeah. Matter of fact, I wouldn't be at all surprised if he asked me to be his girlfriend tonight."

She studies me for a moment, her mouth hanging open. "You've got to be kidding."

"Why is that so hard to believe?"

"Well, I mean, you and him are pretty different. And that's an understatement."

"So what? Do you think a couple have to be exactly the same?"

"Wait a minute. Are you telling me you're going to say yes?"

"I didn't say that."

She throws back her head and laughs. "Oh my God, you *do*—you have a thing for Mr. White. That's hilarious."

"Don't be stupid. He's the one who has a crush on me."

"And you're loving it!"

"Shut up. God, you can be such a pain in the ass sometimes."

"So you're telling me you don't have any interest in him at all?"

"Not that way."

"Okay. Whatever you say."

"Well, that's what I say. And if you tell anyone else any different, you'll wish you hadn't."

We ride in silence for a while. I'm still a little infuriated with her, but finally I have to ask the question—"So, Gillis, huh? He really has a thing for me? Why didn't you tell me?"

"I did. In about seventh grade. You just laughed at me."

It's hard to make the concept fit in my brain. I have to admit, it's kind of flattering, even if Gillis is an idiot, but I also can't help feeling sorry for him. After all, I know how it is to carry around a crush on someone year after year without them showing any interest back. That's one thing I don't plan on doing again.

Brianna drops me off in front of the bowling alley, and I tell her not to wait. The place isn't doing much business. Padgett is sitting behind the front counter reading a big, fat book, but he looks up and smiles when he sees me walking toward him. "Hey, Ceejay, you ready to do some bowling?"

"Yeah, right. Sign me up for a league."

It's stupid but all of a sudden I'm nervous. I've never had The Talk with a guy before. I have no idea what I'll say back to him.

He closes the book and goes, "I'm glad you got here early. I've really been wanting to talk to you."

I'm like, "You have?" But inside I'm all like, What if I accidentally say yes when he pops the question?

"Yeah," he says. "Although—I have to tell you—I was a

little nervous about how you'd react. Here, come back into the office with me."

There's a small office behind the front counter. Inside, he pulls a chair over so I can sit next to him at the desk. With the paperwork piled up, the bowling plaques on the walls, and the musty smell, it isn't exactly the most romantic place in the world.

"So," he says. "There's something I've been thinking about for quite a while, but I wasn't really sure about it till now."

"Really? What's that?"

"Well, remember when Bobby was talking about how things could take a long time to kill a person and how he planned to be the first one to take Angelica up even if she crashed?"

"Sure," I say, thinking this is a pretty strange lead-in to asking me to be his girlfriend.

"Well," he goes on. "I've been doing some research, and I'm ninety-nine-point-nine percent sure that Bobby's problem is something called post-traumatic stress disorder."

"What?" That's all that will come out of my mouth. I'm completely stunned.

"Post-traumatic stress disorder," he repeats. "PTSD for short." He goes on to explain how he read all about it in a couple of books and on about six different Web sites. It's a mental problem, he tells me. People get it when they've gone through something so horrendous their minds have trouble dealing with it. Their chemical balance gets thrown out of whack. They get depressed and anxious, can't sleep well, and have a hard time relating to others. Sometimes their brains will replay the terrible thing they went through over and over, and they can't shut it off. "Here," he says, "let me pull up one of the Web sites." He starts clacking away at the keyboard on the desk.

But I'm like, "I don't need to see any Web site. You think some online idiot knows more about my brother than I do?"

"No, really," he says. "This is a valid Web site. PTSD, it's the real deal."

"What are you saying?" With just a few words, he's completely obliterated all my stupid, wimpy, nervous feelings about him going romantic on me. "Do you think Bobby's some kind of mental defective? You think he needs to go to a shrink? Because that's a load of crap. I don't care how bad it got in the war, my brother's way too tough to let it drive him nuts. You've been hanging out with Captain Crazy too much."

It's weird. I have to fight back the tears. I don't know if it's the strangeness of life lately, or if it's just the disappointment of having Padgett ambush me like this. All this time he's lulled me into thinking he's Mr. Supportive, and now instead of asking me to be his girlfriend, he lays this theory on me about my brother being a nut job. I'm not going to let him see me cry, though. I don't let anyone see that.

"Look," he says, "there's nothing to get defensive about. No one said anything about your brother not being tough. You have to be tough to deal with something like this. You have to have character. It's a battle."

"What kind of battle?" I say. "A battle against crazy?"

"There's all kinds of battles, you know. Everyone has something they have to fight their way through. What I'm saying about Bobby is he's still at war, only it's in his mind now. And we're his army. We're going to help him fight it. The first thing we need to do is talk to him about getting into therapy. I'll even drive him into the city for it if that's what he needs."

"You're not driving him anywhere," I tell him. "Bobby doesn't need to yammer about his feelings to some psychotherapy wimp with a ponytail. It's just stupid. Yeah, maybe Bobby's partying too much, but a lot of people party too much. He'll settle down."

"You call what he's doing partying?" He stares into my eyes. "I thought partying was supposed to be about fun. He doesn't look like he's having fun to me. He looks like he's trying to drown something out. That's exactly what happens with a lot of people who have post-traumatic stress disorder."

"You make it sound like he's running away from something. I can tell you right now Bobby never ran from anything in his life."

"What are you so angry about? I'm not the enemy here."

"I'm not angry. I'm just sticking up for my brother."

"Of course you're angry. Ever since I've known you, you've had a chip on your shoulder about half the time, and it's getting old. I know your brother got a screwed-up deal, getting shipped off to war the way he did, but you can't be mad at everything. That isn't going to get you anywhere."

"Really? Maybe I should just lie down and die, huh? Let people walk over me like a worm in the dirt. Is that what you'd do?"

He shakes his head. "This is exactly why I held off talking to you about this. I knew you'd overreact."

"You think I'm overreacting?" I pop out of the chair and look down on him. "How about this? How about I just walk out of here and leave you to your stupid Web site and your stupid books. And if that seems like an overreaction, then you don't have to bother talking to me again."

"Come on," he says. "Sit down. Just read what this Web site has to say."

But I'm not about to do that. Without another word, I stomp out of the office and through the front door of the bowl-

208

ing alley. In the parking lot, I drop my phone twice before I finally get a call through to Brianna.

"How's it going?" she asks. "Did he pop the question?"

"It's not going," I say. "Everything's shot to pieces. One hundred percent."

33

Okay, no more of this *Padgett* business. That's what I tell my-self. He's back to being Mr. White again—from here on out. I was so stupid, walking into that bowling alley thinking he was going to ask me to be his girlfriend. But that's not really the point. The point is no one's going to brand my brother as crazy. I've seen how people treat the captain around here, and I won't stand for anyone treating Bobby like that.

That's my thought process as I walk into my house that night. I'm so wrapped up in it I just vaguely hear Dad call my name. The second time, he makes sure I hear him.

"Ceejay, come in here. I want to talk to you."

I walk into the living room, where he's standing in front of his favorite chair. He tells me to sit down on the couch. Of course, at first I'm thinking I'm in trouble as usual, but as soon as we both sit down and I get a good look at his face, I know it's something else.

"Is it Bobby?" I ask. "Did something happen to him?"

Dad shakes his head. "It's your grandmother."

I know it's creepy, but when I hear that I'm relieved. Not that I actually want something bad to happen to Grandma, but she hasn't really been first on my list of worries.

Dad goes on, "She's taken a turn for the worse. Your sister came home and found her collapsed in the backyard."

"Is she—"

"She's still alive but I'll be honest—it doesn't look good. Lacy couldn't get her to wake up and had to call an ambulance. It was a stroke. She's in intensive care. I imagine all the treatments she's been going through took their toll on her. We just found out about it a half hour ago. Your mother's heading up tonight and we'll go tomorrow."

I hate to sound like a self-centered idiot, but I can't help thinking this isn't a good time to leave town. Me and Uncle Jimmy and Jerry are just starting a job for the school board, a big one. They need me. But more important than that, I don't want to leave Bobby alone with the captain right now. I'm afraid they'll just bum each other out. And I sure don't want Mr. White showing up and spouting off his PTSD nonsense.

But there's no use in arguing. Even with all the reasons I have to stay, nothing trumps dying.

After Dad finishes explaining our plans for tomorrow, I head upstairs to tell Mom I'm sorry about Grandma and all that kind of thing. A couple of her bags sit open on the bed, mostly packed, and she's standing across the room digging something out of her dresser. At least that's what I think she's doing at first. But she's not moving. Her shoulders are slumped, and her hands grip either side of the top drawer as if she needs to keep herself from falling. In the mirror on the wall, I see her face—eyes clamped shut, her bottom lip bowing tightly against the top one. Deep lines crease her forehead. Tears on her face.

This is the mother I thought could smile through anything. The whole time Grandma's been sick, Mom's acted like better times are bound to come back around, like Christmas or your birthday. But not now. There's no fooling anyone, least of all herself.

I don't know what to do. I mean, obviously, in a situation like this, you're supposed to go over and hug your mom and come up with some kind of words of comfort, something all concerned and Hallmark-cardy, but I'm not the hugging type. More than anything, I just want to hurry down to my room, maybe come back later when the crying spell is over, but she catches a glimpse of me in the mirror.

Immediately, her hands flit to her face to wipe off the tears, and she turns around. The smile is back, a sad, sheepish one, as if she wants me to know she's just being silly.

"Ceejay," she says. "I didn't know you were back."

"Yeah, um, I just got home a minute ago."

She goes over to the bed, picks up a blouse to pack into one of the open bags. Her hands are shaking. "I guess your dad talked to you about what's going on." She's trying to look busy, avoiding eye contact.

"You mean about Grandma?" I say. Like it could be anything else.

"I want to get up there as soon as I can," she says. "Lacy has been doing what she can, but . . ." Her voice trails off. The blouse she's been trying to fold isn't cooperating, and finally she lets it drop to the bed. "I don't know what's the matter with me," she says. "These old hands just won't do right." She tries

212

a little laugh, but it doesn't work either, and she sits on the bed and begins crying again.

"Here, let me help you get that stuff packed," I tell her. I guess I could sit on the bed beside her, but it's more natural for me to go to work on something instead.

As I finish packing the bags, she stares down, nervously twisting her wedding ring. "It's funny," she says. "You don't know how you'll feel about something like this till it's staring you in the face. Mama and I haven't always seen eye to eye over the years, but it wasn't always that way. Things were so different when I was a little girl, and now I feel about like I've turned right back into that little girl, and I don't want her to leave me."

"It's okay," I tell her, and immediately I feel stupid for saying it. But that's what people always say—*it's okay*—when nothing could be further from the truth.

"I used to think she could do no wrong. I thought the worst criminal in the world could show up at our front door, and it wouldn't matter. My mother would keep me safe. Then Dad died. I was just the same age you are now, Ceejay. He died and everything changed."

Somehow I never thought of it like that—my mom being my same age when her dad got killed in that car wreck. Jesus. What that must have been like to go through. The strength it must've taken. Since I was twelve or thirteen, I thought of Mom as nothing but sugary sweet and cheery to a fault, but now I can't help wondering if maybe I underestimated her.

"Maybe it's selfish of me to wish we had more time," she says. "After all, these last couple of months have been so miserable for her. I don't know how she had the courage to get through it like she did. One afternoon when I was driving her

213

home after one of those awful treatments, she told me she knew the end would have to come, but she was going to do everything she could to make her life count, what there was left of it. A lot of other people might have given up, but not her."

"And I'm sure she's not ready to give up now either," I say.

She looks up at me. "That's right," she says. She stands, walks over, and wraps me up in a hug. "The women in this family don't give up easy, do we, Ceejay?"

"We sure don't." I hug her back, and it's weird—for once I actually feel like I am a part of a long line of women in this family. Like I'm tied to them somehow instead of whirling around off to the side on my own.

34

The next day Dad has to go to work for a couple hours in the morning, so it's after ten o'clock before we're ready to load up and get on the road to Grandma's. Drew's holed up in his room with the Xbox, so I have to holler several times for him to get his butt downstairs. Finally, I barge into his room to haul him out by force if I have to.

"Five more minutes," he says without even looking at me.

"Five minutes nothing." I rip the controls out of his hands. "You're coming right now."

"Why do I have to go?" he whines. "It's not like I can't take care of myself around here."

"You're coming because you have to support Mom. Don't you get it? Her mother's dying. So Dad's going and I'm going and you're going and we're going to support Mom one hundred percent."

"Oh, all right," he says. "But I won't like it."

"That's okay. You don't always have to like everything."

On the drive to Davenport, it's Dad and my big sister Colleen in the front seat and me and Drew in the back. Colleen starts going on about how her husband Jason's grandpa had a stroke, and he's doing just fine now.

"People get over strokes all the time," she says.

"That's right," Dad says. "All the time." But he doesn't sound so certain.

"They probably didn't have a stroke and cancer both," I say, and Colleen's like, "Now don't be negative, Ceejay. We need to keep Grandma in our prayers, and everything will work out."

I start to argue about the prayer deal, but decide maybe it's not such a bad idea. I could at least try one for Mom's sake. So in my head I'm like, God, I know maybe I'm not the best person to do the asking, but could you get things to turn out all right with Grandma? Plus, since we're talking, could you look after Bobby while I'm gone? He needs it.

I open my eyes and look out the side window—fences, rolling hills, cows. If God was listening, he doesn't show any sign of it.

When we finally reach the hospital after the long drive, the parking lot is scorching hot. It's been over a hundred degrees for five days straight. The sky is as frayed and faded as ragged denim, and the sunlight explodes off the windows of the parked cars. I'm thinking it should be dreary and raining for the kind of business we have here, but somehow this seems even more depressing.

Inside, we wind through the halls till we come to the intensive care unit, where Grandma's supposed to be. There are two

216

rows of people in their beds, some with drapes pulled around them and some right out in the open with all sorts of hoses hooked up to them. They're dying, I guess. This is the first time I've been around something like this. When my step-grandpa died, we just went up for the funeral and came home. There was nothing to it. But now death is hanging around like some kind of big, fat cop who doesn't know anything but rules.

Drew's like, "This place is weird," and I pop him on the back of the head.

"Grow some manners," I tell him.

Grandma, Mom, and Lacy are nowhere in sight, and I can tell by the look on Dad's face he's thinking the same thing I am—we got here too late. Dad asks a nurse where Grandma is, and it turns out she's been moved to a room on the third floor.

"Well, that must be good," I say. "She must be better."

The nurse mumbles a long *uhhhh*, and looks at Dad.

"Oh, I see," he says.

As we walk away, I'm like, "What is it? I mean, if they moved her to another room, she must be better, right?"

"Not necessarily," Dad says.

"Why else would they move her?"

He stops and looks me in the face. "Because there's nothing else they can do for her here."

When we walk into Grandma's room, Mom and Lacy look up from their chairs on either side of the bed. They're obviously drained. Mom's hair is actually a little bit messed up, and Lacy looks like she hasn't slept in about a month. Grandma's unconscious, has been since yesterday, and looks even more shrunken than the last time I saw her. Tubes run from hanging bags down to her arms. More tubes help her breathe. This doesn't look like anything you come back from.

When Mom starts to get up, Dad tells her to stay there—he knows she's tired—but Lacy pops up, comes straight over, and hugs me.

"I'm glad you're here, Ceejay."

I'm thinking, Jesus, first Mom and now Lacy. Will the hugs never end? But the weird thing is that it really isn't so weird. It actually feels natural to hug her back. Like all the distance that usually wedges itself between us has collapsed. She needs a jolt of strength from someone, and I'm her sister, so it's only right to give it to her.

Colleen goes into her story about her husband's grandpa again, and Mom's like, "That's right. People do come back from strokes." But she's like Dad—it sounds as if she doesn't really believe it will happen this time.

The room is small and really crowded with all of us in there, so Dad persuades Mom and Lacy to go to the cafeteria for a break. Drew goes with them, leaving me and Dad and Colleen behind. At first I can't help but wonder what the deal is—why do people gather around and watch someone who doesn't even know you're there? But as Colleen and Dad do their small-talk thing, I watch Grandma and start thinking maybe on some level she is aware of us. I mean, even with all our differences, we are family and that counts for something, right?

With her bony arms and hollowed face, she doesn't look like the same plump, angry woman who took my skates away from me and wouldn't give them back. The cancer and the stroke have stripped that away, and now she's just a person. Maybe way down inside, she's still fighting for her life, and I can't help wondering what that's about. There's no hope left, really. None. So what is that thing inside that keeps people hanging on even when everything seems so impossible?

For a long moment, Grandma's breathing stops, and I'm

thinking this is it—she's gone—but then her lungs seem to catch, and the strained breathing starts up again. The fight continues.

That's the way it goes all afternoon. We stay by her in shifts. Finally, at dinnertime, we go out to eat, everybody but Mom. When we return, Mom is standing in the hall outside Grandma's room. She looks stunned, lost.

"I just went out of the room for a second," she says, her voice shaking. "I needed a drink. When I came back . . ." And that's all she can get out before the tears overtake her and she falls into Dad's arms.

"What happened?" Drew says. No one answers right away, so he asks again and I tell him Grandma's gone.

"Gone?" he says. "Gone where? I didn't think she could walk."

I glare at him and shake my head. The truth dawns on him. "Oh, that kind of gone."

Mom's sobbing in Dad's arms. "I should've been with her. I didn't want her to go alone like that."

Dad strokes her back. "Maybe she felt like she couldn't move on with us standing around her," he says. "She might've just been hanging on for us."

Lacy collapses into a chair against the wall. She's not crying. She's just staring ahead, and I swear she looks way older than the day she left Knowles to come up here and care for Grandma. She might even look older than me. I'm no expert about these things, but there's been so much hugging going on lately, I figure I can't go wrong if I sit beside her and wrap my arm around her shoulder. She leans her head against me and grabs hold of my free hand. I'm not sure how long something like this is supposed to last, but I guess I'll keep it up as long as she needs it.

35

The funeral is scheduled for three days later. Mom and Lacy stay in Davenport to take care of the arrangements and look after the house. It's Dad's job to call people in Knowles to let them know what happened. All sorts of food—cakes, pies, even hams—come in from various church people. I figure Miss Big Tits Diane Simmons is bound to show up with a casserole and a giant helping of cleavage, but when I tell Uncle Jimmy that, he says not to worry—Dad doesn't want anything to do with her.

I'm like, "What do you mean? You're the one who told me he's not too old for temptation and all that."

"Yeah, well, I guess I was just really thinking about myself when I said that."

"But I've been watching him," I say. "It's like she has a spell on him. Last time she was over I caught them at the kitchen table, and she was poking a carrot stick in his mouth, all flirty and everything. And he just grinned like a fool. I almost stayed home. It was like I thought I should stay there and be their chaperone."

Uncle Jimmy looked thoughtful for a second. "I wasn't going to tell you this. Your dad told me not to tell anyone, but you need to know it. The thing is Diane Simmons won't be bringing food over at all."

"I wouldn't bet on that."

"It's a fact. Your dad told her not to."

"Why would he do that?"

Uncle Jimmy scratches his chin, weighing whether he should go on, before he does. "Because that last time she came over—the carrot-stick time—she ended up laying a big, wet kiss on your dad when he wasn't expecting it."

"You've got to be kidding!"

He shakes his head. "And not only that, she jammed her hand right down between his legs. He said it felt like she was giving him a physical. He jumped up so fast, he about knocked the table over."

My face burns. "That bitch."

"Yeah," Uncle Jimmy says. "And then she starts laughing and telling him she knows how much he wants it and how she wants it too, and starts unbuttoning her blouse. Swear to God, I'm not making this up. She says she's not expecting anything but a little fun on the side. But your old man, he wasn't having any of it. He laid the law down, told her to march herself right back out to her car and to never come back. Told her he loved his wife and he loved his kids, and he wasn't about to let any big pair of tits mess that up."

"He said that?"

"Pretty much. And I'll tell you what, as a man who has let a big pair of tits lead him down the wrong road too many times, I can't tell you how much I admire your dad for being able to do that. I mean, I might fight and screw and just in general get rowdy, but your dad's a stronger man than I am any day."

Obviously Uncle Jimmy's all proud of my dad and everything, but I'm like, "Really? How much strength does it take just to do the thing you ought to do in the first place? Is that something to be proud of? It's like bragging that you don't rob liquor stores or kick babies."

"You're young, Ceejay," he says. "You don't know. Maybe someday you'll find out."

"Well, I'll tell you this—if she comes back around, she's going to get an earful from me."

He puts his hand on my shoulder. "Huh-uh. That's exactly what you can't do. You can't say anything about this to anyone. Maybe later your dad will tell your mom, but it sure isn't anything she needs to find out about right now. The best thing you can do is just keep it to yourself no matter how hard that is."

I know he's right. It'll be hard, but I have to do it.

I'll have to do something else too, and it'll be just as hard, maybe harder. I've been elected to call Bobby about going to the funeral. Back when we were going to visit Grandma, I knew he'd never go, but a funeral is different. It's like a duty, so I figure I'll have to do my best to talk him into it this time.

When I call Dani's place, he's actually there for a change instead of hanging out with the captain. They had to exchange the engine they ordered for Angelica, and now they're waiting for the new one to come in. The captain is still real down about the situation, but Bobby figures the new engine will change everything. He could go on about that for another thirty minutes, but I have to break in and tell him about Grandma. His response is, "Well, they say only the good die young, and Grandma sure wasn't young."

Now, okay, Grandma was kind of like our adversary all this time, but that's still pretty cold, especially since she just died. It really rubs me the wrong way. I'm like, "Come on, Bobby, don't talk like that. I know you and her had your differences, but she's still Mom's mom. And I think she did change there at the end. Besides, it was pretty intense seeing her lying in that hospital bed looking so frail, trying to hang on just for her family's sake and all. You have to let bygones be bygones at a time like this."

Bobby snorts a laugh at that. "She might've been hanging on for Mom, but she sure wasn't hanging on for you and me. You know how it's always been, Ceejay, you and me, we're different—born into the wrong family. Outsiders in our own home. You're not all of a sudden going to start acting like the rest of them, are you?"

"You didn't see what it was like, the way Mom and Lacy took care of her. It wasn't easy. They're a lot tougher than you might think."

"Okay. Good for them. What do you want me to do about it, cry?"

This is too much. Of course, Bobby and I always talked about how we were different from the rest of the family, but he was never mean about it like this. He wasn't even mad about it. He thought it was funny. Our parents and siblings were just these goofy aliens that didn't understand us. I always figured he still loved them, though.

"No," I say, my voice rising. "I don't want you to cry about it. But I damn sure think you need to come to the funeral. You don't have to come for Grandma, but you should at least come for Mom. It'll be real goddamn shitty if you don't."

There's a long pause. I guess he isn't used to me cursing him.

"Then goddamn shitty is just how it's going to have to be," he says finally. "Because I can't go to a funeral, Ceejay. I just can't. Maybe everyone will hate me. They probably have a right to, but there's nothing you can say that'll make me go. There's nothing anyone can say."

"And so that's it?"

"That's it."

I hate to get beat by anything, but I know I'm beat this time. The only thing left to do is think of a lie to tell Mom so Bobby's absence won't go down quite so hard.

36

Here's the lie—Dani's little boy, Ian, is sick, and Bobby has to stay home with him while she's at work. It's not the best lie in the world, but it has a kid in it, so I figure as soft-hearted as Mom is, she'll play along. Of course, she does, too. When I tell her, she says she thinks Bobby's doing the right thing. She even smiles, but not enough to cover up the hurt underneath. Dad looks like he's ready to explode. He doesn't, though, not this time.

The day of the funeral it takes several cars to get us all to Grandma's church in Davenport for the service. The one I'm in is packed and uncomfortable, and I'm wearing a dress for the first time in about a hundred years. When we get there, the parking lot is already pretty full. Our family walks in together after everyone else has been seated, and in a weird way, with everybody looking at us, I feel like a celebrity. Like one of the stars of death's latest show.

There must be a million flowers at the front of the sanctuary, where Grandma's coffin sits closed. At first, I can't help thinking that seems phony. All these people and all these flowers—surely Grandma wasn't that beloved. I mean, it's a sad day and all, but I saw Grandma around other people, and she wasn't much nicer to them than she was to me and Bobby. But, looking around, I realize most of the people are from Knowles. They're here for Mom, not Grandma. They want to show her she's not alone, and I have to admire them for that.

We take our seats at the front, and after a couple of songs, the preacher comes on and tells us why we don't have to be sad. He talks about resurrection, which is kind of a spooky idea, so I try not to think about it too much. The best part of the service comes when the people who knew Grandma step up to tell stories about her, and if you ask me, Lacy is the best speaker of all. Actually, she kind of amazes me. Grandma's passing hit her pretty hard. It's a wonder she can even get up and try to string a speech together in front of a crowd, let alone get through most of it without breaking down.

She starts off talking about how much Grandma wanted to work around the house, even though she was so frail and skinny. "And then one day we were out in the garage," she says, "and Grandma couldn't have weighed a hundred pounds by now, but she was determined to get that place cleaned up. Boxes were everywhere, filled with a lifetime's worth of stuff she'd packed away. I told her we should probably just toss most of it out, but she's like, 'No, we have to go through it all. There might be important things in there I want to pass on to people.'

"So we started going through boxes, and she came across all these old pictures of my mom and dad from high school and then some of their old wedding pictures too. She started crying when she saw those. They reminded her of how much my parents meant to each other.

"For the next week she worked almost till her skinny little fingers cracked, putting those pictures into a brand-new scrapbook along with some of the other mementos she found in her boxes. It was beautiful. And we'd sit there in the evening together, and she'd tell me about my parents when they were young. She told me she didn't always think Mom and Dad were exactly a match made in heaven. 'Your dad was a little high-spirited,' she said. Which I guess is a nice way of saying he was a troublemaker."

Everyone laughs at that, my dad included. It feels good, a warm, healing kind of laugh that you can only get at a funeral or when something else bad happens.

Lacy smiles and turns a little red but keeps going. "Grandma even told a story about Dad's high school days that he never told himself. And anyone who knows my dad knows he isn't shy about telling stories."

We laugh again.

"It seems he showed up at one of Mom's church softball games while she was playing first base. He might have had just a little bit to drink. He'd been out fishing and wasn't wearing anything but his waders. He was all sunburned and his hair was sticking up every which way, and he was holding a big fish up by the stringer, yelling, 'Hey, honey, I caught a seven-pound bass! I caught a seven-pound bass!'"

That really gets the crowd laughing. Usually, when I hear stories about my dad cutting up in his youth, it sounds corny, but this time I can't help being reminded of Bobby and some of the stunts he would get up to. Maybe I would've hung out with Dad if we'd gone to high school together after all.

227

"So," Lacy goes on, "Mom yells back, 'Well, take it home and put it in the freezer.' But Dad just keeps walking toward the field until someone in the bleachers hollers, 'Get out of here with that fish before I stuff it down your throat!' I guess Dad didn't like anyone threatening him, so what does he do? He rares back and hurls that bass straight into the crowd and hits the guy right in the face. A brawl was about five seconds from breaking out, but Mom ran over from first base and slapped Dad on the side of the head with her mitt and told him if he didn't get out of there, she'd go get a bat. Dad pretty much went home after that. He never did get the fish back."

Now the whole sanctuary's roaring with laughter. When it finally dies down, Lacy looks straight at Dad and says, "So, Dad, how come you never told us that story?"

That tickles everybody all over again. A few months ago I never would've believed my perky mom could slap anyone with a baseball glove, but after seeing how she handled this summer with Grandma, it doesn't surprise me a bit.

"And the thing is Grandma told me she used to be as embarrassed as embarrassed could be by what happened that day. She thought Dad's rowdy ways were rubbing off on Mom, especially when she tried telling Mom she couldn't date him anymore. She said, 'I never knew my little curly-headed girl could get so mad. She stood right up to me and said she was not only going to keep dating your father but, by God, she was going to marry him too!'"

I look at Mom. She's blushing, but her smile shows how proud she is of herself.

"And then Grandma said something I won't ever forget," Lacy goes on. "She said she wished more than anything that she had a picture of that seven-pound bass. She'd put it right on the front page of the new scrapbook because it would remind her of just how strong the love was between my parents. She said she wanted to be that strong as she went through her battle with that stupid old cancer. And she was. She was every bit that strong."

Lacy's voice starts breaking on those last few words, and then the tears hit, but she gets through the important part. It's beautiful. I'd start clapping if that kind of thing was allowed in church.

At the reception at Grandma's house afterward, everyone's hanging out and eating piles of ham, green beans, chicken, and coleslaw. I pull Lacy aside and tell her how proud I am of her, not just for the speech but for the way she toughed it out with Grandma the whole summer long. "You are a badd badass girl," I tell her. "One hundred percent."

"You would've done the same thing," she says.

"I'm not so sure about that."

"Of course you would have."

"But they picked you to go."

"Only because you had a summer job already lined up. Mom and Dad probably figured I needed something to put a little backbone in me. And they were right."

"I'm pretty sure you already had it. Besides, Grandma got along with you a lot better than she would have with me."

"I don't know about that. After you came up to visit, Grandma went on and on about how glad she was to see you. She talked about how much you were like Dad, and that was a good thing because Dad had more steel in him than any ten other men she knew."

"More steel, huh?"

"That's what she said, and she said she could tell you were the same way."

"You really miss her, don't you?"

She looks down. "She changed my life."

I squeeze my arm around her shoulder. "Looks to me like you changed each other's lives."

The rest of the afternoon, we sit around Grandma's living room eating and talking. Everyone seems happy, but it's the kind of happiness that has a deep underground stream of sadness below it, which I discover isn't a bad thing. Relatives meander by, along with church people and strangers from Davenport, but somehow, for once, I don't feel out of place.

Mom sits on the sofa next to me, and I press close against her as she opens the guest book where everyone who went to the funeral signed their names. So many people showed up, we didn't have time to visit them all or even see everyone, and now she wants to make sure she knows who came. Slowly, she browses the signatures, sometimes rubbing her index finger over the ink as if that will make her feel closer to the people who signed there. At first, it seems funny—in a cute Mom way—but then I realize how much it must mean to her when I spot a signature that glows brighter than the others, at least in my eyes. I can't believe I didn't see him in the sanctuary, but there's his name in the middle of the page—Padgett Locke.

37

The next evening I'm hanging out in my room with my phone in my hand. I don't really know why I'm holding it. I just know I've received exactly zero calls from a certain long-haired, skinny guy who works in a bowling alley. No text messages, e-mails, or Facebook posts. You'd think he'd at least call to say how nice the service was or something. Of course, I still think he's one hundred percent wrong about Bobby having some kind of mental disorder. Even if I am a little worn out with Bobby for being weird lately and dodging the funeral, that doesn't mean I'm not behind him.

So why did Padgett—he's back to being Padgett in my mind instead of Mr. White—why did he come to the funeral? Was that his way of apologizing? Or is it because he really does have some kind of romantic feelings for me? Either way, I can't be too mad at him anymore. After all, he probably spent hours online researching that stupid PTSD stuff. You have to hand it to him for that, at least, even if he is way off base.

All this thinking ties my brain into a knot as I pace around my bedroom. Yes, I could call him and let him off the hook for the PTSD deal. I could be the bigger person. But I'm not the one who said someone in his family is crazy. That's something I still can't forget. His dad got messed up on booze, but did I hang a label on him, call him an alcoholic? No. I wouldn't do a thing like that. Still, I could call just to give him a chance to admit he was wrong.

Right as I sit down on the bed, the phone rings and I drop it on the floor like it's a live hand grenade. For a moment, I stare at it, trying to think of something to say in case it's Padgett, but nothing comes to mind. Doesn't matter. It's not him.

"Ceejay, I'm glad you're back in town." It's Bobby and he sounds excited, almost happy, which is not his usual frame of mind these days. "You have to come out to the captain's tonight. We're going to do a little celebrating."

Not a question about the funeral or how Mom's doing or anything, which rubs me way the wrong way.

"I don't see any reason for celebrating right now," I tell him.

But he's like, "It's Angelica, we got the engine mounted. Everything's ready to go."

Immediately, I forget the funeral and Padgett both. "You haven't tried to fly that stupid thing yet, have you?"

"No," he says, "but we've putted around in the yard a little bit. There's a guy down in Sparks who flies one almost exactly like this. He's going to give us some lessons. Come on over, though. We'll let you drive it around the yard. It handles great. Show up around nine. Call Padgett and get a ride."

"I don't really know where he is."

"He's probably at the bowling alley. He was over here help-ing us earlier before he had to go to work."

"Is he coming back over there tonight for sure?"

Bobby doesn't answer that. Instead he's like, "Listen, what-ever you do, don't bring that dick Tillman with you."

"Him? I don't even talk to him anymore."

"Good. And if Dani happens to call, don't tell her about it either."

"Why not?"

"No reason. It's just she's a downer when it comes to the captain. I don't need that. Just come on over about nine or so. Chuck will be here too. You have to hear this engine, Ceejay. It's smooth."

I'm glad Bobby's enthusiastic about something, but I felt a lot better when he and the captain were just welding tin moons and stars to that thing. I still can't picture them actually flying it. Of course, this would make the perfect excuse to call Padgett. I'd just be doing him a favor, nothing else. But the more I think about it, the more I talk myself out of it. He'll just have to find out on his own. And if he happens to show up at the captain's tonight, then I guess that's how things are meant to be.

Brianna's more than happy to drive me out there. She hopes they'll let her drive around the yard, but no way is that going to happen. I don't tell her this, but she's way too big. You could shove a cantaloupe into a teacup faster than she could squeeze that butt of hers into Angelica's seat.

On the way over, she asks what Padgett's up to tonight, and she's not satisfied when I brush it off with an "I don't know."

"You're not still mad at him, are you?" she asks. "I mean, when you told me about him coming to the funeral, you sounded pretty impressed."

233

"I'm not mad at him. I just don't want him going around saying bad things about my brother."

"Yeah, right," she says. "I think you're mad because he didn't end up asking you to be his girlfriend like you thought he was going to do."

"Don't be ridiculous. I was relieved when he didn't do that. It kept me from having to let him down."

She cocks an eyebrow. "Uh-huh, sure."

"You know, Brianna," I say, staring a hole in her. "You irritate the hell out of me sometimes."

She just laughs.

Still, when we get to the captain's, I am a little disappointed that Padgett's VW is nowhere to be seen, but I just tell myself, So what? I'm here to see Bobby anyway. Besides, I have other things to think about right now. Bobby's motorcycle and Chuck's pickup are parked out front, but that's not all—so is Mona's Escalade. No wonder Bobby didn't want me to tell Dani anything about going to the captain's tonight.

"Very interesting," says Brianna. "This evening might have some real possibilities."

"You better not tell Tillman about this."

"Why not?" she says, like she doesn't know.

"You just better not."

This isn't good. Bobby's never been the type to cheat on girlfriends, and Dani is not the person to start on. That girl is a terror when she's mad. But it's not just that. More important, I just don't want Bobby to be that kind of guy—a cheating dog. I've always figured him to have more character than that.

The light's on in the barn, so that's where we head. I'm hoping to see everyone sitting around putting the finishing touches on Angelica, everything innocent and aboveboard.

Wrong. It's only Bobby and Mona. She's standing there, leaning against a support post, her head thrown back while Bobby goes at her neck like a vampire who hasn't fed for a couple of centuries.

Brianna starts to say something, but I grab her arm and yank her away from the door.

Inside, Mona goes, "God, Bobby, let's go somewhere."

"What's the matter with here?" Bobby asks.

"What if the others come back?"

"Chuck isn't going to bring the captain back down here. He knows better than that."

Brianna giggles and I put my hand over her mouth.

"But your sister might show up," Mona says, sounding a little out of breath.

"So what?" Bobby tells her. "Ceejay's caught us before."

"That was different," says Mona, and then for a while neither one of them say anything until finally Mona's like, "Oh God, Bobby, you know what that does to me when you do that. Oh God."

Brianna's eyes go wide, and I grab her arm. "Come on," I tell her. "Let's get out of here."

"It was just getting good," she says, but I'm like, "Jesus, don't be such a psycho perv," and I drag her across the yard toward the house.

"What are we doing?" she says. "If they're not going to fire up the aero-ma-dealy-whopper, why don't we just head home?"

"We'll ride it later. Bobby and Mona can't go at it all night. At least, I don't think they can."

"You know, Ceejay, Bobby better be careful. He's really playing with razor blades this time. I mean, you know Dani. She's ten times meaner than Jace. I'd hate to see what she'd do if she found out about this."

"Well, she's not going to. You understand me."

"Hey," Brianna says as we step onto the front porch of the captain's house. "I'm not going to tell anybody. You know that. But this town's too small to keep something like this a secret for long. Someone will blab it all over the place."

"Well, maybe by then Bobby and Dani will be broken up. I can only hope."

I knock on the front door, and Chuck opens it. He smells like weed and beer, and the whites of his eyes have turned a bright stoner pink. "Hey," he says. "Come on in. I'm glad to see you guys. The captain hasn't been much company."

Chuck's blue ice chest sits by the easy chair, and empty beer cans litter the living room floor. Weird music plays on the captain's ancient cheapie record player. "Have you ever heard this?" says Chuck. "It's the captain's album, *Crash Landing on Pluto*. It's freaky."

I ask where the captain is and Chuck says, "He's in the kitchen hiding under the table. He's on a bad frequency. He thinks all sorts of people are out to get him and shit. I'm standing guard against the Nogo Gatu while Bobby and Mona do their deal."

"Oh God," says Brianna. "This is too weird, Ceejay. Let's get out of here."

She's right—it's weird—but something tells me I need to stay.

"You go ahead," I tell her. "Bobby can always give me a ride home on his motorcycle."

"I've heard that before," she says. "Besides, he looks a little busy to me."

Chuck pats me on the back. "Don't worry. I can give you a ride."

Brianna studies him for a second. "You sure you're all right to drive? You look a little wasted."

He smiles. "Don't you worry. The Chuck-in-ator is never too wasted to do a favor for a lady."

From the other room, the captain calls out, "We need metal shutters on the windows. Did anyone hear me? We need metal shutters on the windows."

Brianna shivers. "That's it. I'm outa here. You sure you don't want to come, Ceejay?"

I tell her I am, and she's like, "Well, good luck. I hope Padgett shows up. Call me later and tell me how it went."

I try to tell her that's not why I'm staying, but she just laughs and heads out the door.

When she's gone, Chuck offers me a beer and I take it. This night definitely calls for a little alcohol. We go into the kitchen to check on the captain, and sure enough, there he is under the table with his dog. The bill of his cap is pulled low and his eyes shift back and forth, but he doesn't look at us. It is creepy, all right, but not in a scary way. Really, you can't help but feel sorry for him. Apparently spells like this set down on him every once in a while.

"You all right under there?" says Chuck, knocking on the tabletop, but the captain just mumbles something I can't understand.

"Poor dude," I say. "How long's he been like this?"

"Days."

"He used to be so up," I say as we head back to the living room. "He was so excited about working with Bobby on Angelica."

"Yeah," Chuck says. He wavers a little, like his balance could give way at any time. "But you know what? I guess we all have our trapdoor inside. You never can tell when it might just go *boom*, and all of a sudden you're kicking at the end of your rope."

237

He looks like he knows what he's talking about from first-hand experience. I've never seen him like this before. "What's up with you?" I ask. "You sound like you're depressed yourself."

"Nothing's up," he says. "I don't want to talk about it. Here, have a seat. I want to play you this song."

"'Sliced Penguins'?"

"No, it's another one. It's just about what I feel like."

He lumbers to the record player and sets it to play the song. It starts off with nothing but an acoustic guitar and a harmonica. Then the lyrics kick in. The captain's ragged voice, only younger, all about some girl with sea-green eyes whose tulip lips tell scented lies. Her house is as dark as a vampire's cave and her backyard's scarred with shallow graves. And then the chorus:

> Oh, take me up to Kitty Hawk
> I'll rise above the shifting sands
> Kitty Hawk, Kitty Hawk
> I'll fly away and never land

While the song plays, Chuck stares at the floor, soaking up the music and words. When it's over, I'm like, "Pretty bizarre," and without looking up, Chuck goes, "Yeah, but I get it. Sea-green eyes, man, I know those sea-green eyes."

He sits there quiet for a moment like he's observing a moment of silence for something that died. Then he pops out of the chair and goes, "Hey, let's take this ice chest outside and get some air. I'm starting to fester."

We step onto the front porch just in time to see Mona's Escalade pulling away, Bobby in the passenger seat. Looks like Mona finally got her way and they're heading somewhere more private. Chuck takes a swig of beer and goes, "I guess it was getting too busy around here for the business they have in mind."

"Yeah," I say. "Me and Brianna almost walked in on them a while ago."

"I'm sure Bobby didn't care. It's always the girl that gives a shit about things like that."

We walk over to Chuck's pickup and sit in the bed with our backs against the cab. Even though it's not completely dark yet, the moon hangs over the treetops, a wisp of a cloud slowly drifting across it. We drink beer and talk, with me holding up most of the conversation. I even tell about the time I spied on Chuck and Bobby while they were skinny-dipping with their girlfriends. Chuck smiles. "I wish those days were back," he says.

"Those were fun times," I say. "I never told you this before, but when I was a little kid I thought you were pretty hot." This is something I wouldn't have said if I hadn't drunk about three beers by now.

Chuck's like, "You did?"

"Oh sure." I go on talking about another time I spied on him and Bobby, but he interrupts me.

"You know what, Ceejay? You have a sexy mouth."

"Very funny," I say, but he's like, "No, really," and touches a finger to my bottom lip. "I never could resist a girl with a wide mouth," he says.

"You don't think I look like a frog?"

He shakes his head and leans toward me. Maybe the beers are responsible for slowing down my reactions, but the next thing I know we're kissing. Tongue and everything. And it feels good. It feels great. My muscles turn to hot liquid. My eyes close and everything else in the world vanishes.

His hands are in my hair and along the side of my face, and mine move along his shoulder blades. I can't believe it. I mean, this isn't stone-face Gillis here. This is the legendary Chuck Dunmire. Even Tillman Grant would kill to be as cool as he was. I say *was* because of Chuck's current loser ways, but still, he's had some of the prettiest girlfriends you'd ever want to see. He's dating Amber Galen, for God's sake. And now here he is kissing me. Like I'm someone special.

One hand moves down my throat, between my breasts, and along my stomach. My skin feels electrified. This isn't exactly the first make-out session I've had, but it might as well be. Chuck really knows what he's doing. He's a master. I don't know if he'll move his hand down farther, but I want him to. I want him to so bad. I don't care about anything else. I just want that moment. I want to discover it, to wash up on it like it's a deserted island and live there, careless and warm.

But my stupid brain won't let me. It takes a big step back. I don't want it to, but it does. If Chuck would just move his hand down now, maybe everything else would shut off, but it's too late. My brain blasts a familiar voice at me. It's Uncle Jimmy talking about how strong my dad had to be to resist Ms. Simmons. "You don't know," he said. "Maybe someday you will."

I guess this is the day, because it suddenly makes sense. When you have something right in front of you like this, and your whole body is telling you to go for it, how can you back away? I mean, Bobby couldn't resist Mona, so it must have practically taken superhero strength for my fat, fifty-one-year-old dad to turn down a chance to roll around with those giant, freckled boobs.

Because it's not just about the sex. It's also about wanting so bad to be someone who matters. Someone who isn't taken for granted or ignored or thought of as less than what you want to be. This wild, powerful tornado is sucking me in and I don't care. I want to lose myself to it. I want it to strip away everything I've thought was wrong with me.

Chuck's fingers slip beneath the waistband of my jeans, and

I try to focus on that, just the roughness of his fingertips against me, but I can't. At the last second, I grab his wrist, thinking, Goddamn you, Uncle Jimmy. Goddamn you, Dad. Why did you have to bust into my head right now? But it can't be helped. Here they are. And not just them but my mom, Lacy, and Grandma Brinker all come crowding in. They're the badasses, not me. I'm a weakling compared to them. Unless I can stop what I'm doing right now, I'll be a cheater just like Bobby turned into, and I don't want to be that.

But then another voice in my head is like, A cheater? Who am I cheating on? I don't have a boyfriend. I can do what I want. All of a sudden it hits me, though. Crap, I say to myself, that damn Brianna was right.

"I can't," I whisper, the heat of my own breath bouncing back to me off Chuck's face.

"It'll be good," he says.

"I know." My voice is shaky and small. "But I just can't."

He presses his forehead against mine. "Sure you can."

"No."

"Why not?"

"I don't know. I guess it's just because there's, like, somebody else."

"There isn't anybody else. It's just you and me."

"No, I mean I think maybe I kind of like have feelings for somebody else."

He pulls back and looks into my eyes. "What are you talking about? You mean you're in love with someone?"

"I didn't say that. I'm not sure I know what love is, but it's something."

"Shit, Ceejay, I'll tell you what love is." He turns his face away. "It's the fucking enemy. Love's a mean-ass cage fighter that'll kick your teeth in." His voice cracks.

241

"What's wrong?" I ask, realizing he's not really talking about me anymore.

He stares at the sky without answering.

"Chuck?"

"It's Amber. She's gone."

"Gone?"

"She broke up with me."

This is hard to believe. Chuck Dunmire, devastated over a girl? And a cupcake twin, no less. I'm like, "I didn't know she meant that much to you."

"She did," he says. "She's the only one. She meant everything."

"What happened? Why'd she break up?"

He lays his head against my shoulder. He's not the hot, legendary Chuck Dunmire that I had a crush on anymore. I guess I should be mad at him for wanting to use me to get over Amber, but I'm not. Instead, a huge wave of warmth for him swells up in me. Not a romantic, kissy-kissy warmth, but more like how you might feel about a favorite stuffed bear when you're a little girl.

"She got pregnant," he says.

"Pregnant? Jesus."

"It wasn't like last time with Layla Evans. I was happy this time. I could see us moving in together and having a kid, and I'd come home and there they'd be waiting on me, you know, happy to see me. I'd even stay on the job this time instead of walking off when I get fed up with the boss. Hey, I'd shovel shit ten hours a day if I had to. Anything, I'd do it."

"Have you told her this?"

"Yeah, I told her."

"What'd she say?"

He closes his eyes. "She said it was too late. She already got the abortion."

"She got an abortion?"

"She didn't even tell me she was going to do it. Didn't ask me one thing about it. You know? I said, 'How could you do that without talking to me first?' And she goes, 'What? Like I'd really have a baby with you? Don't be stupid.'"

"She said that?"

"And so I tried to tell her how much I wanted to be a family with her, and she just goes, 'Are you crazy? I'm not going to have a family with a guy like you.' She said all along we were just a summer thing. She said I was okay to have a little fun with, but she's going to college in the fall and she's not letting anything mess that up."

I pet his hair and tell him I'm sorry, and he goes, "What am I going to do, Ceejay?"

Two months ago, I would have probably told him he deserved what he got. It's payback for the way he's treated girls, and that would've been pretty satisfying to hit him with, but now it's like the mother instinct in me has blossomed all of a sudden, and I know he needs a real answer.

"If you really want to know what to do, Chuck, I'll tell you, but you might not like it. It won't be easy."

"That's okay. I'm through with easy."

I take a moment to gather my thoughts. Sure, I throw advice around all the time, but this time is serious. "All right, then," I say when I feel like I know where I'm headed. "Here's what you do—you take all these hard feelings you have about losing Amber and the baby, and you turn them in a different direction. Because I've got news for you, Chuck—you already have a baby. You have a three-year-old girl over in Sparks with

Layla Evans, and that girl needs her dad. That girl needs to walk into a house and know you're happy to see *her*."

"I don't know about that," says Chuck. "Layla doesn't want to have anything to do with me. I'm sure she has another dude by now."

"I'm not saying you'll get Layla back. This isn't about you, Chuck. Forget about you. Focus on that little girl and what she needs. Everything will change from there."

"You think so?"

"I do. I really do."

He raises his head and looks me in the eyes. "You know, Ceejay, whoever this guy is you've got a thing for is real lucky."

"I don't know about that."

"No, I mean it. You're something else." He brushes my hair back from my face. "You mind if I give you one more kiss just for good measure?"

I have to smile at him. You can't help but like Chuck. "Okay, just one."

It's a good kiss. I'm sure he's not even capable of kissing bad, but it doesn't matter now. I've been inoculated against feeling passion for him. This kiss is nothing but good practice. Except just as he's finishing up, a pair of headlights shine on us. My first thought is Bobby and Mona are back, but I'm not that lucky. It's Padgett's VW pulling up instead.

38

The headlights flick off, and for a moment the VW sits there idling. I wave with my free hand, but my other arm is still wrapped around Chuck's back. I'm hoping at least Padgett didn't see the kiss, but that's doubtful. The back of the pickup is facing directly toward the road leading up to the captain's house. The headlights beamed straight into our faces. I pull my arm free and start to get up, but the headlights flip back on and the VW begins backing up.

"Padgett," I call. "Hey, wait a minute." But he turns the car around and heads back toward the main road.

I'm like, "Oh, crap. Come on, Chuck, we have to catch him."

"What? Why?"

"Don't ask questions. Let's just go."

As Chuck fires up the truck, he looks at me and goes, "This isn't the dude you're hot for, is it?" And I'm like, "Yeah, you got anything to say about it?"

"No," he says. "Not a thing. Except like I said before—he's a lucky guy."

On the highway, it's not hard to catch Padgett—he's not exactly the fast and the furious in that VW of his—but getting him to pull over is another story. I have to yell and wave and do everything but flash my boobs at him before he finally stops on the shoulder of the road.

I tell Chuck to wait in the pickup, but he's right behind me as I walk up to the VW. Padgett rolls down the window. "What are you guys chasing me for?"

"Why'd you drive off?"

He looks away. "It didn't exactly seem like you two were in the mood for company."

"Hey, we were just talking. Chuck's girlfriend broke up with him, and I was giving him some advice."

Padgett's like, "I know. I saw what kind of advice you were giving him. I'm sure he's a much better kisser now."

I'm like, *What's he got to be mad about? He* sure never tried to kiss me. He hasn't even called in the last couple of days.

"Look," says Chuck. "She's telling you the truth, dude. She was just giving me some advice. I'm the one that laid the kiss on her. She didn't ask for it or anything."

Padgett goes, "It didn't look like she was asking you to stop either."

So Chuck goes, "Quit being such a crybaby. You're the one she's crazy about, not me."

I knew letting Chuck out of the truck was a bad idea.

"Shut up," I tell him. "You're not helping. Go back to the truck and let me talk to him."

"What's the matter?" says Chuck. "What'd I say?"

"Just give us a few minutes alone, okay?"

He's like, "Whatever," and heads back to the truck.

"What was he talking about?" Padgett says. "Did he say you're crazy about me?"

"Don't pay any attention to him. He's wasted times ten."

"So that's not what he said?"

"Look, I don't want to stand here talking with him back there staring at us. Why don't you get out and we'll take a walk."

"A walk? Where, down the side of the highway?"

"We'll just walk down to the bridge and look at the river and then come back."

He stares through the windshield for a moment.

"Come on," I tell him. "What do you think I'm going to do, pull a chainsaw on you or something?"

Finally, he's like, "Oh, all right," twists his key from the ignition, and gets out of the car. The bridge isn't but a couple of hundred yards down the road, but the weird tension between us makes it seem longer.

After an awkward silence, I go, "This is going to be hard for me. I'm not a big apologizer, but the first thing I want you to know is I'm sorry about the way I acted the other night when you were telling me about that traumatic stress stuff."

"Post-traumatic stress disorder."

"Yeah, right. It's just I'm real protective when it comes to Bobby. He's always been like the most important person in my life, pretty much."

"I wasn't trying to say anything bad about him. You know? I mean, if you're protective, you should want to know what's wrong with him. He needs professional help."

"But it's just so ridiculous—my brother with a mental

disorder. Anyone who could think that doesn't know him one bit."

He starts to come back with something to that, and I realize I'm getting mad all over again, so I cut him off. "Look, I don't want to argue about it anymore. What I want to say is I'm glad you want to help. I think you're wrong, but I appreciate how much trouble you went through doing research and everything. That was really nice of you, and I shouldn't, you know, put you down for that. Okay?"

He says okay, but I can tell he still wants to push the issue. We finally reach the bridge and stand there leaning against the guardrail, looking at the river. The light from the moon swims along the surface of the water below. The air is warm, and the smell of the woods is thick and heavy.

"So," I say, "were you mad about me and Chuck?"

"Mad? Why should I be mad? I just didn't want to interrupt you guys, that's all."

"You seemed mad."

"Well, I'm not."

"He did kiss me," I say. "But it was just one of those things that came out of the blue. He was wasted and feeling bad about getting dumped by his girlfriend and needed someone to make him feel not so bad about himself. That's all that was. I feel sorry for him, but I don't have any, like, *feeling* feelings for him."

"You don't?"

"No."

He looks toward the river. "That's good."

"Really? You think it's good?"

"Yeah."

"Why?" I'm bound to get him to admit he has feelings for me, even if I have to squeeze it out of him.

He keeps staring at the river.

"Well?" I say.

Without looking at me he says, "I talked to my father the other day."

"Wait a minute. Are you changing the subject?"

"I'm just trying to explain something." He runs his fingers through his hair. "The thing is my dad had a big relapse, got arrested for DUI again. It looks like he may be going to jail for a while."

"I'm sorry." I reach over and squeeze his wrist. "So now what's going to happen?"

"Well, for one thing it means I won't be going back to the city this fall."

"Oh yeah?" I try not to sound too happy about it. I mean, yes, I hate to hear his dad had a relapse and all, but at the same time I'm pretty thrilled Padgett's staying around a little longer.

"Yeah," he says. "I won't be doing all those things in the city we used to talk about. I won't be doing anything."

"That's not true. We'll do plenty of stuff together right here. The city will still be there later on."

"Maybe," he says, still staring off at the river. "But I have to tell you I've been thinking, and I just don't think I can do, like, a real relationship. I mean, look at what happened with my parents. Why would I want to get involved in a disaster like that?"

Wow. You can't help but hurt for a guy when he says something like that.

So I'm like, "Hey, all relationships aren't a disaster. My parents' sure isn't. They've lasted pretty well. I'm not saying it was always easy, but they toughed it out when they had to. Come on, you're the guy wearing white. Take your own advice and have a little hope."

He lets out a faint half-laugh and half-sigh. "Maybe I should start wearing blue instead." He brushes his long hair back from his face. "Anymore, it seems like all this hope business is just a way of kidding yourself, pretending something good's going to come when you don't have any way of knowing if it will. Like a dull painkiller to keep you from seeing what life's really about."

I study him for a moment. "Then forget hope," I tell him. "Screw it. You don't need hope. What you need is valiance. When everything goes dark, you keep going anyway. That's what you do."

He looks at me, a skeptical smile cocking one side of his mouth. "Valiance, huh?"

"Damn right," I say. "That's what you can wear white for now. Like the white knight, the way he keeps fighting with dragons breathing fire right in his face."

"That's all right for you," he says, looking away. "You've got valiance to spare, but where am I going to get any?"

"What are you talking about? You had to have plenty of guts just to be you in a town like this."

"I don't know about that."

I step closer to him. "Let me ask you something."

"What?" He doesn't make eye contact.

"Here, look at me."

"Okay," he says. "What's the question?"

"Just this," I say, and, without giving myself a chance to chicken out, I lean in and kiss him, hard, putting everything I just learned from Chuck into it and then some.

When I pull back, he stares at me for a second, then says, "Ask me again."

This time everything inside us breaks loose. Our hands get into the action, mine moving up and down his back, and his tangling in my hair. It's different from how it was with Chuck. There's more than just the sexual thing. I'm gravity-defying,

250

like a rocket burning full-force into space, the moon and the stars fracturing around me and falling on all sides.

"What does that do for your relationship-disaster theory?" I ask when we stop to get our breath.

"What theory?" he says, and comes back for more.

I could stand there kissing on that bridge till my lips wear out. It crosses my mind that the Tip-Top Motel isn't too far away. If we pooled our money, we could probably get a room. But a strange noise brings us back to reality. Something is coming down the highway, but we can't tell what. Then Padgett recognizes the sputtering sound.

"Crap!" he says. "It's Angelica. The captain's trying to fly her down the road!"

39

It's more like he's bouncing than flying. The tires skip on the road, then he's a couple of feet in the air, then another skip and he's four feet high. As he gets closer, we see Chuck running behind the captain, but he's so wasted he keeps falling down.

"This isn't good," Padgett says. "He hasn't even had any flying lessons."

We both run up the highway, waving our arms and yelling for him to stop, but he never looks our way. His cap is turned backward and his goggles stretch so tight his face takes on the wild determination of a comic-book character. He's hollering something I can't understand at first, but as he gets even with us it comes clear: "The Nogo Gatu are here! The Nogo Gatu are here! Evacuate! Evacuate!"

The aero-velocipede dips low again. It isn't exactly going

to break the sound barrier, so, running hard, we can actually keep pace, but what good is that? It's not like we can tackle the thing.

"Captain," Padgett yells, "cut off the engine. Cut off the engine."

Fat chance. Instead, the captain whooshes up to almost six feet, the highest he's been yet, and heads across the bridge, coming back down, and nearly banging into the guardrails before making it to the other side.

Behind us, Chuck's huffing and puffing, his nose bloody from falling down on the road. "I tried to stop him," he shouts. "The dude's totally flipped out."

"Hurry up," calls Padgett. "We're going to have to grab hold of it somehow."

I'm like, "The whole thing will crash if we try that," but he's already sprinting away from me.

"We don't have any other choice," he calls over his shoulder.

So there we are, running down the road with the captain in front of us, gaining speed, rising and dipping, veering left then right, Angelica's nose aiming upward at one moment, her tail end scraping pavement the next. As we catch up to him, he's about five feet off the ground, but we have a bigger problem than just finding a place to grab hold of.

In the distance, a pair of headlights rounds the curve in the road and heads our way.

"Oh hell," says Chuck. He's even with me now, and all three of us are gaining on Angelica.

"Captain, you gotta come down!" hollers Padgett. "You gotta come down."

Padgett reaches for Angelica's frame, but as soon as he does, she wafts up and away from his grip. "Come on, Chuck," I yell. "You have to grab it. You're the only one tall enough."

Chuck leaps once and misses, then tries again, and this time he loses his balance and crashes to the pavement.

The headlights blaze closer. There's no way we can stay in the road. We can only hope the captain will fly high enough to dodge the car or that the driver will see us in time to stop.

With the car a couple hundred yards away, the captain glides up to his highest altitude yet, maybe ten feet, but he only stays there for a moment before swooping back down. The headlights bear down hard, but at the last moment, the driver must spot what probably seems like a low-flying UFO. Brakes squeal, the car fishtails, the front end veers off the road and smacks into a highway sign.

At the same time, the captain dips low and tilts to the left. The tail end of the car juts into the road, and the nose of the aero-velocipede heads straight for it like a dive bomber.

"Pull up!" yells Padgett. "Pull up!"

But it's too late. Angelica's wheels plow into the car, snapping against the rear fender, her belly scraping across the trunk. From there she bounces through a fence and digs into the alfalfa field on the other side, the motor sputtering out as she rocks to a stop.

Only as we run toward the scene of the crash do I realize who's in the car—Dani. She must have been heading home. After ripping off her seat belt, she throws open the car door and starts screaming, "What the hell are you dumbasses doing out here? You could've killed me!" She looks like a ninja assassin coming at us. "See what you did to my fucking car!"

The car is pretty banged up, both from the highway sign and the aero-velocipede, but we don't have time to stand around doing a damage estimate. The captain could be seriously hurt, maybe even dead. Padgett reaches him first, with me and Chuck right behind.

"Are you all right?" Padgett says. "Captain?"

The captain raises his head. "Whose side are you on?" he asks, the weird fear in his eyes magnified by the goggles.

"We're on your side," says Padgett, and the captain goes, "I've got to get out of here. They're coming. They were in my house. They got in through the electrical outlets. I need to get up high enough. They can't get me up there."

"Here," says Padgett. "Let's help him get out of this thing."

We unstrap the harness and ease him out of the seat, but he can't stand up. His leg isn't broken or anything. It's just nerves. He's shaking all over. Even his beard seems to quiver as we help him sit down.

Standing on the other side of the fence, Dani yells, "I called the cops. They're on their way, so don't any of you think about trying to get out of here. It's a crime to leave the scene of an accident, you know."

Just then another pair of headlights rounds the curve, and Dani's like, "Oh, hell no. Now they're going to ram my car from the other side."

"Maybe it's the police," I say, and she's all, "How stupid are you? I just called them ten seconds ago. Get your butt over here and help me wave them out of the way."

So both of us are standing at the rear of her car waving, and sure enough the driver sees us, slows down, and stops on the shoulder of the road. The passenger door opens, and who do you think steps out? It's Bobby. He looks back into the Escalade and goes, "Stay in the car, okay?" But does Mona do it? No way. She steps right out and walks into the glare of the headlights, everything about her looking expensive as a weekend in Palm Springs, even her tan.

I'm thinking, Crap, you just had to make sure Dani knew you were here, didn't you?

Bobby goes, "Ceejay, what happened? What are you doing out here?" But before I can get a word out, Dani's like, "Hold on a minute. Hold on just one minute now. What are *you* doing riding around with this bitch?"

Bobby stops and stares at Dani like he can't remember exactly who she is. "You got me there," he says, scratching his head. "Maybe if you give me a couple of minutes, I'll come up with a good lie."

Dani's eyes go wild and she's like, "You bastard," and charges him, fists flying. She's pretty quick too, and Bobby can't get a good grip on her wrists before she slugs him a couple of hard ones on the jaw. Even with him holding on to her, she's not done. She's cussing and squirming and kicking so bad, there's nothing to do but pin her down on the pavement. "I'm gonna kill you!" she screams. "I'm gonna kill you and that bitch and your sister and everyone here!"

I've never seen anyone as mad as that. There's nothing Bobby can do but keep her pinned down until Officer Dave and Officer Larry pull up with their red lights flashing. Jesus, I tell myself, maybe we'll all get sent into the army this time.

40

It's weird—sometimes you can tell how much you care about something by how mad you get over it. Not so long ago I was all ticked off at Captain Crazy and wanted the cops to haul him off to jail, and now here I am ticked off because the cops *are* hauling him off to jail. Why should I care? If it wasn't for the captain, maybe Bobby and I would have hung out more, just him and me, maybe even moved in together, but the fact is I do care. I let Officer Dave and Officer Larry know it too.

I'm like, "Surely you don't go around arresting everyone who gets into a car wreck." But Officer Dave says this isn't exactly your average accident. They aren't sure what the charges will be, but from surveying Dani's car, Angelica's broken frame, and the captain's crazed face, they figure it won't be hard to come up with a whole list of crimes he's guilty of.

I practically beg them to let us take the captain home, but they won't go for it. They even look me over and say, how do they know I wasn't the captain's partner in crime, along with everyone else there?

Padgett steps up to play defense attorney, arguing that we tried to stop the captain. "Look at his bloody nose," he says, pointing to Chuck. "He must have fallen down five times trying to catch him."

The cops study Chuck for a second, but they don't seem convinced. Most likely they've seen Chuck with a bloody nose before.

They're more understanding about Bobby. Dani launches into how he attacked her, but when Mona steps up and explains how Dani was the first one to come fists swinging, the officers exchange looks that say they know what's going on, and they'd just as soon not get in the middle of some nasty lovers' quarrel. The crash is already more than enough to deal with.

We all have to go down to the police station so they can fill out a report. Except Mona. I guess when you own an Escalade and Coach purse, you don't have to be bothered with the legal system. Of course, Bobby's anything but happy to have the cops ordering him around. From the look in his eyes, I can tell things are on the verge of going very, very wrong, so I walk up and take his hand. "Come on," I tell him. "Maybe we can convince them to let us take the captain home."

He relaxes a little. "All right, Ceejay, I'll go, but we have to haul Angelica back to the captain's first."

I let Padgett explain that deal to the cops. He's less likely to lose his temper if they don't like it. They don't. "No one's going anywhere right now but down to the station," says Officer Dave. "You can pick up that hunk of junk tomorrow."

Padgett looks at Bobby. "That'll work. Nobody's going to mess with it out here tonight."

"They'd better not," Bobby says.

When we finally make it to the cop shop, they herd me, Bobby, Chuck, and Padgett into a blank-walled room where we have to sit around in uncomfortable metal chairs. Dani gets a separate room to herself. One by one we're called into a cramped office to give our statements. I'm the last one in, and it's pretty obvious by now Officer Dave has figured out we're telling the truth. He nods while I rattle off my story, jots down a few notes, then tells me to go wait in the other room and we'll all get to go home in a couple of minutes. Which is a relief. I thought they were going to be dicks about it. Maybe they feel guilty about helping to get Bobby sent off to the war after all.

But out in the hall, Bobby's facing off against Officer Larry—Bobby in his T-shirt, jeans, and boots, and Officer Larry with his starched blue uniform, his silver badge glinting in the fluorescent light. Bobby's demanding they let the captain go home with us. This was just an accident, he growls. You don't throw someone behind bars for a traffic accident.

But Officer Larry tells him no way is the captain going home tonight. "This isn't just about being a public nuisance this time," Officer Larry says, his face flaring red right up to the borderline of his short black hair. Cops hate it when somebody tries to tell *them* what to do for a change. "This is property damage and endangerment of life and limb."

Bobby's fists clench at his sides. He's been about to explode ever since the cops showed up, and it's up to me to defuse him yet again. I walk up and stand next to him and ask Officer Larry if they've called the captain's brother. He says they have.

"That's all right then," I tell Bobby. "I've seen this a million

259

times. The captain's brother comes down and gets him out in about two minutes."

Officer Larry looks like he wants to say something, probably about how that's not going to happen this time, but he glances at Bobby and thinks better of it. Instead he's like, "That's right. Just let the captain's brother handle things. You go ahead and take off. If you have any questions, you can call up here tomorrow."

"Thanks," I say. "Come on, Bobby."

Bobby stares at Officer Larry a moment longer, just to let him know this thing isn't over, not by a long shot.

I touch him lightly on the back. "Time to go home. I think we're both probably worn out."

"Home?" He looks at me, not in the eyes, just down at the top of my head. "Too bad I don't have any home to go to. I'm pretty sure Dani would shoot me on sight if I showed up back there."

"That's all right," I tell him. "You're coming home with me and sleeping in your old room."

"I don't think that's a good idea."

Chuck steps up from behind. "Don't worry, dude. I still have plenty of room on my couch for you."

"That's okay," Bobby says. "Take me out to the captain's. I'll spend the night there."

Padgett knows it hurts me to hear Bobby say he'd rather go to the captain's than home with me. I mean, if he'd rather do that now, when will the time ever come when he'd want to share a place with me?

Padgett takes hold of my hand and squeezes it. "Let's all go out to the captain's," he says. "We need to haul Angelica back anyway."

41

The next day, at lunch, I get Uncle Jimmy to loan me his truck for an hour so I can drive Bobby over to Dani's to rescue his stuff while she's at work. Actually, he owns so little, he could probably haul everything off on his motorcycle, but the truth is I just want to spend time alone with him.

As we drive away from the captain's, I do my best one more time to argue him into giving his old room a try—just long enough so he can get a job and save up for a two-bedroom rent house—but he's not going for it.

"The parents' place is too small for me now," he says.

"What are you talking about?" I ask. "It's bigger than Dani's ratty old trailer."

"I'm not talking about physical size, Ceejay. I'm talking about the psychological size. I can't be squeezed in like that.

I can't have people looking over my shoulder thinking about how I'm supposed to be or who I used to be or what's wrong with me. You know? I have to have some breathing room."

"Maybe it won't be like that," I say. "Give the parents a chance. Sit down and have a conversation for a while. I think they really do want to make up for how they let you get a bum deal. Even Dad. Maybe he is actually more like us than we've given him credit for."

"But that's just my point," Bobby says, looking out the side window. "He thinks I'm like him. But I'm not. I'm not like anybody anymore. Except maybe the captain. That's what I figure I'll do—I'll move my stuff over and stay at his place."

It hurts all over again to hear Bobby talk like he prefers the captain over me, but I'm not about to admit it. "The captain? How can you live in the middle of all that junk he has out there? What you need to do is start thinking about getting your own rent house."

"I'll feel right at home in the middle of a bunch of junk," he says, like he himself is just a piece of junk somebody threw away. I have no comeback for that. I'll just have to wait. He'll see—he's not like the captain at all.

At Dani's, the gravel driveway is empty, which is good. I'm hoping we can just get in and out with no hassles. But just as Bobby goes to stick his key in the front-door lock, the door swings open in front of us. It's Tillman.

"What are you doing here?" he asks, his chest jutting out like he's ready for trouble.

"Us?" I say. "We're just here to get Bobby's stuff. What are you doing here?"

"Mom dropped me off when she had to take Dani to work because her damn car won't drive." He stares at me like it's my fault.

"Look," I say, "I didn't ask you how you got here. I asked you *why* you're here."

"Oh, I don't know. Maybe because Dani figured she needed someone to stand guard over the place. Looks like she was right."

"So what? You're going to tell us we can't come in?"

"That's right."

Bobby snorts out a laugh. "Yeah, right. Get out of the way, little man. All I want is what's mine and then I'll leave. Gladly." He steps forward. Tillman puffs up like he's getting ready to defend his sister's grand, sparkling trailer, but Bobby stares him down and he gives way.

There's not much to gather up, just what will fit in Bobby's duffel bag, but it still takes too long, what with Tillman yammering at us the whole time like an obnoxious dachshund. He says he told Dani that Bobby wasn't worth a damn and how it didn't take long for Bobby to prove him right. Maybe if Jace had swung a little lower with that baseball bat, he says, Bobby would've been in the hospital instead of causing his sister grief. All the while he's shooting off his mouth, Bobby just goes about sorting through his things and stuffing them into the bag, but I can't keep quiet.

"What happened to you, Tillman? After all these years of us being friends, you go and turn against me like we never even knew each other. Don't you have any loyalty to anyone?"

"Hey," he says. "I am being loyal—to my sister. Who are you being loyal to, your brother? Can you really tell me he treated Dani right? No. Listen, I'm not the one who changed. I'm not the one who started hanging out with the damn town crazoid, helping him make his totem poles or whatever. You want to see someone who's changed, look in the mirror."

"You don't know what you're talking about." I get right up

in his face. "About my brother or the captain. I'll tell you this—the captain has more sense than you ever had. Or ever will have. He just sees things in a different way. But you, you're too narrow-minded to understand that."

"Yeah, right. The captain has so much sense the cops won't even let him go back home. The dude can't even take care of himself."

"What are you talking about? The captain's brother's going to get him out of jail just like he always does."

"That shows how much you know." He smiles a creepy little self-satisfied smile. "The captain's brother is the one who doesn't want him going home. Dani called up there today to make sure they weren't letting him out, and the cops told her his brother's having him put in a home. They're going to juice that dude up on meds until he can't say his own name. He's not going to be a problem for anyone from here on out."

That gets Bobby's attention. "What are you talking about, you little liar?" he says, staring Tillman down.

Tillman's like, "Calling me a liar isn't going to change anything. Your boy's done. Over and out and down for the count."

"Yeah?" Bobby says, his face about six inches from Tillman's. "We'll see about that."

He walks back, grabs his bag, and goes, "Come on, Ceejay, let's get out of this dump."

"Yeah, get on out of here," says Tillman, "so I can fumigate the place before my sister gets home."

We're just about to walk out the front door, but Tillman can't resist shooting another poison dart at us as we go. "One more thing," he says. "I'd keep checking over your shoulder if I was you, Bobby. Dani made another phone call this morning— to Rick Nichols. Told him all about you and Mona. I don't think he liked the idea of you messing around with his wife too much. He wants to have a little talk with you. And you know what? Rick's the kind of guy who's likely to bring along more artillery than just a baseball bat."

Bobby stops and sets his duffel bag down by the door. "Well, Tillman," he says. "You know what I think about that?" He grabs the little gold lamp from the end table next to the couch. "Here's what I think about that." He steps toward Tillman and cocks back the lamp at the same time. Stumbling backward, Tillman jerks up his arm to guard his face. But Bobby doesn't hit him. Instead, he swings the lamp hard in the other direction, shattering it against the wall, then lets what's left drop to the floor.

He hoists up his duffel bag and slings the strap around his shoulder. "Have a nice day." He smiles and walks out the door.

42

Tillman wasn't lying. I hoped he was making up that business about Captain Crazy getting stuck in some kind of home, just saying it to get to me and Bobby, but when I call Padgett, he knows the whole scoop. The captain's brother, Richard, isn't vouching for him anymore. He says the captain's not just a danger to others but to himself, and he's sticking the captain in Oak Grove, the old folks' home on the edge of town. The old folks' home! Jesus, the captain's only sixty-four.

On top of that, you'd think Richard would at least choose Autumn Crest. I mean, as far as old folks' homes go, Oak Grove is the worst. I've been there. Brianna's big sister Karina works there. She's not a nurse or anything. She's like the night-shift queen of bedpan swappers, spoon feeders, and colostomy-bag changers. It's disgusting, but other than that it's a pretty easy

266

job. Me and Brianna go over every once in a while at night and play Hearts with her in the cafeteria between rounds. Sometimes Brianna even sneaks weed in to her.

The building is a long rectangle made of ugly yellow brick. It looks like a stick of rancid butter with window air-conditioning units plugged into it. As soon as you walk in, the pee smell hits you right in the nose. Old folks in wheelchairs are parked all over the foyer like plants that someone set out in the sun. One time I walked in and this old lady with sores all over her legs hollers, "See anything you like?" And then she starts cackling like it's the funniest thing since *I Love Lucy*.

And there's the old man who tried to escape. Karina says they caught him rattling the emergency exit door several times and ran him back to his room. Then one day he made it. No one knew he was gone till his daughter showed up to visit. Karina had to come in on her time off and help look for him. They called the cops in too. Finally around eight o'clock in the evening, they found him in the woods sitting in the middle of a creek with his pants down. He told them he just wanted to get clean.

So you can see why me and Bobby and Padgett are pretty outraged about the captain ending up in there. He should be at his home in the country with the anti–Nogo Gatu sculptures protecting him. The aero-velocipede's busted—what harm can the captain do now? It's nothing but another railroad job, just like they railroaded Bobby off to the war.

That evening we try to visit, but Richard's there and doesn't want us around. He calls us *enablers*, like that's a bad thing. Says we should have known better than to help the captain build something like the aero-velocipede.

"At least we're there with him," Bobby says. "What do you do? You drop off some food, give him a hard time about shaping up his life, then leave. You never listen to him. You never even give him a chance to let you know who he is. You're way too busy telling him who he ought to be."

Richard looks down the hall. I can't tell for sure, but it seems like Bobby might have hit a sore spot. "How long have you known my brother?" he asks wearily. "A couple of months? I've tried to help him my whole life."

So I'm like, "Yeah, but you never had us before. We're ready to step up and take some of the load off you."

He nods, but he doesn't seem convinced. I guess I don't exactly appear like your standard health-care provider. And to tell the truth, I'm only ready to take on the chore because of Bobby.

"Look," Richard says. "My brother's resting right now. Call me tomorrow and we'll see how he's doing. If he's up to it, we'll see if maybe he can have some visitors."

We agree to that, but when Padgett calls the next day, Richard tells him the captain's still not ready to see anyone. The same thing the day after that. Bobby's getting tired of it, says it's bullshit. "We need to *make* that asshole let us see the captain. I don't care if we have to pound it into him."

Pound it into him? Now he's talking about beating up an old man? That's not the Bobby I used to know. He was the one who kicked the butts of guys who talked about pounding old men. I have to steer him in a different direction fast.

"Do we really need Richard's permission?" I say, a perfect idea suddenly striking me. "We don't have to go during visiting hours at all. We can wait till after midnight and get Brianna's big sister to sneak us in."

I halfway expect Bobby to keep going on about pounding Richard, but instead his eyes do what they rarely do anymore—

light up. "A sneak attack?" he says. "Hmmm. That could actually work. Yeah, I like it. That's my Ceejay, brilliant as always."

This is more like it, I tell myself. Now I have something I can actually do instead of sitting around waiting for life to change. When I lay out the plan to Padgett, he's up for it right away—it's the start of the misfit revolution, he says—but Brianna takes some convincing. She doesn't want her sister to get fired—and I can't blame her for that—but this is an emergency. Besides, if Karina can get away with smoking weed on her shift, then I'm sure she can handle a little thing like sneaking us in. Finally, Brianna agrees and calls me back later to say Karina's in, but she wants a little something in return—a little weed ought to do it.

That evening, I tell the parents I'm spending the night with Brianna, and she, Bobby, and I load up with Padgett in his VW. As planned, it's exactly 12:08 when we pull up to Oak Grove, and Karina's waiting at the front door to let us in. Even though she's older, she's not as tall as Brianna. She might weigh just as much, though.

"Okay," she whispers as we walk inside, "Brianna, you come with me and act like you're just here to play cards. The rest of you, be real quiet. The captain's room is number twenty-three, down that hall. Make sure you don't disturb Mr. Kuykendall in the room next door. He's a light sleeper and gets real cranky if somebody wakes him in the middle of the night."

It's eerie creeping down the half-lit hall. Our shoes squeak on the freshly mopped floor, but there's nobody around to catch us. The night nurse is in the office, and Bridget, the other aide, is making her rounds down another hall. The plan is for us to stay with the captain for one hour and then sneak back out during the next round of bed checks.

At room twenty-three, I slowly twist the doorknob, but still it makes a click that sounds so loud it might as well be a gunshot. We look down the hall. No one's around to hear anything. Except, of course, Mr. Kuykendall in the next room. I pause for a moment before opening the door, letting the silence take everything over again.

Inside, the captain's bed sits in the middle of the room. It has a high metal railing along the side to make sure he doesn't roll onto the floor. From his point of view, it probably seems like he's in jail. There are a couple of chairs and a chest of drawers, but nothing to make this look like anyone's home. You might think Richard would've put some plants or flowers in there, at least, but no such luck for the captain. He lies there stiff as a mummy, wrapped tight in his sheets, a white strap with a silver buckle across his stomach.

"Damn," Bobby whispers bitterly. "They've strapped him in like he's Hannibal Lecter or somebody."

As we gather round his bed, his eyes open. He stares at us, but his face is blank. No sparkle of the Yimmies or dark fear of the Nogo Gatu in his eyes. Nothing.

"Captain," whispers Bobby. "It's me. It's Bobby. We came to visit you."

Still nothing registers in the captain's eyes.

Padgett leans over him. "Are they treating you all right in here?"

The captain's mouth opens, but no words come out.

"We hauled Angelica back to your house," I tell him. "She's a little cracked up but nothing we can't handle."

"We'll get her fixed up in no time," Bobby says.

The captain still looks at us as if we're strangers.

"They've got him all doped up," Bobby says. "He's practically a zombie."

"What's that smell?" asks Padgett. "Something stinks." And Bobby's like, "Jesus, it's shit. He shit himself, and they just let him lie here in it. What kind of place is this?"

I'm like, "Maybe I should go down and get Karina," but Bobby says no way—that'll just get us kicked out.

"Well, we can't let him stay like this."

"We're not going to," Bobby says. "Here, help me get this thing unstrapped. We'll take him into the bathroom and get him cleaned up, and then we're going to spring him out of this hellhole."

Padgett and I look at each other. We're just teenagers. We know we don't have the authority to do anything like this. But I guess neither of us was ever the kind to let that stop us before.

"Whatever you say," I tell him. "You're the commander."

"Come on," says Bobby. "Let's go."

While we wrestle with the strap and the sheets, the captain looks on blankly. A car shows about as much emotion when mechanics are working it over. Once we get him up, helping him to the bathroom is a whole new challenge. His legs barely work. He stares down at them as if he's not sure what their function is.

"You can do it," says Bobby. "One foot in front of the other."

Finally, we get him in the bathroom, and Bobby cleans him up while me and Padgett strip the sheets off the bed. None of this is a pretty chore. I can't help thinking about my mom and little sister. They helped Grandma like this for a long time. Some people wouldn't do it. It'd be beneath them. But our family has more guts than that.

The captain's clothes are in the closet, and it takes all three of us to get him dressed. As we work on him, he finally perks up a little. The smallest trace of a smile tugs at his lips. "I used to have clothes just like this," he says.

We're about finished with him when the door opens behind us. We're startled so bad, everyone but the captain practically jumps out of their shoes.

"What are you doing?" It's Brianna.

"Where's your sister?" Bobby asks her. "You're supposed to be keeping her busy."

"She's still in the cafeteria playing Hearts with Bridget. Why does the captain have his clothes on?"

Me, Bobby, and Padgett trade glances. "Look, Brianna," I say, "we have to get him out of here. He doesn't belong in this place."

But she's like, "Wait a minute. That's not part of the deal. You were just supposed to visit with him. You can't take him off the grounds."

"He was lying here in his own shit," says Bobby.

"I don't care," Brianna says. "You take him out of here and my sister will get fired. Not to mention you'll probably get arrested for kidnapping."

Padgett tries to take the logical route with her. "No one's going to get arrested," he says. "All we want to do is haul him back to his own house and let him come down from whatever drugs they've pumped him up with. Once Richard sees that it's better for him to stay at home, everything will work out."

"Yeah? Well, what if it doesn't? You don't know what's going to happen. He might do something twice as crazy. He might kill himself."

"We won't let that happen," I say, but she's like, "What are you going to do, live there?"

Bobby walks over and puts his hand on her shoulder. "Listen, Brianna, I want you to understand this—the captain's dying right here. Maybe not physically, but his soul is. Look at him. Everything that makes him the captain is gone, hollowed out, like a jack-o'-lantern. That's the worst thing there is right there. Worse than killing himself. So think about that, because we're taking him out of here no matter what. You can go tell your sister, you can tell the nurse. I don't care if we have to fight them on the way out, but we're getting the hell out of here with the captain right now."

She studies the captain for a moment. Her face softens. "Okay," she says. "But you better get him out pretty quick before the next bed check. I'll go try to make sure no one comes down this way."

Bobby hugs her. "Good girl."

We give her enough time to get back to the cafeteria before we hoist the captain up from the bed. His legs still don't work all that great, so while Bobby leads the way, me and Padgett help the captain shuffle across the room and out the door. The way his legs wobble, it's like trying to teach a hundred-and-seventy-pound baby how to walk.

In the hall, I lose my grip on his arm and we both end up crashing into his neighbor's door. From inside the room comes a loud shout—"Hey! Who's out there?"

"Oh crap," says Padgett. "We woke Mr. Kuykendall."

Mr. Kuykendall isn't finished either. "Nurse!" he yells. "There's somebody trying to break in here! Nurse! I don't pay my good money to have transients knocking on my door at all hours of the night!"

"Jesus," says Bobby. "We better get the hell out of here. Let me get hold of the captain. Padgett, you go ahead and make sure nobody's looking."

Bobby loops the captain's right arm around his shoulder, then hoists him up and carries him down the hall like a big bundle of laundry, Mr. Kuykendall still barking angry-old-man curses behind us.

At the end of the hall, Padgett stops, peeks around the corner, then holds up a hand to stop us. The first thought that flashes through my mind is Brianna told her sister what we're doing, and now everybody who works there is ready to come down on us like a squad of Nazis. But I should know better. Brianna's too true blue for that.

A moment later, Padgett waves for us to come on and then scurries ahead to hold open the front door. Outside, we dash for the VW, Bobby bringing up the rear, the captain still in his arms. I open the passenger door, and me and Bobby climb into the back, squeezing the captain between us to keep him propped up.

"Are you okay?" I ask him.

He shakes his head. "Buoyancy is the number-one rule of thumb," he answers regretfully.

Bobby pats his knee. "Don't worry, we're taking you home."

Padgett cranks the ignition. "Should we wait for Brianna?" he asks, and Bobby tells him no, we have to get the hell out of here now. But I'm like, "Wait a minute. We can't just leave her stranded here. Besides, her sister's expecting her to leave with us."

"Okay," says Bobby. "But if she's not out here in five minutes, I say we hit the road."

Exactly five minutes later, Brianna walks outside.

"Did they suspect anything?" I ask as she opens the car door. "Did they hear Mr. Kuykendall?"

She sits in the front seat. "Everything's okay for now. But Karina's not going to like it when she does the next bed check and finds that empty bed."

"Don't worry," Bobby tells her. "I'll buy your sister a whole bag of weed to make up for it—shit, I'll buy her a pound of it— but for right now, let's step the hell on the gas."

As we pull out of the parking lot, relief sweeps into my chest—for a second. Then I see a pair of headlights flick on in the parking lot of the nursery across the street. We head west and so do the headlights.

"Don't look now," I say, "but I think someone's following us."

43

At the first intersection we come to, Padgett slows to a stop, and Bobby's like, "What are you doing, dude? Blow the stop sign. There's no one coming."

"But what if it's the cops behind us?" Padgett says.

I stare out the back window. "I don't think it's the cops. The headlights are too high off the ground. It looks more like it must be a truck." Then a bad thought hits me. "Or it might be a Hummer."

Brianna looks at me. "Crap—a Hummer?"

"Who cares if it's a Hummer?" says Bobby as we pull away from the stop sign. "It could be a Mack truck for all I care."

I'm like, "Yeah, but the thing is—Rick Nichols is the only one in town who has a Hummer." I'm thinking I might prefer the police to Mona's husband. Everybody knows the dude is jealous to start with, but if Dani really told him about Bobby and Mona, like Tillman said, then he could turn straight-up deadly.

Bobby doesn't seem worried, though. "How would that dick even know where I was? I mean, it's not like I'm a regular at Oak Grove."

Brianna's still looking over the seat, a sort of sick expression on her face.

"What?" I ask her. "You know something, don't you?"

"Maybe," she says, casting her gaze down toward the floorboard.

"What'd you do?"

"I sort of told Tillman what we were doing tonight. But I never thought in a million years he'd call Rick Nichols about it. I didn't even think Tillman knew Rick."

I'm like, "God, Brianna, why did you tell Tillman? You know he's got it in for Bobby."

"Hey, he asked me what I was doing tonight and I told him. It's not like I'm used to lying to him about stuff, you know."

I look out the rear window again. The headlights are closer. It's pretty certain they belong to a Hummer.

"What should I do?" asks Padgett. "I can't outrun him in this piece of junk."

"Pull over," says Bobby.

"What?"

"Pull over. If this dude wants trouble with me, I'll be glad to give it to him."

I'm like, "Wait a minute, Bobby. This might not be like with Jace. Rick Nichols—you don't know him—he could have a shotgun in there."

"So what?" Bobby says. "What's he going to do, shoot me? Who cares? Pull over, Padgett."

But I'm like, "Don't do it, Padgett. Keep on going. They can't do anything to us while we're driving."

"They could run us off the road," Brianna says.

"Pull over," Bobby demands. "Pull over right now, or I'm going to jump out the door."

Padgett checks my face in the rearview mirror. I nod. What else is there to do? Bobby has his mind set. But the terrible thing is I know Rick Nichols has every reason to come after Bobby. Bobby knows it too. He just doesn't care.

Before we're even completely stopped, he bursts out of the car, strides back, and stands in the middle of the road with his arms folded across his chest. The rest of us, except for the captain, are right behind him when the Hummer squeals to a stop about twenty yards away. I expect Rick to throw open the door any second but he doesn't. The motor revs and the headlights glare at us, but nobody steps out.

When my eyes get used to the brightness of the lights, I see Rick isn't alone. Two other black silhouettes sit in the car with him. It's easy to tell one is Tillman, so the other must be Dani. She's probably muttering in Rick's ear, telling him all the havoc he needs to wreak on Bobby. In the dark, the three of them look like soldiers of the Nogo Gatu.

Finally, Rick rolls down the window and yells, "I ought to run you down, you son of a bitch."

I'm like, What a creep. If they'd just get out of the Hummer, we'd take them down with no problem, but Rick's too much of a coward.

"Go ahead," Bobby yells back. "Tromp that pedal."

The Hummer creeps forward before stopping again. "This town's sick of you trying to ruin people's lives around here," Rick shouts.

"The whole world's sick, as far as I can see."

278

"You aren't fit to walk this earth anymore."

"I know it," Bobby tells him. "So why don't you go ahead and do what you have to do."

I'm like, "God, shut up, Bobby. He's jealous enough he might do it."

Rick guns the engine, but the Hummer stays put. "You don't want to test me, asshole. I'll run you over in a second."

Bobby looks at his watch. "A second's up, buddy, and I'm still standing. If you want to see me start shaking, then you might as well leave because that's not going to happen."

I know Bobby's calling his bluff, but this is getting too crazy.

"You think you're some kind of big war hero?" Rick says. "That's not what anyone else thinks. Everybody around here sees you as a loser who got kicked out of the army."

From the backseat, Dani yells something at Rick, but I can't tell what it is. Then he revs the engine again, only this time he jams it into gear and the Hummer bucks forward, stopping about five yards away. Still, Bobby doesn't move. "Come on," he hollers. "You got a soldier's vehicle, do a soldier's job. Just give it one more hard stomp on the gas, and it'll all be over with."

"I'll break you in half," Rick yells back, "if you don't promise to stay away from my wife right now. Promise on your mother's life, and we'll end this with maybe only one broken leg."

Bobby snorts out a laugh. "Sorry," he says. "I don't have any promises left in me."

"I'm not kidding!" Rick yells.

"Yes, you are," Bobby tells him. "You're kidding yourself. You can't do it. Not with a real human standing in front of you. You know why? Because you'd have to give up being human yourself, and once you do that, there's no coming back."

The engine growls, but the Hummer stays put, and from inside, Dani's voice rings out, "For Christ's sake, you wimp. If you can't do anything, I will." And in the next second, the door swings open and she charges out. At first, she's only a black ghost behind the headlights, but from my angle I can see the pistol in her hand. She raises it and fires one shot over Bobby's head, then another. The noise blows through me like a lightning bolt.

Brianna's like, "Jesus, holy crap!" and drops to the pavement. Inside the Hummer, Rick goes, "Hey, nobody said anything about guns. I didn't throw in with shooting anyone."

A couple more shots fire, and me and Padgett drop next to Brianna, but Bobby stays put. "Come on, Dani," he taunts, "you're a better shot than that."

She keeps coming. She's in the blaze of the headlights now, and I see the rage on her face. She's practically demented. She squeezes the trigger again and again, each shot zinging over Bobby's head. "Kneel, you bastard," she screams. "Kneel down or I'll blow your face inside out."

"Do it," Bobby says. "Don't just talk about it."

She's right in front of him now, her arm sticking out stiff, the gun only a couple of feet away from his face. I'm afraid she's gone wild enough to do it, and I start looking for a way to maybe make a charge at her.

"I don't let anybody cheat on me." She spits the words at him. "I don't take that kind of disrespect."

But she can't pull the trigger.

Instead, she flies at Bobby, swinging both the gun and her empty fist. She tries to knee him in the groin, even tries to bite him, but he wrestles the gun away, and she crashes butt-first to the pavement.

Rick and Tillman burst out of the Hummer, but they're not about to make any kind of rush now that Bobby's holding the pistol. Me and Padgett pop up and start toward Bobby, but he does something that freezes us both in place—he jams the barrel of the gun up under his chin.

"Okay, Dani," he says, his voice flat, emotionless. "Let's hear it—do you want me to pull this trigger?"

"What?" she says, sniffling, tears streaking her face.

"You heard me. Just say the word, and I'll blow what's left of my brains out."

She sits there on the pavement staring up at him. I look from him to her, then from her to him. It's my brother here— the hardest guy I've ever known—standing in front of me holding a gun to his head. The reality of it burns my eyes, my face, my brain. But I can't do anything. He's too far away.

"Bobby," I cry. "This isn't funny."

"I'm not trying to be funny," he says. "It's a simple choice. What's it going to be, Dani? Do you want me to pull the trigger or not?"

She wipes her nose with the back of her hand. The rage bleeds out of her face. She looks more like a confused little girl. "No," she says finally. Just that—*no*.

Bobby lowers the pistol, and the bad air in my lungs releases in one sudden rush.

"I didn't think so," he says. "Next time you people want to come after somebody, you better make your minds up about what you're really prepared to do." He sticks the pistol into the waistband of his jeans and heads back to the car. Dani, Tillman, and Rick do nothing but watch him go.

As he climbs into the backseat with the captain, the rest of us follow him in, and Brianna moans, "That was insane. You know that, don't you? What would you have done if she said yes, go ahead and shoot your stupid head off?"

But Bobby just goes, "You better hit the gas, Padgett. Get us the hell out of here. They'll probably call the cops and tell them we have the captain. That's the only thing left they can do to me now."

44

The moon is hiding, but the porch light washes across Captain Crazy's front yard and glints on the sculptures. Padgett parks next to the fat boy, and as soon as he cuts off the engine, Brianna goes into the same rant she's kept up ever since we left Dani, Tillman, and Rick on the highway—"Take me home. Get the captain into the house and then get me out of here. I don't want to have anything to do with the police."

I'm like, "Calm down, Brianna. We don't even know if anyone called the police."

"Yeah, right," she says sarcastically. "I could tell how happy Dani and Rick were for us. They're on our side all the way."

"Look," Bobby cuts in. "As soon as I get the captain up to the house, I want all of you to leave. This is my operation. You guys will just get in the way."

"Hey," Padgett says. "He's our friend too. Whatever happens, I want to be here."

"Me too," I agree. "One hundred percent." But Bobby insists we need to get gone and let him handle the situation the way it needs to be handled. He quits grappling with the captain, trying to dislodge him from the backseat, and stares us down. "No reason for anyone else to get in trouble. I know what I have to do and it doesn't involve you."

Me and Padgett argue back, and Brianna keeps up her *I want to go home* whine until we're making nothing but noise. Then the chatter stops as the captain steps out of the car without any help. A look of relief melts the ragged edge of confusion from his face.

"Ah, the fat boy," he says, gazing at the sculpture. "The fat boy's here. There's a true frequency rising."

"That's right, Captain," Bobby tells him. "Everything's cool." Then to the rest of us he says, "He's going to be all right. He just needed to see his own place. Look, Ceejay, you and Padgett take Brianna home. You can come back afterward if you want."

Brianna's like, "That's the best idea I've heard yet," and Padgett goes along with it. But me, I'm not leaving Bobby to face the cops by himself, especially with that pistol in his waistband. He gets frustrated with me, but there's nothing he can do. I'm sticking with him and that's that.

Padgett's like, "Wait a minute, I'm not going and leaving you here," but I walk over and squeeze his hand. "I'll be all right. I need to talk with Bobby, just me and him."

He hesitates, searching my eyes, then leans over and kisses me on the forehead. "All right, Ceejay. I trust you to know what you're doing. But I promise you I'll be back just as soon as I drop Brianna off."

284

"Thanks." I give his hand another squeeze for good measure. I want to kiss him too. I want to kiss him hard, but the moment has taken that option away.

By the time he and Brianna leave, Bobby has already helped the captain to the porch. He eases him into the rocking chair in front of the window and tells me to watch him while he goes inside.

"Don't you think we ought to put him in bed?" I suggest, but Bobby's like, "No, I'm not taking him inside."

"Why not? He needs to sleep off those meds they polluted him with."

Bobby turns and stares me down, exasperated. "Because we're not staying here, that's why. We're taking the captain's truck and getting the hell out of here."

"What? Where are we going?"

"Not you. Me and the captain." He flings open the door and marches inside with me right behind him.

"If you're going anywhere," I tell him, "I'm going too."

"No, you're not."

"Wait a minute," I say to his back. "I've stuck with you through this whole thing. You've been trying to shut me out ever since you got out of the army. You've shut the whole family out. I'm not going to let you do it anymore."

He stops in the doorway to the back hall. "Look, Ceejay," he says, his face stern. "This is something only me and the captain can do."

"You're going to have a hard time stopping me from coming. I'll jump in the back of the truck if I have to."

"Then I'll pull over and yank your ass out and make sure you don't get back in. I'll tie you down if I have to."

I look at the pistol in his waistband. "You better put that thing up."

"I don't think so," he says. "When things get down to the nitty-gritty, it might come in handy."

"What things? What are you planning on doing, Bobby? Tell me."

He looks away and rubs his hand across the side of his face. "All I'm saying is if the cops catch up to us, we're not coming back. We're not coming back no matter what."

His meaning hits me like a disease, like stomach cancer. "You mean you think you're going to shoot it out with the police? Is that what you're talking about? Because that's the stupidest thing I ever heard."

"Yeah? Well, you're young, Ceejay. You don't know shit yet in your life. You've seen what they want to do to the captain. He doesn't want to go on living like that. And I don't want to live like I have been either."

"You know what? I'm tired of you telling me I'm young and I won't understand. You just try me. Explain this one thing and maybe I'll shut up—what happened to you in the war, Bobby? What changed you? You've been such a dick since you've been back. It's like you're drowning, and you're trying to pull down everyone else around you."

"You think you can understand?" He shakes his head. "Words can't even say it." He walks over and sits in this giant overstuffed chair, the one with the cedar tree and deer tapestry draped over it. He looks like he's crouching in a forest, a weariness about his body that seems to come from everything wrong in the world weighing him down. "People think they know what war's like," he says. "They send you over there, and they think they know how it'll be because they've seen the movies, they've played the video games, they've seen the news, but they don't know. And then we come back, and they don't know how that is either."

He's right. I can't help but think of the times I played paintball and thought I was doing it just the way Bobby was doing things in the war. It was stupid. I can see that now. I walk over and sit on the arm of the sofa across from him. "Maybe that's true," I say. "I can't understand that. I guess no one can completely understand everything someone else has been through. But that doesn't mean I can't be on your side. It doesn't mean I can't at least listen and—I don't know—just be there."

"But you can't be there, Ceejay." He stares at his hands folded between his knees. "Sometimes what happens takes you somewhere else, takes away who you are, even. Maybe it's one big thing or maybe it happens little by little. You go into the army and they make you a soldier, and it gets into your bones and your bloodstream. It's the air in your lungs. The heat in your brain and the taste of the words in your mouth. Then they ship you off to another planet a million miles away. It's not like this planet around here—green alfalfa and lakes and marigolds and shit like that. And that place gets in your bones too. You're shipwrecked there and it's on fire. It's salt and ashes. Flies buzz at you like shotgun pellets. There's no water and your tongue's turned to dust and every other person has diarrhea. That's where I live now, Ceejay. You can't live there with me."

I have something to say, but it won't come clear in my mind. It's trapped under something. It's like the person I've always been is holding down the person I want to be.

"You remember me telling you about my buddy Covell?" Bobby smiles a hollow smile.

"Yeah, the guy from Texas who lived on a ranch? Wanted to be a stand-up comic?"

"That's him. Good old Covell." He stares over my head. "He loved getting on the road. Everyone else hated it because you had to have total focus on everything around you one hundred percent of the time just to keep alive, but Covell loved being on the move. Loved the wide-open spaces most of all.

"So one day we're on the street driving through town, the sun torching us like it's about three feet above our heads. We're moving so slow you'd think we were stuck behind a parade of senior citizens. That's how Covell put it—a parade of senior citizens. Then he starts riffing on old folks, especially his grandpa who claimed he was descended from some famous Wild West sheriff. It was hilarious. He goes into his grandpa's voice and shows me how he'd draw his pistol in a gunfight, all shaky and in slow motion. I was laughing my ass off."

Bobby smiles at the memory but only briefly.

"Then all of a sudden—*fwoom!* An IED goes off under a Humvee, two Humvees in front of us, blasting the back end off the road. Just like that. One second I'm sitting there thinking Covell ought to be in the movies with Will Ferrell, and the next second everything goes crazy. The guys in the bombed truck pile out—carrying a couple of wounded—and run for the vehicle in front of us. Our orders are to back the hell out of there, but there's a jam-up behind us. Can't back up and can't go forward. Sniper fire peppers down from one of the rooftops. The people on the street are rushing everywhere, trying to get inside or into an alley. Except these three hajji.

"They're running straight for our vehicle, their clothes fluttering white in the sun, like ghosts in the daytime. It looks like one of them is carrying something, but with smoke and fire and the chaos of the street, it's hard to tell for sure. We're yelling for them to stop, to stay back, to find cover, but they keep coming toward us. I swear I see something glinting in the hand of the one on the left, and then Meyers yells, 'He's got a bomb, he's got a fucking bomb,' and someone else is like, 'Light those motherfuckers up,' and that's when Covell fires. I mean, sure, Covell's a comedian, but he's someone you want on your side, too, when the shit flies. He's got your back, and that's what it's all about. It doesn't matter what anyone else thinks of the war, if you got your buddy's back, you're doing your job.

"So as soon as Covell pulls the trigger, the rest of us do too, and it's like *bam, bam, bam, bam,* and those three hajjis—those three *men*—drop to the pavement. One, two, three. It's like someone cut their fucking power off, like someone threw the big-bad switch. They're over."

He pauses, looks down at the pistol in his waistband, then goes on. "People think they know what it's like to shoot someone. They think it'll be easy. You just squeeze the trigger like in the movies, like on the video game, but they don't know shit. There's no taking anything back. There's no starting over."

He shakes his head. And in just that little gesture, I see the war in a different way than I ever saw it in my head before. *No taking anything back*—those aren't just words. They're a scar.

"We didn't have time to think about video games and that crap, though," he continues. "As soon as the vehicle behind us clears out, we go zipping backward as fast as we can. Me and Covell, we're still looking at those men on the ground, trying to see what the one dude might have been carrying, but it's too crazy to make anything out. We never did find out either. We were on the road for two days after that, and no one could tell us. Meyers said we just did what we had to do. We yelled for them to stop, and they didn't. Case closed. But that wasn't good enough for Covell.

"He couldn't stop thinking about it. Neither could I for that matter, but it was worse with Covell. The thing kept playing over and over in his mind. When he went to sleep, which wasn't often, he dreamed about it. Then he started seeing them in the dark, those three men. They talked to him, told him their names—Shadrach, Meshach, and Abednego.

"'You know who Shadrach, Meshach, and Abednego were?' he asks me, this paranoid look in his eyes. I'm like, 'No,' and he goes, 'They were three Jewish dudes from the Bible who lived in Iraq a long time ago. This king ordered his soldiers to pitch them into a fiery furnace, but instead of the flames taking them, the soldiers burned up instead.'

"I'm like, 'Dude, those guys were Muslims, not Jews,' but he says, 'That's just the point, man. Don't you see? You can't really know who people are underneath unless you're God. It was just a boom box he had in his hand. That's all they had. It was Abednego's. He just bought it down the street and was taking it home to give to his daughter.'

"I tried telling him—I said, 'Covell, you can't know that,' but he just nodded and said, 'He told me, man. He told me in person.'

"After that, I tried getting Covell some help, talked to anyone I could. I mean, I had to have my buddy's back, right? I told them Covell was having problems, couldn't sleep, had hallucinations. They were just like, 'He's going to have to suck it up.' That's all. Suck it up."

He looks down at his hands. They're trembling. "I didn't know what else I could do. It's not like I could throw him in a truck and run away. Where could we go? So one night I'm asleep—finally I'm asleep—and Covell gets up and walks out across the sand, kneels down facing west, toward Texas, gouges the barrel of his rifle into the soft spot under his chin, and blows the top of his head off. That was it. Gone. I tried to do what I could, but it wasn't enough. The flames took him down, and they're taking me down too."

I understand Bobby's obsession with coming to Casa Crazy

now. He sees Covell in the captain, and he wants to do here what he couldn't do over there. And it crashes down onto me how hard that must have been for someone like Bobby. Nothing he knew about fighting—left hooks, right crosses, upper cuts, ducking punches, and taking the enemy to the ground—were any good for a deal like what happened with Covell. All that isn't any good for what the captain's going through, and it's no good for what I have to do now either. What I learned from Bobby about fighting won't work if I want to help my brother get through this. I need a whole different kind of *BADD*, the kind Lacy and my mom and even my dad showed me this summer. That's just as important as anything else in this kind of battle.

A weird quiet spreads through the room. It's like a presence, like the ghosts of Covell, Shadrach, Meshach, and Abednego all together. They've come for Bobby. They want to carry him away, and there's no one here but me to stop them.

"I'm sorry about your friend." My voice feels like it's welling up from some strange place, somewhere it's never come up from before. "I wish I could've known him. There's a lot of things I wish. I wish Grandma didn't get sick, I wish Tillman was still my friend, I wish you never went away and the war never happened. And I wish I could understand exactly what you're going through now. Maybe it's this thing Padgett told me about—post-traumatic stress disorder. He's read all about it, and—"

"I know what PTSD is," Bobby says, wearily, as if the term itself is one more thing weighing him down.

"Well," I say, "I don't know if it's that or something else, but I get it that you've changed. I didn't want to believe that. You know? I just wanted to believe we'd go back to being Bobby and Ceejay just like before you left. I know that's not possible now, but I'm still on your side. It doesn't matter if you're never like you used to be—I've got your back. One hundred percent. Just like Mom and Lacy had Grandma's back during her whole battle with cancer."

Then a terrible thing happens—tears start flooding from my eyes. Actual tears! The last person I want to cry in front of is Bobby, but I can't hold them back. I'm afraid if I keep talking it'll only get worse, but I can't stop now.

"You should see Lacy," I say, wiping the stupid streaks from my face. "She's so strong. I used to want to make her like me, but now I want to be like her. So that's what I'm going to do, Bobby. I'm going to have your back no matter what it takes, and so is the whole family. And Padgett and Chuck and the captain."

Bobby shakes his head. "Look, Ceejay—"

"Hold on. Just hear me out. The other thing is that you can't give up on the captain. I don't care how hopeless things look, you have to keep going. That's what people do. They keep going. And you're good for the captain. You're the one who's kept him on track these last few weeks. I mean, we all have to have his back too, but you have to be the leader because he's not going to make it without you. You have to be the one."

Bobby starts to interrupt again, but I keep charging ahead. "You might think you aren't any good now, that you can't do anything, but you're wrong. You just have to look at things different. You know what the strongest thing is I've seen you do since you've been back? It's not fighting Jace or playing chicken with a stupid Hummer. It was tonight when you cleaned the captain up like you did. That was big time right there, Bobby. Big time."

He smiles at that. It's a sick, sad smile, but it's a smile.

"See, that's what you can do—you can live here with the captain and look after him, make sure he takes the right kind

292

of medication or whatever it is he needs." It isn't easy to say. I know it means letting go of my dream of us ever sharing a place together. I hate to lose that, but it's the only thing I can think of to keep Bobby from losing himself. I'll just have to stay at home with the parents, and maybe that's okay. Maybe I've held my grudge against them for too long anyway.

I keep plowing forward. "We'll convince Richard that's the only reason we took the captain out of that crappy home, so he'd have someone to take care of him who didn't treat him like a damn stray dog at the pound. I'll talk to Richard for you. Mom and Dad will vouch for you too. I know they will. I thought for a long time they weren't on our side—and maybe they do screw up sometimes—but they are on our side. We'll make it happen. We've got to. We've all got to have each other's backs, just like Covell always had yours."

Bobby's staring me in the face now. Tears well up in his eyes too, but I'm not sure what they mean. Is his mind changing, or does he just regret having a big bawl-baby for a sister?

Before he can say anything, the sound of a car pulling up outside distracts him. My first hope is that Padgett has come back, but that hope dies as the red police-car lights carousel against the window curtains, and the siren lets out a single shrill burp. Bobby's hand goes for the pistol.

"Listen, Bobby," I tell him, trying to make my voice as hard as I can. "If you go out there and start waving that pistol around, I'm coming too." I know I'm taking a gamble. He might charge out there anyway, but that's a chance I'll have to take.

"I'll follow right behind you," I tell him. "And whatever happens to you is going to happen to me. So you can make up your mind right now. Are you going to give up on yourself and me and everyone else, or are you going to keep on going?"

Bobby stares hard into my eyes, but before he can say

anything, the front door swings open. It's the captain. He has that Nogo Gatu shadow in his eyes. "They're coming," he says. "We can't stop them now. Nothing floats. The air is filled with the wrong kind of metal."

Outside, car doors slam. Bobby stands up and slips the pistol from his waistband. For a long moment, he stands there holding it by his side like something nearly too heavy to carry. He looks at me, and I have nothing left to tell him beyond what I can say with my eyes. He nods, then sets the pistol on the end table.

"You know what, Ceejay?" he says. "You're one hell of a sister."

"And you're one hell of a brother," I tell him.

He walks to the captain. "It's going to be all right," he says. "Screw the metal in the air." He gazes into the captain's face, then hugs him to his chest. "I'm going to look after you now, Captain. We're going to fight the goddamn Nogo Gatu together. Okay? I don't know if we'll whip them, but we'll put up the biggest fight you ever saw."

45

Not long after Officer Dave and Officer Larry herd me, Bobby, and the captain into the front yard, Richard shows up too, flies out of the car, and charges over as fast as a stiff-legged man his age can charge. At first he's furious, wants us arrested, but he backs off when I describe the rotten condition we found the captain in at the nursing home.

"Nobody on the staff was paying any attention to him," I tell Richard. "He'd crapped himself and nobody cared. He was just lying there, doped up, stinking up the room. You know who cleaned him up?" I squeeze Bobby's arm. "My brother. He cleaned the crap off him, got him dressed, and made him feel like a person again."

Richard looks at the captain, the captain nods, and the

anger starts to ease away from Richard's face. "You did that?" he asks Bobby.

"Somebody had to."

"Well, you should've called me. It's not up to you to take him out of there."

"I don't like that place," the captain cuts in. "It smells like death in there."

"Listen," says Officer Dave, "you want to press charges, we'll take them down to the station."

Richard stares at his hands as he rubs them together, then looks up. "I don't guess I'll press charges. At least, not this time."

"How about your brother?" Officer Dave asks. "Should we haul him back to the home?"

Me and Bobby stare at Richard. He has to know what we think of that idea.

"No," he says. "Not right now. I'll take him home with me for the night."

"What about after that?" Bobby asks.

"We'll just have to wait and see."

Now is not the time to argue about how the captain should stay home and let Bobby look after him. No doubt getting Richard to warm up to the idea is going to take some crafty maneuvering on our part. Even as wrought up as he is, Bobby understands that.

As he and I sit on the porch watching the cops, the captain, and Richard drive away, I slap his knee and say, "You know what we have to do, don't you?"

"No, what?"

"We have to go talk to Dad. We have to get him to go over to Richard's and help us lay out our plan about you moving in here."

Bobby watches the taillights disappear around the curve in the road. "I don't know about that. Dad's not likely to take to the idea any better than Richard."

"You might be surprised," I tell him. I'm not sure whether I'm right, but I'm ready to give Dad the benefit of the doubt.

46

The next evening Bobby shows up at home for dinner. The parents are beside themselves over this. Mom's been flitting around the kitchen like a housefly ever since I told her he was coming. Dad hit the yard work with a vengeance, even though all he said when he first heard the news was, "It's about time."

Dinner goes fine, a little awkward, but I expected that. Everyone just has to get used to each other all over again. Mom keeps trying to dish more food onto our plates, Dad tells a string of jokes I've heard before, and Drew sits there staring at Bobby like some kind of action hero has landed at our table. No mention of Bobby getting kicked out of the army. Not yet anyway.

When dinner's over and Drew has gone outside, me and Bobby lay out the plan. I've thought through my part over and over, and it makes total sense, but when we get it all out there,

Mom's first reaction is, "Oh, honey, I don't know. That sounds like a big responsibility."

"I know it is," Bobby says. "I've dealt with bigger."

"You know you're not going to cure this man, don't you?" Dad says. "The most you can do is keep him out of trouble, and that won't be easy, to say the least."

"That's okay," Bobby says. "The captain's a good man. I just want to try my best to do what's right for him."

Mom looks at Dad, waiting to see what he's going to say, but he doesn't have an answer right away. Maybe he's thinking Bobby's not up to the job, that anyone who gets himself kicked out of the army can't handle responsibility like this. I don't know, but I can't let him make the wrong decision this time.

"You know, Dad," I say. "When Grandma was sick, you told me how important it was to stand behind family. Well, that's all Bobby's asking you to do now. That's it. Just stand behind what he needs to do."

Dad stares into my eyes, his forehead furrowed. Then, after a long pause, he claps his hands together the way he does when his mind is made up. "All right, then. I'll give Richard a call and see when we can go over for a talk."

"Great," I say. Me and Bobby exchange grins, and Mom smiles one of her worried smiles that looks like she's about to swallow her teeth.

As we walk away from the table, Dad wraps his arm around Bobby's shoulder and says, "I'm proud of you for wanting to take this on. You're just the kind of man I always hoped you'd be."

"I don't know about that," Bobby says.

"I do," Dad tells him. "And don't you worry about that general discharge from the army. They're the ones who ought to be ashamed, not you. You gave everything you had."

Bobby doesn't say anything back. He just nods.

Dad wraps his other arm around me and goes, "Okay, General Ceejay McDermott, it's time to get down to the next mission. We're going to talk some sense into Richard Monroe and get this situation with the captain straightened out. And I guarantee you—no one's going to stop us till we do. Isn't that right?"

"No doubt about it," I say.

47

Padgett's wearing his white painter's pants and cap and a white long-sleeved T-shirt. Only this time the T-shirt isn't completely white. On the back is a silk-screened picture of a knight battling a dragon. I designed the dragon and he did the knight. We're a pretty good team at this silk-screening business. And just above the picture, in flaming red, is the word *Valiance*.

"This is going to be a great day," he says, slapping the steering wheel of his old VW for emphasis. "The misfit revolution is in full swing now. Who knows where it might lead."

"Yeah," I say. "Maybe we'll even convert the jocks to the misfit side."

He laughs. "That would be perfect."

It's one of those ideal late-September days—deep blue sky,

zero clouds, a light breeze blowing through the open windows, and a bright but not brash sun looking down on everything.

We're cruising along a narrow gravel road that cuts through the countryside just off Highway 9. Following behind us is the family van, packed full of McDermotts. All but Bobby. He's coming right behind them in the old lime-green truck with the captain and Richard. Angelica's cinched down in the back.

Today's the day—the first-ever flight of the aero-velocipede.

Everyone's excited—well, Mom and I might be more nervous than excited—but everyone else is hyped up about how great it's going to be. Even Richard. Yes, it's true. I think he's pretty much in love with Angelica, or at least infatuated. It took him a while to come around, though.

Of course, it wasn't easy to talk him into letting Bobby move into Casa Crazy to look after the captain, but we did it. Or mainly Bobby did it, by digging down deep and laying out the whole Covell story all over again. At the end, he told Richard, "I know you understand what I'm talking about because you and the captain lost your own brother in Vietnam. You know what that means. I'd do anything to bring Covell back, and I'm sure you'd do anything to bring your little brother back. But we can't, so we have to do what we can for the ones who are still here."

That hooked Richard right there. He tried to act like it didn't at first, but I could tell it did. When he finally laid down the rules about how it was going to be if Bobby moved in, the main one was that Bobby and the captain could never try to fix up Angelica to fly again. Bobby agreed, but the captain didn't take it well.

Bobby did a good job of keeping him on his meds, but the captain just seemed bummed all the time. Not Nogo Gatu bummed, but like he didn't have anything to look forward to.

So Bobby and Padgett and I went over to Richard's and persuaded him to at least let the captain work on the thing. We swore we wouldn't let him try to fly it—we'd even keep it chained up in the barn—but Richard wouldn't budge. At least until I told him we wouldn't even think about working on it unless he was there.

I don't know if it was the wine that we kept him supplied with, or if it was just that weird bonding thing guys do when they work on something mechanical, but the next thing you know, Richard's one of the guys. He's hammering at the frame and flashing screwdrivers around like an ancient Samurai. Not long after that, it's pretty much settled—someone's going to have to fly it. And, of course—against my wishes—that someone is Bobby.

So now here we are—Aviation Day. Angelica's ready for the sky. Painted silver and red, she's so pretty you'd swear she could recite poetry. As we turn down the road that runs along the side of the field, cars are already parked on both shoulders. Just about everybody we want to see has shown up, along with quite a few kids from high school we don't have much use for. They just want to see something—anything—different happen around Knowles for a change. I wouldn't be surprised if some of them are hoping to witness a huge, flaming crash.

"Here's our big chance to get popular," Padgett jokes as we park next to the barbwire fence. "You could probably sign autographs just for being Bobby's sister."

"Yeah," I say. "And who knows? Maybe you and me will end up getting voted Weirdest Couple this year."

He laughs. "That's my girl. Always aiming for the stars."

As the lime-green truck pulls through the gate and onto the field with Angelica in the back, the crowd swarms around. Dad helps Bobby, Richard, and the captain unload the aero-velocipede while the rest of the family looks on, glowing with excitement. Lacy's so confident, she probably believes Bobby could fly to the moon and back. Mom has one of her worried smiles going. Some people may think she's phony for always being so perky, but I've come to see beyond that. Her smiles are like Padgett's white outfits. She puts them on to inspire other people. It doesn't matter if her heart is breaking—if her own mother is dying—she'll lift one of those smiles up as high as she can. I guarantee it takes more strength to do that than any muscleman with a giant set of barbells ever had.

Of course, Uncle Jimmy and all the other relatives on my dad's side are there. Uncle Jimmy even has a date with him. I don't know if she's a keeper or someone he just woke up next to this morning, but he holds her hand and grins at her like a junior high boy with his first crush.

And then there's Chuck. He's beardless now but as merry as ever. He has his little three-year-old girl Amanda with him. She's riding on his shoulders. He actually took my advice about trying to be a dad to her. Amanda's mother, Layla Evans, walks just behind them. She doesn't look so thrilled about the situation at first, but when her little girl beams a smile down and says, "Look at me, Mommy, I'm the highest one here," Layla busts out a grin twice as big as her daughter's. I can't help but feel proud of the part I played in the change in Chuck. Maybe this is a part of what the misfit revolution is really about.

There are a few people missing. Of course, Dani and Tillman aren't there. Too bad about Tillman. I don't know if we'll ever be friends again. And Mona's nowhere to be seen either. I guess it would be too much to expect her to dump the Escalade and Coach purse and big house in Summer Gate for a guy who goes to the city for therapy once a week and whose biggest ambition is to fly a crazy sculpture around.

Gillis pops out of the crowd and comes our way, all smiles. "Well, if it isn't the Dirty Duo," he says. "You mean you two still haven't broken up?" That's Gillis for you. It'd kill him to say something nice about Padgett and me. Guess I can't blame him. He's different when Brianna shows up, though.

It's the new-and-improved Brianna. I don't know if it has anything to do with Bobby giving her a hard time about her look, but she's ditched the all-black Goth girl outfits for senior year. No more nose ring or scary makeup. I like the change. It fits her better.

"Wow," Gillis says. "Brianna. Looking hot, girl."

She looks down at him. "Forget it, leprechaun. You and me? It's never going to happen."

"Give it time," he says. "I might grow on you."

"Yeah," she says. "Like a tumor."

"Listen to that," I tell Padgett. "The romantic tension is so thick you couldn't cut it with a chainsaw."

"Ugh," Brianna says, and slaps me on the arm. "Come on, let's go over and talk to Bobby."

We push our way through the crowd that's gathered around Angelica. Richard and the captain are checking her over as Bobby and Dad talk. While Mom is probably more worried than I am about this flying deal, Dad is completely behind it, says he may take her up himself one of these days. He even went over to Sparks a couple of times with Bobby to sit in on the flying lessons. Of course, Dad doesn't know what I know—that Bobby sat on the captain's porch right in front of me that one night and talked about how Angelica was a Russian roulette machine, and as long as she got up in the air, it didn't matter if she crashed. I have a hard time shaking that out of my head, but I tell myself Bobby didn't really mean it. Besides, he's different now.

After giving Angelica one last thorough inspection, Richard and the captain tell Bobby she's good to go. He puts on his black helmet, his goggles, and his gloves, and then lets everyone in the family hug him before he goes up. I'm the last in line. It's the best hug I've had from him since he got back. I don't want to let go.

"Okay, Mr. Pilot Man," I tell him. "I don't want to see you trying any daredevil stunts up there."

He steps back and smiles. "Me? Daredevil stunts? You know I'd never do such a thing."

"You better not. You have too many people who love you around here to go trying stuff like that."

"Hey, what's not to love?" he says. Then he leans in and whispers in my ear, "You're my number-one girl, and you always will be."

After that, it's all business. He climbs into Angelica's sparkly blue seat, and Richard and the captain strap him in. "Remember," says the captain. "You have to get on the right vibration level. Buoyancy is key."

They fire up the engine, and I know there's no turning back now. Dad clears the crowd from the flight strip, and the captain stands out front and counts down from ten. At zero, he waves his hand and jogs out of the way.

Angelica chugs across the field, slowly at first, then picks up speed. She rises from the ground then bumps back down three or four times as the engine whines louder.

"Yeah, Bobby!" shouts Chuck. "Let 'er rip, buddy!"

His little girl waves her arms and squeals happily.

Angelica bounces a couple more times, then begins to rise steadily. She's going twice as fast as what the captain was doing in her that night on the highway. Twenty feet up, thirty feet, forty. Everyone in the crowd cranes their heads as she climbs. They look like flowers following the sunrise.

At the end of the field, there's a patch of small cedars, and Bobby clears them easily as Angelica soars farther and farther into the perfect blue sky. Cheers bust out all around. If any of the kids from school were hoping to see a crash, I guarantee they've forgotten that now. Everyone's whooping and hollering. Everyone's on Bobby's side, willing him to stay in the air.

From the look of pride on my dad's face, you'd think Bobby was the first astronaut headed to Mars. I know Mom still has to be worried, but she's shoved every trace of it off her face so that it can't infect anyone else. My sisters, my little brother, the uncles, Gillis, Brianna, and Padgett all look up with expressions of pure, glorious triumph. The captain smiles broadly, but it's a regular-person smile now. With all the medication he's been taking, he hasn't seen the Nogo Gatu in weeks, but he doesn't see the Yimmies anymore either.

Angelica makes a wide circle high over the field. She and Bobby look so small, so light, it's like gravity has nothing to do with them anymore. It's beautiful the way she soars, the sunlight glinting on her decorated frame. I know why Bobby wanted to fly her now. I know why the captain did. It's free up there.

Still, I want Bobby to stay over the field. Don't fly over the trees anymore, I plead with him in my mind. You can't land that thing in the trees. But my ESP must be broken because the next thing I know he's soaring far out over the woods, farther away than we'd planned on him going. Come back, my mind shouts to him. Come back.

This time it works. Angelica turns and begins to swoop lower. But she's still above the spiny tops of the trees. "Give me your binoculars," I tell Padgett, and rip them from his hands almost before he can get the strap loose from around his neck.

Angelica's coming down more steeply, but she's still too far away for me to get a good look at Bobby, even with the binoculars. What can he be thinking? He hasn't even been up that long. It's too soon to try to land now.

Closer and closer he comes. Lower and lower. It looks like Angelica's wheels might clip the treetops. Pull up, Bobby, my mind shouts. Pull up. He doesn't, but misses the trees anyway. Now he's heading straight our way, the sound of the engine growing louder but not loud enough to drown out the cheers from the crowd.

Finally, I get the binoculars zeroed in on Bobby's face. I hope to see a look of ecstasy, the pure joy of knowing he's beyond the flames that pulled Covell down, but that's not his expression at all. Instead, his mouth is set in a straight, hard line, his eyes completely focused. His hands grip the controls as if they are part of the machinery of life itself. Every molecule in his body and all the energy in every one of those molecules strain toward one purpose—to keep on going.

He whooshes low over our heads, waving at us as he does. The cheers boom louder than ever. Then he starts climbing again, flying like he was born knowing how. He soars higher and higher, freer and freer, the sky welcoming him like a favorite son.

"Wow," says Padgett. "He's a flying ace already."

"You should've seen the expression on his face," I say, leaning into Padgett's side. "He is one hundred percent B-A-D-D."

He wraps his arm around me. "You do pretty good at that yourself."

"Yeah," I say, staring into the sky. "I guess it runs in the family."

ABOUT THE AUTHOR

Tim Tharp lives in Oklahoma, where he writes novels and teaches in the Humanities Department at Rose State College. In addition to earning a master's degree in creative writing from Brown University, he has also spent time as a factory hand, construction laborer, psychiatric aide, record store clerk, and long-distance hitchhiker.

Tharp is the author of *Falling Dark*, for which he won the Milkweed National Fiction Prize, and two young adult novels: *Knights of the Hill Country*, which was an ALA-YALSA Best Book for Young Adults, and *The Spectacular Now*, which was a National Book Award finalist in 2008.